Praise for the Novels
of Jessica Barksdale Inclán

The Instant When Everything Is Perfect

"Inclán shows us women we recognize from our families, our neighborhoods, even from inside our own thoughts. *The Instant When Everything Is Perfect* resonates with universal yearnings."
—Jean Reynolds, author of *A Blessed Event*

"A compassionate look at a mother and daughter caught in a time of transition. But neither of the strong women in this moving story behave exactly as expected. Inclán's portrait is heartfelt and honest: She sees the strength of women and the bonds of family as Mia Alden and Sallie Tillier move through a time of difficulty and change, stumbling again into unexpected hope and, ultimately, passion."
—Elizabeth Letts, author of *Quality of Care*

Walking with Her Daughter

"As Inclán delves into one woman's pain as she reconciles loss with a new life, she grants readers insight into the resiliency of the human spirit in a touching and very human story." —*Booklist*

"Inclán writes powerfully and movingly about Jenna's enthrallingly triumphant battle with grief." —*Romantic Times* (4½ Stars, Top Pick)

continued . . .

Written by today's freshest new talents and selected by New American Library, NAL Accent novels touch on subjects close to a woman's heart, from friendship to family to finding our place in the world. The Conversation Guides included in each book are intended to enrich the individual reading experience, as well as encourage us to explore these topics together—because books, and life, are meant for sharing.

Visit us online at www.penguin.com.

One Small Thing

"Endearing . . . touching and realistic . . . intriguing."
—*Publishers Weekly*

"Each of [Inclán's] three previous novels has expounded on the large emotional issues that can tear human relationships apart. . . . Where Inclán excels as a writer is in tapping into each character's inner thoughts and feelings." —*Contra Costa Times*

When You Go Away

"This is by far Inclán's most daring novel and evidence of a rapidly developing talent that nimbly manipulates the tragic aspects of human nature to produce a book that is true to life in its heartbreaking quest for hope." —*Booklist*

"Muted, poignant drama with an immensely appealing depth, plain grace—and echoes of Inclán's *Her Daughter's Eyes*." —*Kirkus Reviews*

The Matter of Grace

"[An] engaging, down-to-earth second novel. . . . Inclán has a sharp, compassionate feel for how women look at relationships, sex, and marital issues; her female characters are strong and well-drawn. . . . The twists and turns of Grace's story will keep readers guessing until the final chapters." —*Publishers Weekly*

Her Daughter's Eyes

"A debut novel as gutsy [and] appealing . . . as its heroines. But it is the plight of the teenage sisters, in all their clever foolishness, that strikes at the heart." —*Publishers Weekly*

"A modern-day depiction of familial disintegration with offbeat twists and luminous sparks of hope." —*Booklist*

"Well-written, thoughtful. . . . Inclán never condescends and never judges, preferring to let her subtly drawn people speak for themselves. . . . The understanding portrayal of her teenaged heroines—stubborn, careless, and fiercely honest—is remarkably astute."
—*Kirkus Reviews*

"An exquisitely poignant look into the heart of a troubled family."
—*New York Times* bestselling author Deborah Smith

"Poignant, sharply introspective, and thought-provoking. Every parent of a teenager and, indeed, every teenager should read this work with care."
—*New York Times* bestselling author Dorothea Benton Frank

"Haunting, compelling . . . takes the reader on an emotional roller-coaster ride." —*New York Times* bestselling author Kristin Hannah

OTHER NAL ACCENT NOVELS
BY JESSICA BARKSDALE INCLÁN

Her Daughter's Eyes

The Matter of Grace

When You Go Away

One Small Thing

Walking with Her Daughter

Jessica Barksdale Inclán

The
INSTANT
WHEN
EVERYTHING
IS PERFECT

CONVERSATION GUIDE
NAL
ACCENT
INCLUDED

FICTION FOR THE WAY WE LIVE

NAL Accent
Published by New American Library, a division of
Penguin Group (USA) Inc., 375 Hudson Street,
New York, New York 10014, USA
Penguin Group (Canada), 90 Eglinton Avenue East, Suite 700, Toronto,
Ontario M4P 2Y3, Canada (a division of Pearson Penguin Canada Inc.)
Penguin Books Ltd., 80 Strand, London WC2R 0RL, England
Penguin Ireland, 25 St. Stephen's Green, Dublin 2,
Ireland (a division of Penguin Books Ltd.)
Penguin Group (Australia), 250 Camberwell Road, Camberwell, Victoria 3124,
Australia (a division of Pearson Australia Group Pty. Ltd.)
Penguin Books India Pvt. Ltd., 11 Community Centre, Panchsheel Park,
New Delhi - 110 017, India
Penguin Group (NZ), cnr Airborne and Rosedale Roads, Albany,
Auckland 1310, New Zealand (a division of Pearson New Zealand Ltd.)
Penguin Books (South Africa) (Pty.) Ltd., 24 Sturdee Avenue,
Rosebank, Johannesburg 2196, South Africa

Penguin Books Ltd, Registered Offices:
80 Strand, London WC2R 0RL, England

First published by NAL Accent, an imprint of New American Library,
a division of Penguin Group (USA) Inc.

First Printing, February 2006
10 9 8 7 6 5 4 3 2 1

FICTION FOR THE WAY WE LIVE

REGISTERED TRADEMARK—MARCA REGISTRADA

LIBRARY OF CONGRESS CATALOGING-IN-PUBLICATION DATA
Inclán, Jessica Barksdale.
The instant when everything is perfect/Jessica Barksdale Inclán.
p. cm.
ISBN 0-451-21753-5
1. New York (N.Y.)—Fiction. 2. Young adults—Fiction. 3. Friendship—Fiction. I. Title.
PS3559.N332I57 2006
813'.6—dc22   2005009003

Set in Adobe Garamond
Designed by Ginger Legato

Printed in the United States of America

For Jesse

ACKNOWLEDGMENTS

As always, to my readers, thank you.

My biggest thanks go to my mother, Carole Jo Barksdale, for being brave, for sharing her experiences with me, and for hanging in there.

I must thank my readers Julie Roemer, Keri DuLaney, Marcia Goodman, Gail Offen-Brown, and Joan Kresich. As always, your ideas and comments help me to tell the story I'm trying to tell.

And I thank the boys, all three of them, Mitchell, Julien, and Jesse.

Mia

Mia Alden is running late because she worked out too long at her club, showering fast and almost bolting out of the locker room without combing her hair. As she passes the last bank of mirrors, she stops and looks at herself. Her mother, Sally, will be very disappointed with her if she shows up at the hospital looking wet and spiky haired, her face sticky with lotion. So even though Mia knows that her toilette will force her to speed on the freeway all the way from Monte Veda to Walnut Creek, she opens her bag and pulls out her comb, her blusher, her lipstick, smoothing and brushing herself into a decent picture, one her mother will approve of.

Sally Tillier, Mia's mother, has never left her house without lipstick on, her hair brushed, her clothes neatly pressed. Sally takes walks around her retirement community neighborhood, wearing carefully ironed pastel blouses and khaki pants. Mia, who manages to care and not care about what people think about her, often shops at the Safeway in ripped sweatpants and paint-spattered T-shirts. Sometimes (especially now, because she's on sabbatical from her university professorship) she goes to the post office and bank without combing her hair, her short hair a bright blond whirl on her head.

She cringes when she runs into someone she knows, which is often, because she and her husband and two boys live in the town she grew up in. Most of Sally's old friends still live in Monte Veda, as do Mia's former Girl Scout leader, Sunday school teacher, and many of her friends' parents. And there they all are, it seems, at the post office every time Mia runs in to mail a manuscript to her agent or editor, all of them wanting to know the story of her adult life and eager to tell her about their children, the children who are now adults like Mia.

Mia is not a natural beauty. She is the kind of person who can become beautiful when she puts on the right clothes (the kind that shape and smooth her round flesh). She is fond of dark jersey knits and raw silk. She can draw her face into a kind of stunning glamour that washes off at night. When she talks to crowds, she moves fluidly, and every semester, one or another of her students falls in love with her. Mia imagines that when the semester is over, they must wonder what kind of sick enchantment came over them, something powerful enough to develop a crush on a slightly overweight, middle-aged woman.

Her husband, Ford, says she is a cutie, or, at least, he used to. She can't quite remember the last time he said those words, holding her tight, whispering, "You're my little cutie."

Maybe this is what happens to all long marriages, she thinks. They simmer into friendship, no matter what you do. When she asked Ford a couple years back to go to counseling because things seemed flat, he said, "What do you think we're supposed to act like at this age?"

Maybe he just couldn't sustain the habit of endearments. After all, he met her twenty-two years ago when she was thin. At the post office, she's not cute, not even close.

But today, Mia decides that her mother's appointment is not the time to test Sally's patience, so after a wild, fast drive, she sits in the exam room with her mother. Her hair is in order, her lips slightly red and shiny, her eyelashes darkened, her cheeks rosy. She wears black jersey knit pants and a red sweater that, she realizes, shows some cleavage. Now, in an exam room full of medical drawings of mastectomies, she wonders if cleavage is insensitive.

Sally is on the examination table, which is a table unlike any Mia has ever seen. Or, at least, it's set up differently, the back raised high to support the patient's back, the sitting area small. In another galaxy, Sally would seem ready for takeoff, the only thing missing from her sitting position a headset and space suit.

Sally rests her feet on a footstool, clutching closed her hospital gown that hangs huge on her small frame. Even though the cancer is not making Sally feel ill, she seems to have lost weight since last week, her face tight and drawn and gray, the bones just under her thin skin. But though tired, she's still elegant, crossing her long, thin legs on the table, hitting the back of the table with her left heel, as if the repetitive noise will keep away feeling.

Mia has tried to do her best to keep her fear in check ever since Sally called last week.

"I've got bad news," Sally said. "It's cancer."

Without warning, Mia began to cry, saying, "Mom. Oh, Mom. This is— I don't like this."

"Now, really," Sally said, her voice crackling and tight, the voice she used throughout Mia's childhood when there were fights and squabbles about clothes or the phone or the car. All three sisters knew that once Sally spoke like that, her words were a noose that could squeeze tight.

So Mia stopped crying, leaned against the wall of her kitchen, and listened to Sally's plans, everything already divided up into time squares that would be dealt with in precise chronological order.

This is just one of the reasons why Mia believes she's a changeling, a baby wrested from her natural mother and given to a woman of opposite temperament and body type. For months at a time, Mia doesn't live in chronological time, immersed in her stories and novels and poems, thinking about them when she's teaching at the university or at a movie or making dinner.

"Don't bug Mom," she heard her older son, Lucien, say once to his younger brother, Harper. Mia was sitting on the couch in the living room, a pillow on her lap. She'd been walking somewhere—to her bedroom or the kitchen—and just stopped and sat down to imagine what her characters might do if . . .

"Why?" Harper said.

"I think she's writing," Lucien said.

If Mia still lived at home, Sally would have said, "Don't just sit there. Go clean your room."

It's not just the temperament issue. There's also the parade of physical differences. While Mia's younger sisters, Katherine and Dahlia, are tall, wide hipped, small breasted, long legged, fine limbed, delicate like Sally, Mia is like the Polish relative everyone forgot about. She is shorter than her mother by two inches, full breasted, short legged. Her wrists and ankles are strong and thick, her fingers round, her body smooth with flesh.

Mia has studied her mother's and sisters' bodies since she was nine, noting all the differences. Their collarbones are prominent, straight from throat to shoulder. Hers are arched. Their necks are long and elegant; hers short and full. Their faces are round; hers oval. Their feet narrow; hers wide. Their eyes are so brown they are almost black; hers are gold. Her hair is curly and blond; theirs is straight and, at one time, jet-black. Sally went gray at thirty-nine, Katherine and Dahlia following suit. Mia's blond hair is still blond, not a wiry gray hair on her head. Her mother and sisters are nearsighted, all wearing glasses since childhood. Mia has 20/15 vision, is able to make out an exit sign from a half mile off.

Sally was a chemist before marrying David, Katherine is a pathologist, Dahlia an accountant. From as far back as anyone can remember, Sally's relatives have been doctors or physicists or scientists or business people. Mia writes novels, short stories, and poems, and teaches literature and writing. She's the "creative one," a phrase that is always spoken in hushed tones around holiday tables.

And because her father died when Mia was nine—just when she began to see how different she was—his family is lost to her, all of them dead before David died, nothing but old letters and death certificates and tombstones, no one left to spearhead a search for long-lost cousins across the country. A few old photographs show large women tucked into corsets filled to capacity, their noses—like Mia's—slightly large. But there are no pictures of collarbones or ankles or wrists; these ancestors wrapped in dark silks and muslins from neck to foot. The mystery of who Mia is died with them all.

"I wish he'd hurry up," Sally says, her dark eyes turning to the nasty slits that in former times would send all three girls running to their rooms. "This hospital. Killed your father. Killed him dead. And this doctor? Groszmann. I hate that name. He spells it funny, though. Anyway, I know too much German to like it. Your grandfather was one hundred percent German. He never had an accent. Not that I remember."

"Mom," Mia starts.

"The least he could do is be on time." She clutches at her robe.

Sally doesn't look at Mia as she speaks, and for the millionth time, Mia wonders how Sally could have possibly given Mia her name. *Mine.* It has always seemed to Mia that Sally should have waited for Katherine to use this possessive name. Katherine is the favorite, and she's not even the baby. Already, Sally's been boasting about how Katherine read the slide of her biopsy, finding flaws in this hospital's report. Certainly, around the time of the operations, Katherine will fly in from Philadelphia and move next to her mother's bedside, as if she had been in Mia's position all along—through the first appointments with the breast surgery nursing coordinator, the surgeon who had initially told Sally that the mass looked "just fine," and now this appointment with the plastic surgeon.

Katherine will read the chart, say, "Why did they do that? I'm going to ask right now."

She will order the nurses around and then resort to flirting with the doctors—male or female—to get the information she needs. For the moment, that instant, she will be the strong daughter, the able daughter, because in a crisis, Sally won't look too closely at her. Katherine keeps herself far enough away from Sally to avoid too much attention, to avoid being seen. Katherine is bisexual, though Sally does not know this or pretends not to know it, despite the long years of Katherine coming home alone for vacations and holidays, or having excuses for why she can't visit at all.

Dahlia will be at Sally's condo with her two children, Matt and Mike, her husband, Steve, staying at home in Phoenix to mind their accounting business. Dahlia, the youngest, will clean and cook and buy new sheets for Sally's king-sized bed. She will stay just long enough to get Sally comfortable and then leave, soon followed by Katherine, who will bark out orders in her modulated doctor voice, a voice she must have developed during med school because she certainly doesn't have to worry about how her patients, all of them dead, will react now. Mia will bathe her mother and take her to the toilet and clean her wounds.

"Mom," Mia says, "it's just a name. Groszmann is very common."

Sally rolls her eyes. "I don't want this. I want them cut off and be done with it. Over. Finished."

"You haven't even watched the movie. You don't know what the doctor will say, either," Mia says.

"I don't need to know what he says. I know how hospitals work. Don't forget how I had to be on top of everything with your father. Doctors don't read slides the way they should. They don't pay attention. They don't care."

"That was a long time ago—" Mia begins.

"Some things never change," Sally finishes, looking hard at Mia.

There is a quick knock on the door and then it opens slowly. Dr. Groszmann comes in, almost apologetically, as if he's interrupting something very private—or he isn't sure he belongs. Mia understands this stance immediately and finds herself blushing. A blush that starts on her chest and pushes its way up to her forehead. She smiles, hoping that the doctor will imagine she is always this color. Or maybe he will think she's just run in late, flushed from trying to find parking and running up three flights of stairs.

But he is blushing, too, and even though she can't see her own face, Mia thinks that they both must be the same rosy red.

Sally shuffles on the table, her gown crackling, and she flashes her dark, mean eyes at him.

"My appointment was supposed to be at three thirty."

Dr. Groszmann stops looking at Mia, and his face becomes even redder. "I'm sorry. We're a little backed up today."

Mia thinks to say "A rush on reconstruction?" But she doesn't because she can't find her voice. She looks at her red Giraudon shoes.

"Mrs. Tillier." He looks at the chart and holds out his hand. Sally's eyes widen and she looks up at him and shakes his hand. In that second, Mia can see how scared she is. Mia is scared, too.

Since her mother called, Mia hasn't wanted to think of what cancer means, what it has always meant to Mia, ever since she was nine and her father died.

How can her mother really be sitting here with cancer? Can it be possible that her mother might die from it? Even though Sally is prickly and very different from Mia, Sally is constant, the voice Mia hears in her head despite herself. She's the first person Mia calls when something good or bad happens.

"Well, yes," Sally says, pulling back her hand, adjusting her gown. "Who else would I be?"

Dr. Groszmann turns to Mia, his face paler now, his mouth in a slight smile. His skin is smooth except for a trio of wrinkles at the corner of each eye. She wonders why he doesn't slip into a colleague's office and get shot full of Botox during his break. Wouldn't anyone working in a plastic surgery office be tormented by the tyranny of perfection?

She can feel her stretch marks under her sweater. Her thighs spread onto the chair, both prime candidates for liposuction.

"I'm Mia Alden. Her daughter."

"The pathologist? It's here on the chart that the slides went to a daughter." He seems excited, just like all left-brained people are when they hear the call of their own. Like Mia's whole family at Thanksgiving or Christmas talking about beta-blockers or nanotechnology.

Mia shakes her head. "No, not the pathologist. I'm just a writer. I'm not on the chart."

Dr. Groszmann—it only says R. GROSZMANN on his white lab coat—blushes again and holds his hand out to her. His hands are red and slightly dry looking, almost painfully so—probably from washing before and after surgery—but strong and soft. Mia lets go quickly.

"Nice to meet you."

"Thanks." Mia sits back in her chair, and R. Groszmann sits on his stool, opening the chart again and then looking at Sally.

"So you are going to have a bilateral mastectomy?" He asks the question. It isn't a question at all, but fact. Sally stares at him.

"There's only cancer in one breast," he points out.

Sally shakes her head. "I'm not coming back here in five years and going through this again. Dr. Jacobs said she herself might do the same thing in my position."

The doctor crosses his legs. "I understand. So have you given any thought about what you'd like to do in terms of reconstruction?"

Mia can't help it. She touches one of her breasts. She likes her

breasts. At this point in her life, Sally's breasts have turned into little more than two nipples with a pad of flesh underneath them,
barely an A cup. Maybe a double-A. For many years, Mia wanted
her mother's breasts—or her sisters', really. Both Dahlia and
Katherine have perky little breasts, the nipples just at the rise before the downward turn. Teenaged breasts. Katherine, of course,
hasn't been pregnant or nursed a child, so some of her uplift is
from lack of use. But Dahlia returned to her prepregnancy shape
within weeks of weaning both the boys. And neither she nor Sally
has the crosshatch of silvery stretch marks that Mia does.

But Mia would miss her breasts, the way material hugs them,
the way they are always there when she looks down. She can still
see her boys on her left nipple, the one she weaned them both
from. It wasn't on purpose. She just must have started their last
suck on the right, and then put them on the left, their toddler
mouths latching on for that final time.

She looks down now and can see first Lucien and then Harper,
eyes closed, tongues tasting the last milk.

Ford likes them too, sucking and kissing them when they make
love. One amazing night, he began sucking them when she was
asleep, and she woke to an orgasm from his pulling, tugging lips
alone. When she's awake, though, she is sometimes annoyed by his
suckling, wondering why it's men who have this solace all their
lives, but women are weaned from comfort before they can even remember it.

"I'm not going to be talked out of having them both come off."

"I—" he starts.

"Both off. And then I want some nice breasts. I want to look
okay in a T-shirt."

Sally has always laughed about her breasts, saying they were
barely there. Now and then, she turned to Mia at a picnic or dinner party and whispered, "I'm not even wearing a bra. Imagine
that."

Now, Mia thinks, she'll have to take her mother to the lingerie department at Nordstrom to buy some bras. Maybe some with a little underwire and lace.

Dr. Groszmann smiles, writes something in the chart, reads a little more. "Have you seen the reconstruction movie?"

Sally waves her arms. "Of course, they were out of everything down at Health Services. They said they'd call, but they never did."

Dr. Groszmann nods, his eyes flicking to Mia and then back to Sally.

"Let me go over your options," he says. Mia leans in, wanting to know the options, too. Dr. Groszmann sits back and looks at Sally. He is very good-looking, but a bit thin. A runner. A workaholic. Too thin for her, of course. It's possible she weighs more than he does. What does she weigh now? One hundred fifty? She doesn't get on the scale these days. In fact, the last time she got on the scale was in the week before Harper was born—more than sixteen years ago—and she tipped the scales at 197. He weighed ten pounds, twelve ounces, but still. One hundred ninety-seven.

Dr. Groszmann weighs what? Maybe 160. Probably less. He would get lost in her bones and flesh, pulled down into her vortex. He'd be sucked into her and made invisible. They'd have to send the search-and-rescue hounds, she thinks, almost laughing. She puts a finger to her lip and avoids the doctor's gaze.

"There's immediate reconstruction, which would commence the moment the mastectomy was over."

Sally nods, the immediacy attractive to her. Mia watches her mother's lips, sees them twitch in an almost smile at the word. Immediate. Like everything should be. Tears should be over immediately. Grief? Gone. Worry? Vanquished in a second. Move, move, move. You don't know if you want the dress, the boyfriend, the college, the job? Well, forget it.

"Delayed reconstruction can take place weeks, months, if not years after the mastectomy," Dr. Groszmann continues, detailing the potential drawbacks to both the immediate and the delayed. And as she listens, Mia realizes she's lived in the drawbacks. Too soon; too late. Too fast; not quick enough. She's been like Sally and then too much like herself, stuck in the fear of moving at all.

"You're telling me the skin could die?" Sally asks. "The skin could die?"

"It's a rare complication, but yes." Dr. Groszmann looks at Mia. "The skin gets its nourishment from the chest wall. If there is an expander between them, sometimes the skin can react. And if this reaction necessitates treatment, that could put off the chemotherapy. And if you are going to need radiation—which I think is unlikely—I won't be able to do an immediate reconstruction at all."

"So what do you recommend?" Mia asks, knowing she is supposed to be asking questions. That's her official role here, the witness, the advocate.

Dr. Groszmann looks at her, his eyes tired but very blue. He pushes his long brown hair (nicely tied in a ponytail) away from his forehead. In that second, Mia blushes again. He sees her, and his skin pulses rose.

She looks at her red shoes.

"Your mother," he begins, and then turns to Sally. "You seem to be a very practical person. What I'm hearing from you is that your lifestyle is more important to you than time spent in recovery. You like to walk in your neighborhood. You want to travel. To be with your grandchildren. Reconstruction on top of a mastectomy will necessitate a longer recovery. And we haven't even talked about the stages or types of reconstruction. My recommendation, based on hearing what you've said to me and to your surgeon, is a delayed reconstruction. After your treatment for breast cancer. When you have time."

Sally leans forward, listening closely. Mia tries to pay attention, too, focusing on the doctor's face, listening to his words. She's here to pay attention, to ask smart questions, to help her mother make the right choices, but what she really wants to do is ask the doctor questions such as "Are you married? Would it bother you that I am?"

She wonders what is wrong with her. She wonders if she's insane. Here she is, fighting the urge to flirt with her mother's plastic surgeon. Her poor mother is sitting on this funky table, her left breast filled with moderately differentiated infiltrating and *in situ* ductal carcinoma. Breast cancer that has spread, and breast cancer that is waiting to spread.

"Fine," Sally says, her voice flat. "I'll have a delayed reconstruction. But I want to know everything. Everything about it. And don't tell me to watch the damn movie. The woman down in Health Services seems to be functioning on half a brain cell."

Dr. R. Groszmann smiles again and almost winks at Mia. Mia feels the heat in her body and shifts on her chair. He leans back against the cabinet filled with gowns and boxes of tissue and cotton balls and latex gloves, and begins talking.

જી

After he is done telling Sally everything, Dr. Groszmann asks her to take off her robe. He pulls a measuring tape from a drawer in the cabinet and scoots closer to the examination table. All of this, the position he takes in front of her mother's bent knees, the way his face is directly in front of Sally's breasts, seems too intimate. Sally's long, lovely back is arched, her head turned toward the window, her breasts as perky as they've ever been, nipples erect.

Mia is uncomfortable suddenly, sad, though she knows that she shouldn't be. Her mother would be the last to want someone else's hands on her body. Sally doesn't need a man to tell her she is beautiful, but just seeing the evidence of a life untouched this way makes Mia want to jump out of her chair and run out of the room. Her left leg starts to twitch; the plastic back of the chair digs in her back. She doesn't understand how her mother can live in this beautiful body and not long to be touched, to show it off, to enjoy the connection with someone else. Maybe Sally pretends not to care that for thirty-three years she's been alone, but it makes Mia want to throw herself down and weep.

In another universe, Dr. Groszmann brings his lips to Sally's nipple and sucks, pressing his face and forehead into her chest. In that same universe, Sally smiles, pulls him close, and somehow they manage to fold this table into a place they could lie on. In this universe, Mia is not in the room, just as she was never in the room when Sally pulled her father close. In the thirty-three years since David died, Sally has—as far as Mia knows and, of course, she might be wrong—never sat in front of a man like this, her breasts pushed out, her nipples tingling, her head bent away in supplication. Even though this is an exam, an important one, Sally's willing body makes Mia want to cry, to call out for the doctor to notice how beautiful her mother is, Sally's skin pale and unmarked and lovely. She wants to tell Dr. Groszmann to worship her, to lower the table, to make love to Sally right now, but, of course, Mia doesn't. She looks at the floor, not wanting to see her mother's swan beauty, her untouched flesh, her imperious smile.

Dr. Groszmann makes comments to Sally, but Mia adjusts her gaze, noticing the pigeons outside the window, the building opposite, the gray sky hovering over the dry hills.

❧

Out in the hall, Sally stands next to Dr. Groszmann's medical assistant, arranging for future appointments. She is supposed to watch the movie and then come back to tell the doctor her firm decision. Sally needs to decide soon, because her cancer surgery is in two weeks, and if she changes her mind and wants an immediate reconstruction, there will be further measurements.

Mia leans against the wall, moving out of the way when a clerk pushes a basket full of charts past her. She looks down at the charts, the folders held together with colored tape, the names written with dark black pen. So many sick people, all reduced to words. Soon her mother will turn into a chart like this.

"She's a great candidate for reconstruction."

Mia gasps, looks up. Dr. Groszmann stands next to her, a chart in his hand for another patient, another cancerous breast.

"Oh, that's good news. Good news is nice." Mia breathes deeply, trying to hold the wall of blood urging itself up her chest again.

"Yes," he says, pushing his hair back, a habit, Mia can see, because there's not a strand out of place. He looks at her and then cocks his head toward the hallway. "Well, see you next week."

He holds out his hand again and Mia takes it, his skin already familiar. She blinks and considers how even if she weren't married, she would never, ever sleep with a plastic surgeon. Her stretch marks chide her. Her thighs laugh. Her wrinkles crow.

"Right. Next week." She lets go of his hand, and he walks down the hall. He turns back to her, and she sort of smiles, sort of moves her hand in a wave. Then he knocks on a door and begins all over again what he did in the room with Sally. Another blush. Another mother/daughter wanting answers.

"Christ," Sally whispers, taking Mia's arm as they walk toward the exit into the waiting room.

"What?"

"Crap HMO. They hire the most illiterate to run the show. Doctors don't do anything to keep the boat afloat. Did you see that girl's teeth? Crooked and brown. Obviously no dental plan here."

"Mom," Mia says, pulling her mother to a standstill. "Did you get your appointment?"

"Yes, of course. Do you think I'd leave here without it?" Sally starts walking again. "It's Monday, if you can believe that. And I have the blasted movie to watch before then. You need to come watch it with me. I'll make popcorn. We can pretend we're having fun."

Mia looks at her watch. Harper will be home from school. Of course, that doesn't mean much now that he is sixteen, can drive himself to his tutor and drama practice, but she still needs that cut-off time of three thirty, a way of telling everyone she has to leave, running from curriculum meetings or lunch dates or shopping trips. And when she gets home, Harper is usually not there, any-way, so she pours herself a glass of wine and reads the mail.

And though Mia knows this is wrong, she needs to get away from Sally. From this hospital and all its problems. From the cancer.

"Harper is home, Mom. I'll come get the movie tomorrow. We have till Monday."

Sally opens the door and they walk past the seated women.

"Eleven percent," Sally mutters as they stand in front of the elevators.

"Eleven percent what?" Mia asks.

"Women who will get breast cancer. You need to make sure you check yourself. Every month. Don't forget the mammograms. And ask for a sonogram. After the doctor thought he felt a lump, that was the way they found mine, you know."

The elevator doors open and they walk in. Five years of mam-mograms didn't catch Sally's cancer, though; her breasts small and dense, the flesh the same color on the film as the cancer hiding in her milk ducts.

"I feel fine," Sally announces. A man next to her raises his eyebrows.

"Of course you do, Mom."

"I don't feel like I have this glop growing in me. You know, that's what the surgeon said. She said, 'Look at this gloppy stuff.' "

The doors open on the second floor and the man rushes out. Mia slaps the CLOSE DOOR button.

"Katherine would know why it's gloppy, Mom."

"I wish she were here now," Sally says, her voice a sigh. Mia swallows, knowing well the sound of that longing.

"She'll be here for the surgery. So will Dahlia."

"Yes, I know."

The doors open into the lobby, and they leave the elevator.

"I hate this place," Sally says, looking at the scuffed carpet.

Mia takes her mother's arm, knowing that they will hate it even more before this is over.

❧

When Mia gets home, Harper has already left for his math tutor's. She stands in the kitchen, staring at the counter, smiling as she imagines his afternoon routine. He's left a frozen burrito wrapper there, and the TV remote is on the dining room table. She can see the ghost of his after-school self sitting there, watching the History Channel, biting into the burrito without looking at it.

Unlike Lucien, Harper is a child of habit, though no one would know this from looking into the hump of clothes, papers, books, and magazines on the floor of his room. But he's methodical in terms of what he does when he comes home, the minutes he spends eating, watching TV, sitting on the toilet with a book, doing homework, playing computer games. Mia can tell time by the sound of him in the bathroom in the morning, by his hard-heeled walk on the hardwood floor, coming into her bedroom to say good-bye.

Maybe he became this way because for his whole life, his brain has misfired on him, turning words backward, numbers upside down, making whole sentences his teachers speak undecipherable. She used to think that Harper in a classroom was like herself in the Paris metro, speaking French so horribly that she ended up buying a week pass when all she wanted was a ticket to get her to the Gare du Nord.

He's been in the resource class since second grade, and now even though he gets good grades and reads for pleasure, he knows that failure can come up suddenly and pull you down without warning.

While sometimes Mia wants to weep when she thinks of what Harper has gone through just to learn how to read and add and multiply and type, most of the time she thinks of him like a lion, running through life without fear despite the thorn in his paw.

Lucien is not like his predictable brother, instead a wild boy, lazy and brilliant, reading all of James Joyce as a freshman and flunking algebra twice. He majored in LSD and marijuana until his sophomore year, when Mia and Ford admitted him to an outpatient rehab program that the entire family went to for a year. Now he's at a very liberal college in Washington State, majoring in literature and writing a novel. He calls her to talk about Ayn Rand, Richard Brautigan, and Nietzsche; he calls to ask her for money. He smokes only cigarettes now, though, and his written grade reports from his teachers are admiring. After reading phrases in the reports like "he might consider writing book reviews for a little side income" and "extremely productive" and "strong poetic voice," Mia imagines that Lucien is finally happy, able to stop seeking the thrill that the drugs gave him.

Both her boys are beautiful, dark and tall and slim like their father, even if their brains seem to be like Mia's.

Mia breathes in and then the phone rings. She looks at the clock, knowing it must be Ford, calling her from his car, stuck somewhere on the Bay Bridge or in the Caldecott Tunnel. Traffic lately has become his way of life, forcing him to pull over in Oakland or Emeryville for a drink while the rest of the suburban folk idle and swear in lines of hot cars. But it's not Ford.

"How is the old girl?" Kenzie asks.

"Fired up. Bitchy. Complaining." Mia takes the phone to the dining room table and sits in Harper's seat. Kenzie's phone is scratchy, as if Mia's best friend is calling her from a cave. Kenzie calls her from everywhere she can get a signal, though; tops of ski-resort runs, the Eiffel Tower, a river in Colorado. Mia met Kenzie during Mia's first teaching class at Cal, Kenzie at the time working in the public relations office at the university. She came into Mia's fiction workshop for photos of students hard at work.

"Oh, come on!" Kenzie said to Mia's students. "Character development can't be that serious. Your teacher looks harmless enough. Smile, for God's sake! The camera won't bite you."

Now, as a freelance photographer, Kenzie travels all over the world and always wants to share everything with Mia, regardless of where she is. Mia sometimes thinks that since Kenzie took the photograph of Mia that ended up on her first book jacket, they are bound for life, connected through eyes and image.

"Well, that's good. That's great, really. What did the doctor say?"

"Where are you?" Mia asks.

"In the basement. Something's gone wrong with the plumbing again."

"Oh." Mia sighs.

"Well?"

"He was nice. Gave her the options. She has to decide by next week, when she goes in for her second appointment."

"Was she scared?"

Mia closes her eyes, trying to forget Sally's horrified face when Dr. Groszmann told her about the side effects of immediate reconstruction.

"Yeah. It's not really as easy as they've made it sound. You know, go in, come out with perfect breasts. There are a lot of steps."

"I'm sure it's horrible, but I'd go Dolly Parton."

"What?"

"I think she should get giant ones. Make up for all those years of flatness. I would."

Mia shakes her head and spins the TV remote on the smooth oak table. "No, you wouldn't. You like running around without the iron hands of a Jogbra. You like your sexy boyish look in a white T-shirt."

"You're right. But I'd think about it."

Kenzie shrieks, says, "Hold on," and Mia can hear running water. As she waits, she wonders how to bring up what happened in the doctor's office besides the reconstruction talk. All these years, Kenzie has told her date stories, but Mia has never started off the conversation, never had anything to say. Never embarrassed herself like she did this afternoon, her face turning the color of sunburn whenever Dr. Groszmann spoke to her.

"God," Kenzie says, back and panting slightly. "Plumbers. So, what else happened? Then I've got to go."

"Well, the doctor was nice."

There is a hitch in the conversation, and Mia can almost hear Kenzie smile. "My God! You slut."

"I know. It was sickening."

"What does he look like?" There is a bang, the sound of metal on metal. A door slams.

"Too thin, too long-haired, too soft-spoken."

"You want him. Shit! There's a foot of water in here. Goddamn it. I've got to go. Listen," Kenzie says, and Mia listens. "Are you there?"

"You told me to listen."

"Smart-ass. Sally girl is going to be fine."

"I know," Mia says. "She always has been before."

"I'll call you later. First I need to swim out of here. Bye."

Mia clicks off the phone and stares out the window at the bird feeder. A flock of angry purple finches screams at each other, and Mia wonders if she should take the feeder down. Last year, she got rid of the hummingbird feeder because of the aerial wars two males engaged in the entire summer, buzzing right by people on the deck, swooping past with their high-pitched needle-beaked whines. Despite everything she knew, she couldn't help but imagine a guest lanced through the cheek by a bird drunk on sugar water. So she took down the feeder, pretending not to notice the two males sitting on opposite branches for weeks, waiting.

She stands up and walks over to hang up the phone, the plastic suddenly heavy in her hand. Of course, Kenzie is right. Sally will be fine. She has to be. Both doctors think there is little chance the cancer has spread to her lymph nodes, and the cancer has taken years to grow, a slow, plodding cancer. Even Katherine agreed. When Mia complained to her sister that the surgeon was going to wait three weeks to operate, Katherine sighed.

"Oh, don't get dramatic. That cancer is going nowhere."

"How can you tell? Can't something escape right now and sail up into her lymph nodes and get spread around just like that? How can anyone say one little cell isn't going to make giant headway in three weeks?"

"Look, I read the initial path report. Carefully. This cancer isn't going to be more than stage one, stage two at the most."

"How can you tell that from a piece of paper?" Mia asked.

Katherine sighed again and started talking in that condescending, slightly exasperated doctor voice Mia hated. She talked about aggregate dimensions of the sites and surgical margins and mitotic activity. After a few minutes of this, Mia gave up and decided to believe her sister. Why not? Sally was Katherine's mother, too, and if Katherine thought it was okay to walk around with cancer in her milk ducts, who was Mia to argue?

Mia walks into her room and stares at her bed. Since she's been on sabbatical, she hasn't taken one single afternoon nap. Not one. Usually during a semester, she would find herself sneaking in here at three, falling down on the bed, and sinking into a deathlike slumber until Harper came home. Since she isn't reading student papers or going to meetings or driving to campus, she isn't tired in the afternoons anymore. But today, her body feels like someone has scrubbed it clean with steel wool, her insides jittery and quaking and trembling. As she stands at the foot of the bed, she has sharp, quick worries about Sally, then Ford. There seems to be more wrong than what's on the surface, than what's obvious. Her heart races. Her eyelids ache. Her stomach pulses. With her coat still on, she sits down and then lies down, closing her eyes against the afternoon light. In a minute, she is asleep.

Her dream makes no sense because she does not play baseball or like baseball or think about baseball, not ever. The game is as far from her mind as the NASDAQ or quantum physics. But in this dream, she is on a team that has recently hired a player with a disability. Someone tells this to Mia and she nods, knowing about disabilities. She thinks with a sudden, quick pain about Harper and his reading difficulties, and turns to look at this person in left field. She can feel her gasp in her head and body. This person is covered tightly in some kind of white plastic wrap. Underneath the covering, Mia can see this person move, arms and legs shifting. In a way, the movements of this person's body under the wrap remind her of what her stomach looked like in late pregnancy when the babies turned, a wall of arm pulsing across her abdomen.

Suddenly, a ball cracks off a bat and flies high. It's headed right toward the wrapped person, and somehow the person catches it. She watches the person, her gaze coming closer and closer to him, his very body making her feel like she's trapped and suffocating. But she can't stop watching. All his body parts seem to scrabble around inside the wrap as he tries to find the ball. And then there is stillness. The person has found it, a round lump under the wrap. Mia finds herself moving closer to the person, staring at the ball right there on the person's chest, when suddenly, she is the one in the wrap, she is the one that can't see, can't hear, can't move freely, and then she wakes, gasping, her heart pounding against the cage of her ribs.

❦

Ford and Harper are at the table, finishing the last of the chicken Peloponnese. As Mia picks up the empty dish from the table, Ford smiles, but his eyes focus on the kitchen wall as he talks.

"That was really good," he says, twirling a fork on the table, his face vacant.

"Thanks," she says, taking a plate to the sink and turning on the water. But what she really wants to say is "Where are you?" What Mia wants to know is what he won't tell her. But because this weeknight family dinner is rare—he's often traveling for business during the week—she doesn't want to start something they can't finish, pulling Harper into the mix.

"Mom?" Harper says.

"Yeah?"

"I need twenty dollars. My English class has adopted a family in Oakland."

Ford sits back in his chair and looks at Harper. "Don't you usually do that at Christmas?"

"Mr. K. forgot. So we decided to do it for Easter." Harper puts down his fork. "Oh, not Easter. We have to call it a spring break gift. In case they're, like, Muslim or something."

Ford puts his hand into his back pocket and pulls out his wallet. He arrived home late, as he often does these days, and he's still in his suit pants and white button-down shirt. His tie curls like a snake on the kitchen counter next to the colander. His dark bangs stand up straight from his forehead.

"Here." He slides a twenty across to Harper.

Harper nods, his eyes on his plate. "Thanks."

"I wish someone had adopted us when we were in college. Or even later. We could have used a benefactor," Mia says, thinking about the apartments they lived in, the worst one just after Harper was born. The plumbing drained right into the ground below the house. Mold grew like wild green hair in Mia's shoes in the closet.

Ford shakes his head and wipes his mouth. "You are such an exaggerator. It wasn't that bad. Don't make this into a scene for one of your novels."

She knows he doesn't like to think of those days, so long ago and so different from how they live now. In fact, when she brings up the stories of the shabby apartments and the horror of months with thirty-one long days between paydays, he quickly changes the subject. But back then, surrounded by moldy shoes and parades of ants coming up through the floorboards, how could either have imagined this house in Monte Veda, Ford's wonderful job with Baden Randolph Myers? When Lucien was a toddler and Harper a baby, how could they have envisioned Mia at the university and then an author? Maybe they had dreams, but the reality was night school and buckets of dirty cloth diapers, disposable too expensive to buy.

And strangely, they are living the dream they both conjured up so long ago—two healthy children, a nice home, plenty of money, great careers. But somehow, they forgot to think up later dreams, other goals, future plans. What is the story for their old age? What are their plans for five, ten, twenty-five years from now? It's as if the plot of their lives stopped, leaving them where the sequel should begin.

Mia opens her mouth as if to ask, but then thinks of Sally and David. Maybe it's best to let the future stay a blur. In case it doesn't even show up.

Harper finishes eating and stands up. He unfolds forever, his body long and lanky, the tallest Alden boy, taller than Ford. He is on his nighttime path: homework, IMing his friends, shower, sleep. He doesn't seem to notice his parents, but he touches Mia's shoulder as he passes her at the sink. Her baby. Her last baby, a man now.

"So, how was it?" Ford asks, his elbows on the table. "What's your mom going to do?"

Mia sighs. "She has to decide by Monday. But it looks like she'll wait to heal from the first surgery before she goes ahead with the reconstruction."

"Does the doctor seem good?" Ford takes his last sip of wine, stares at the empty glass, and then pours another to the top of the thin crystal glass.

"He's nice." She shrugs. She looks at her husband. His shirt-sleeves are rolled up, the neck of his shirt open. If she were to squint, he would be the young man she met her sophomore year of college, the one who rode his bike in winter, wearing shorts. He would be knocking on her apartment door, asking if he could borrow the phone, he and his roommate upstairs too poor to get one for themselves.

He was the first man to want her so aggressively, asking her out over and over until she said yes. And if she'd been disappointed with how it felt to be with him in bed, everything else about him made up for that lack of feeling. His kindness, his warmth, his desire for her, his commitment to their "unwanted" pregnancy of Lucien. What a wonderful father he was, is, always has been, to both boys.

Sometimes before bed, Ford undressing slowly in their room, sighing about something from his day, Mia wants to ask him where he is. "Where have you gone?" she wants to say. "Who are you now?" She wants him to ask her, too. Maybe she would tell him then how she feels, but his sighs pass without her saying a word, and then they are in bed and then they are asleep.

But she knows she really doesn't have to change anything about their marriage. It could go on for years just like this. He is a good man, a lovely man, even if most of the time she feels as if she is sleeping with her brother.

Once Kenzie said, "It's a myth that one person can give you everything you need. Is one person supposed to keep you mentally and physically challenged at all times?"

"That's the way we've decided it should be."

"There's always self-love, sweetie," Kenzie said, laughing. "There's always a quickie at the Harlot Hotel."

Mia snorted. "There's not a lot of support out there for going elsewhere for sexual pleasure. We call that adultery."

"So? And anyway, here's the other thing. Honesty is overrated. Don't forget that. Say it over and over to yourself before you leave the house in the morning."

Now as Mia looks at Ford, she knows that if she ever tells him the truth, if she ever says, "You know, Ford, I love you so much. But I want something. I'm not sure what it is, really. A feeling. A pulse. I think I want to go outside our marriage for sex. You mean well, but you just don't do it for me," she knows it would kill him.

Ford takes her hand. "It will be okay. Your mom will be fine."

She looks at her husband and hopes he's right. She hopes it all will be okay.

T W O

Sally

S ally stares at herself in her bedroom mirror. She's taken off her blouse and her bra and turned on all the lights in the room. Now she stands a foot away from the mirror, looking at her breasts. She lifts up one arm, watching her breast rise, seeing the pale white smoothness of her underarm. Then she drops that arm and lifts the other, the healthy breast bouncing up, this underarm just as pale.

Her breasts seem exactly the same as always, not much different since she weaned Dahlia. The nipples are large, brown, distended, the flesh below them saggy. *Droopy* was the exact word the plastic surgeon in *Breast Cancer: Understanding Your Treatment Options* used to describe the downward press of gravity on flesh.

"Observe how the healthy breast droops," the doctor intoned, as if being cancer-free wasn't enough to exclude the breast from criticism. "And now here's a photo of how we matched the healthy breast with the reconstructed breast. Look how symmetrical."

A red laser dot circled the areola. That's something Sally has learned during cancer. How to pronounce areola. Maybe she's never actually said the word—was there a need?—but she thought *air-e-O-la,* like some kind of musical note. Instead, when the doctors talk about the areola complex, it's *oh-ree-la,* the musical note's sour twin.

On and on the photos went, but none showed the patients' faces, so it was hard to determine if the breasts matched the women. Sally knows that at sixty-six, she doesn't want a pair of perky little packages riding under her sweater. How ridiculous would that be? All the men at bridge would stare at her during the rubbers, unable to bid. On her walks, poor widowed Dick Brantley would stare at her even more than usual as she bent down to pat Mitzie, his cocker spaniel.

But maybe that wouldn't be so bad. Sally likes Dick, enjoys his deep voice saying, "Hey, ho, Sal," when they pass each other on the street.

She shakes her head, pushing away for now her flirtatious fantasy of Dick. She has to think. What she wants, really, is for the doctors to figure out how to suck the offending goop out of her breast and let her go on with what she has. Her flesh. Her nipple. The droop that she earned.

Sally looks down at her left breast, wondering why it betrayed her. And then she laughs, full of her own self-pity. Why would a breast betray her? It was she, most likely, who betrayed her breasts, taking those flipping hormones from the time she was forty-five until the day of the cancer diagnosis. She ignored the reports, the warnings, telling a concerned Mia just last year, "It works. Why stop? Everyone is panicking."

Now, two weeks since her diagnosis, having stopped the hormones, she's awash in hot flashes, burning through the night in sweat, her hair thinning even before she can start chemotherapy.

"Christ," she mutters, picking up her bra and putting it on. Her left breast doesn't even hurt, not even from the biopsy she had two weeks ago. She feels fine, wonderful, as if she could do two laps around the neighborhood in less than an hour; as if she could do all of Florence or Rome or Paris in one day. There is no evidence of illness except on a slide and in her chart, and for a second, Sally wonders if she could run away from the words that the doctors wrote down to tell her what she is. A cancer patient.

Downstairs in the kitchen, Sally cleans up her popcorn mess. Somehow, she's never quite figured out how to time the popcorn right, so she burns one bag for every bag she can eat. The air smells like char, a slight haze of smoke clinging to the kitchen ceiling. Sally opens a window, and dumps the unpopped kernels into the trash. Her fingers are shaking, and she suddenly slides down to the floor, her breath quick and harsh and full of tears.

David, she thinks, *come help me.* But then she shakes her head, swallowing back her sadness. It's impossible. He died before they even invented microwave popcorn. And, anyway, he doesn't know a thing about cancer. Sally's the one who studied up when he was sick. He couldn't help her at all.

When David died of cancer, it happened so fast. Spring turned into summer without Sally noticing. Before she knew it, it was one hundred degrees and David was in the ground. Now she can't even remember what she did in those few short months, except for driving to and from the hospital. She must have taken care of her girls, cooked, cleaned, ironed school clothes, fed the dog, watered the yard. But she has no memory of anything but the corridor outside David's hospital room, the slick linoleum, the smell that jammed itself down her throat—cotton sheets washed in water too hot, ammonia, alcohol, plastic, rot.

And then, like that, it was over, life pushing on, and Sally had to keep going. She didn't want to, but how could she stop? She had three girls, nine, six, and three. There was the insurance money to figure out, the will to go through, and David's clothes and belongings to deal with. Before she knew it, the children were a year older. Then two, then ten, all Sally's worries of the future shielding her from the present. Mia was in college, suddenly pregnant, her life gushing way past the predictable lines Sally and David had imagined for her when she was little. At least Katherine never did anything like that, complicating her life so quickly, and Dahlia had followed Sally's suggestions perfectly, waiting exactly two years after graduating before marrying Steve, who from all accounts still seems perfect for her. So when did Sally have the chance to think about David and illness and death? By the time the girls were out of college and into their own lives, Sally's life with David seemed like a dream she'd once had, a book read long ago on a summer beach, the memory soaked with sun and forgetfulness. But it was a book she still couldn't put down.

Sally wants to cry but there aren't tears. Just pain. Her throat hurts; her head aches. The smell of the burned popcorn makes her nauseous. For a second, she imagines this is what the chemo will be like, her body full of sickness, all her cells trying to regenerate, clawing to life.

"Christ," she says, rubbing her face and pushing herself up slowly. "Holy cow."

Everything in her feels heavy, wrong. Did David feel this way? If so, he never told her, never complained. Oh, how he must have hurt.

Sally slaps the counter. "Enough!" She closes her eyes, waits, and then opens them and looks out the window. The red bud tree her gardener, Rigo, planted last year has lost the last of its pink flowers, the green fan-shaped leaves open toward the afternoon light. Sally needs air, light, sun, so she puts the popcorn bowl into the dishwasher and leaves the kitchen. She's going to take a walk. She'll put on her turquoise pants and even slather on sunscreen, though the light is almost gone from the sky, though wrinkles and *skin* cancer are the least of her worries now.

If she runs into Dick Brantley and Mitzie, she'll smile, say something nice. Maybe she will ask him in for coffee, or maybe he'll want one of the beers she keeps handy for Ford. They will sit in the living room, and she'll listen to his stories about his wife, find out where he's going to travel to next. That's just what she'll do. For good karma, as Mia would say. For plain good luck.

Sally is in bed, sitting up with a magazine on her lap, watching the television in her room. She's popped in the second video, one that her neighbor Nydia Nuñez brought over with a lemon pound cake. This one is entitled *Reconstruction: Not a Misnomer*.

"My son-in-law, he's a surgeon, you know. His hospital made this. I had it for my sister," Nydia said as she handed Sally the cake and the video.

Sally wondered how Nydia found out about the cancer, and then remembered the phone call she'd had to make to Vera Lyons, the head of the home-improvement committee for the complex. Sally knew she wouldn't be able to chair the deck paint choice committee now.

"Oh," Sally said, gripping the cake gently, the hard video against her chest. "How is your sister?"

Nydia waved her hand. "Hers was different."

How? Sally wanted to ask. *How was she different from me? Was her cancer terrible, spread throughout her body? In every lymph node and cell? Was the tumor site huge, over 4 cm?* Sally wanted to tell Nydia that her site is only 1.3, small, so small, just like this. She imagined holding up her fingers to show Nydia the tiny, itsy-bitsy spot. She wanted to run and get the pathology report, shake it under her neighbor's nose. *Look! Tell me! Tell me that I won't be like your sister!*

But instead, Sally smiled broadly, thanked Nydia, and didn't invite her in, promising to return the video after watching the entire thing. Yes, the whole thing.

The breasts on this video are stunning, gorgeous, perfectly shaped. Reconstruction is not a misnomer here, and the narrator does not use the term *mastectomy deformity,* a phrase that made Sally wince throughout the other film.

She learns more about saline implants (silicone is apparently just on the horizon again, suddenly not poisonous or toxic anymore) and TRAM flap reconstruction (they look the best). Because the doctors use stomach fat to create the breasts, the good news with

TRAM flaps is that along with lovely, more natural breasts, you get a tummy tuck in the process. A twofer.

The video whirs on. There are close-ups of the "newly made" breasts, the scars hardly visible; the only difference is in the nipple. No amount of tattooing can bring back a perfect *oh-ree-la* complex. Sally can see that now. But as she watches picture after picture of perfect breasts, she knows she wants to keep her own. She wants to enjoy them as she hasn't since—since David died. She might even want to show them to Dick, to make his millennium.

Sally giggles and looks down at the video box in her hands, turning it over slowly. As she reads the back, she gasps. Beverly Hills. This video was made by a volunteer group for Cedars Sinai Hospital. She shakes her head and then flicks off the VCR. Like her crappy HMO will pay for newly made, perfect breasts. Not in this decade. Even today, she knows that the hospital would kill David all over again, ignoring his symptoms, unable to find the cancer that was crawling around his stomach. Even today, she would be a widow.

Fuck them, she thinks, using Katherine's constant command about Republicans, bigots, racists, the uneducated, the rich, the middle class, people who shop at Wal-Mart.

Fuck them all.

§

After her appointment at the ob-gyn, Sally meets Mia upstairs in the Plastic Surgery waiting room. All Dr. Kirsch wanted to do was follow up with her after she stopped the hormones, but the talk before it was awkward and embarrassing because Sally wasn't sure how to thank him for finding her tumor in the first place, while doing the exam Sally should have been performing all along. When he first found the lump, Sally could make excuses for herself. "It's just a cyst," she said to herself the day she drove home from her appointment. "A little cyst."

But after the biopsy and the terrible results, she is embarrassed, mortified that she missed a lump for a whole year, neglected to do what Dr. Kirsch ordered her to do every month in the shower: *Fingers flat, move gently over every part of each breast. Check for any lump, hard knot, thickening.*

Shame, she thought to herself when she heard the biopsy report, *shame on you.*

So it was with a great effort that she somehow managed to say, "Thank you for doing such a thorough exam on me," and Dr. Kirsch nodded, keeping to himself his refrain of, "Once a month in the shower. Saves lives."

Sally is tired and barely says hello to Mia. After she registers at the desk, Sally sits down hard on the stiff wooden chair. In Beverly Hills, she thinks, where there are newly made breasts, they must have better chairs. Leather. Stuffed. Comfortable.

She pats Mia's knee and then looks at her oldest daughter. Today, Mia looks more pulled together, pretty in the way Mia can be pretty. Her oldest daughter is not beautiful. Not like Dahlia, who managed to get all of David's and Sally's best characteristics: long, thick dark hair; thin, agile body; straight, small nose; wide blue eyes. Katherine is of that model, too, but her face is slightly wider than Dahlia's, her skin not as smooth, her eyes smaller. But pretty. Pretty enough to be married, which she is not. Not even once.

There's more to Katherine's story, Sally knows that. But it's Katherine's to tell, not Sally's to ask.

"Are you okay, Mom?" Mia asks.

Sally shrugs, opens her purse to look for a mint, scraping the soft bottom with her hands. "Darn it."

"What? What's wrong?"

Sally clicks her purse closed. "All I want is a mint."

Mia opens her purse and pulls out a rectangular tin of mints Sally can smell before Mia opens the box.

"Here, Mom. This will wake you right up." Sally takes a mint from the box and looks at Mia. Her oldest girl.

None of the pictures of Mia, with her high school dates, that clutter Sally's hallway—photos of junior proms and senior balls— elicit the oohs and aahs from Sally's bridge friends. None of them say "What a lovely girl," as they do when looking at photos of Katherine and Dahlia.

Even now that Mia is a published author and has done readings at Monte Veda Books to a crowd full of Sally's friends, the comments Sally gets about Mia are in regard to her brilliance and humor and work ethic. At first, the kind of compliments Mia received bothered Sally. She could feel her long-dead mother, Frona, at her shoulder, saying, "She's an attractive girl. If we could just get her to shape up! And that dress, dear. It's not appropriate for this venue. In front of all these people in cotton. My goodness."

Sally often has to shake her mother's voice out of her head, even now, twenty years since Frona died of lung cancer. She can still feel the slice of her mother's words when Sally came down to breakfast over fifty years ago. Sally was experiencing her one and only overweight period, an adolescent push toward flesh, her new woman's body greedy for hips and breasts.

Her mother untied her apron and stared at her, hissing, "Girls do not wear jeans. And certainly not with your hips!"

Not only do her mother's words still ring in her ear, but she can feel the way the stiff denim felt as she pushed the jeans down her plump butt and thighs, the tears in her throat as she tried not to cry.

Even worse, in the past and sometimes, rarely, now, Frona's vitriol slips out of Sally's own mouth, leaving a bruising sentence in the air, one usually directed toward Mia. Frona would cringe at Mia's hips in pants, and without meaning to or wanting to, Sally has said, "There's got to be a way for you to lose weight" and "If you could only get rid of a few pounds."

Sally wants to swallow down those words, take them back. She doesn't know why she keeps hurting Mia this way, hurting this daughter who has always been with her. The daughter who is always there for her. It's as if Frona takes her over like a possessing spirit, uses Sally's brain and mouth for an instant, and then vanishes, leaving Sally to deal with what remains.

And lately, Sally has felt a bruise on her heart for Mia, something she can't really articulate, sensing a sadness in her oldest daughter, a pain that maybe Mia doesn't even notice. Sally isn't sure what could be wrong. Mia seems happy in her life, especially now that Lucien and all his issues are squared away. Ford is a lovely man, so there couldn't be anything wrong with their marriage. But at times—in the car at an intersection or at a lunch in between salad and entrée—Sally bites back words before she begins to say something that might hurt Mia, might be more than she wants to know. Before Frona can come out of Sally's mouth.

Sally pats Mia's knee again and looks up at the television set that flickers all day long in the waiting room. She knows that if she had to have one of her daughters as a mother, she'd pick Mia. In a heartbeat. Even with all her teaching and writing, Mia has stuck with those boys even when Sally herself would have tossed Lucien overboard. How Mia ever dealt with his psychotic reaction to that drug is beyond Sally. What had Lucien thought as the drug pumped through his brain? That everyone was really a musical note that swirled from him? Mia and Ford sat up with him all night and then got him into the program, the rehab that went on and on and on. And really, who knows what the kid is doing now up at that hippie college?

Harper's learning problems? Solved with tutors and therapists and backpacking trips that cost a bundle. And though she could never tell Katherine this, she is glad that Mia is the one who lives nearby, who will go to the appointments with her, who will take notes and ask questions. Despite Frona's voice and her own voice still playing in her head, Sally knows that a small rear end and a handsome skirt are not what are really important.

"So, did you decide?" Mia asks, putting her hand on top of Sally's. "That movie had a lot of options. I think I'd be confused."

Sally looks down at Mia's solid fingers, feels their warmth under her own skin.

"Oh yes. I did. And you should have seen the video Nydia Nuñez gave me. Made reconstruction look like a fairy tale. Came out of Beverly Hills. Not a harsh scar in the batch. Bells and whistles. I was surprised they didn't throw in a face-lift at the same time. Cure everyone's problems all at once."

Mia laughs. "I bet they give you a massage before the surgery. Chai lattes. A pedicure."

"Well," Sally says, "I think I'll be lucky to escape from *this* place with my life."

She is about to say more until she realizes that what she's said isn't funny. It's the truth, the truth that she and Mia have known with David.

"Anyway." Sally folds her arms, feeling her breasts pressed against her chest. "I want a reconstruction, but delayed. Maybe a TRAM flap reconstruction. But later. All that talk about dead skin. Terrible."

Mia turns to look Sally in the eye. Sally sees how her oldest child is getting old herself, tiny lines at her eyes. Who will sit with Mia when she is where Sally sits, ill with something or other? For some reason, she doesn't imagine Ford. Where is Ford? Why isn't Ford with Mia, taking care of her? Sally's heart begins to race until she thinks, *Harper. Harper will be here. Tender-hearted Harper.*

"Are you sure? You know what you will look like for the months until you have the surgery. Not that I thought they looked so bad myself. You told me you were appalled by the scars."

"Deformity."

Mia nods. "Deformity."

Sally uncrosses her arms and pushes her hair back. "I'll get one of those—or two of those—thingies. You know. Prostheses. Slap them in my bra. That will carry me through."

"As long as you're sure, Mom," Mia says. "As long as it's what you want."

Sally opens her mouth to say yes, but then closes it and sits back against the hard chair. What she wants is immaterial here, because none of her wants will be granted. Since her diagnosis, her wants have been sailing in front of her eyes like tiny ships, all with full sails and plenty of headwind. What she wants is for it to be 1970 or late 1969, months before David felt the first twinge of pain in his stomach. She'll block the free radical, chemical, virus, or poison that started his cancer. Or if that's impossible even with all her magic, she wants to come from the future to that date and save him, whisk her husband forward to her time and take him to the swanky hospital in Beverly Hills. She will tell the doctors, in their pretty white coats with their state-of-the-art diagnostic machines, to find the cancer. She'll know, after all, where it will be. She can tell them where to look. And maybe, if she were able to save him, she wouldn't be here now.

Who knew how grief could turn a cell against the body that made it?

A line has formed at the registration desk because the clerk is flirting with a man, taking her time swiping his card and laughing, tilting her head just so to show off her long, lovely jawline. Two women here for varicose vein surgery turn to each other and cluck, clutching their paperwork. The television flickers on, news, all disastrous. The weather will turn, winds will tear down power lines and delay traffic. The president will start another war, either in some underdeveloped country or here, at home, between gays and straights, conservatives and liberals, businessmen and environmentalists. The Congress and Senate will battle over the budget that is so far in deficit, Sally can't even begin to imagine what the number would look like written down. Schoolchildren will lose years in a horrid educational system. Katherine will sit at home in Philadelphia in front of the screen and yell *Fuck them! Fuck them!*

On and on it will go until the nurse swings open the door and calls out, "Sally Tillier."

Robert

Robert puts down the recorder, clicking PAUSE, and stares at the chart in front of him. His last patient, Jackie Lagalante, has just had her final checkup after her TRAM flap reconstruction. It wasn't easy. In fact, when Jackie came in for her first consult and then later, after she'd gone through chemotherapy and radiation, she was thin, her bones like hooks under her skin. But she was a good consumer—she'd watched the videos carefully and saw that the TRAM gave the best results. Breasts that were of her own skin, own flesh, supple and natural.

"I want those," she'd said, the bangs from her wig dipping down over her eyes. "These are the breasts I want."

Robert didn't know what to say except, "You're too thin."

Jackie stared at him, blinking once, twice. "Then I'll gain weight. I'll grow the fat for my own breasts, and you'll move it from my stomach to the right place. I read about it. It can happen."

In his other life, Robert would have said yes immediately, assuring Jackie that all of this, and maybe more, was possible. These new breasts would be shapelier, better formed, and feel better than anything she could get with an implant. And certainly, this newly grown flesh would be cancer-free, not prey to the disease that flowed in her lobes and ducts. He would have extolled the virtues of nipple tattoo and given out the phone numbers of former patients whom she could call for glowing reports on his technique, bedside manner, and wise counsel.

But he was not in his other life now, so what he did was to nod and agree with her plan. They could do it. It would work. And her TRAM flap was, as it turned out, successful. But he didn't promise anything. He never does anymore.

He clicks the recorder back on. "Patient was recommended to continue with her oncological checkups and tests and was told to make an appointment if she notices any tissue loss."

Robert turns off the recorder, pushes his hair off his forehead, and picks up the appointment schedule his assistant, Carla, prints out each morning. Sally Tillier. From last week. Impending double mastectomy. Thin, too, like Jackie Lagalante.

He puts down the schedule, rubs his forehead. Sally Tillier brought her daughter to her last appointment, probably because of something she'd read in a book about having an advocate. Probably the breast surgery nursing coordinator counseled Sally to bring another set of eyes and ears to every appointment. Sometimes Robert wants to open the door wide and shoo the family member/advocate out of the door, hustling them and their little notebooks and tape recorders from his office. Too many eyes, too many ears. But he liked the daughter, felt it in his face when he opened the door, a flush of blood at what? A kindred soul? Someone who might understand what had happened to him? Her face made him want to smile and cry. He recognized her, a complete stranger. "There you are," he almost said. "Where in the hell have you been?"

Robert sits back in his chair, shaking his head. Right. His parted twin walked into one of his exam rooms, just like that. Maybe it was just that the daughter seemed like someone who would never ask for a procedure as trivial as a forehead peel or liposuction or a chin implant. Someone who would never swish into his office, sit down, and talk about having a "little cosmetic maintenance."

He doesn't know what his reaction was all about, but when he'd seen her—what was her name? Had he written it on the chart?—she reminded him of a taste, something like caramel, rich and thick and sweet.

For the first time that day, Robert Groszmann, M.D., is excited to see a patient.

&

He tries not to look at the daughter, Mia Alden, too often. He is conscious of focusing on Sally while she talks, nodding, blinking once, twice, and then turning to Mia for a quick, natural affirmation of Sally's words. Mia is never looking at him, her eyes on Sally's face, but he can tell that she sees his glance, her peripheral vision catching his gaze. Her face seems flushed, high colored. He looks back at Sally, listens, wondering how old Mia is. Her skin shows, as the current lotion ads say, the signs of aging. Small crow's-feet by her eyes, the slight grooves running from nose to lips, lines that will slowly deepen with time. But she has no eyelid droop, no need for a blepharoplasty; no excess skin under her chin. She's had no work done, not ever.

She's not wearing a wedding ring, and there is no tan line where one should be. But her last name is different from Sally's. So maybe she's divorced or separated. Robert stares at his chart, wondering what went wrong with her marriage. Or, he thinks, she just doesn't wear a ring. A choice? She's not old enough to be a hippie, throwing out all social norms. Perhaps she just took it off for today, to send him a message.

She's got to be thirty-eight. Maybe forty?

"So, what do you think?" Sally glares at him, her dark eyes glinting.

Robert pushes his hair back, blinks, reads the actual words he wrote on the chart, and then looks up. "What I'm hearing you say is that you do not like the way a mastectomy deformity looks."

"God, no! All those lumps and bumps in the wrong places."

"Those people," Robert says, "were fat. Overweight. Considerably. You wouldn't have a result like that."

Mia laughs, shifts in her chair. "Lucky it's you and not me, Mom."

Robert swallows, unable to believe he said the word *fat*. Why not *obese*? *Overweight*? Clinical terms. He glances at Mia, who is still blushing.

Sally waves her hand. "It's just so ugly. But I can live with it until I heal from the first surgery. Then I want it done. An A cup, just like we discussed."

Robert writes down what she says, knowing that the appointment is just about over. He won't see Sally Tillier or Mia Alden for months now, not until after Sally has had her mastectomy, undergone chemo or radiation treatments, and healed. Maybe, as sometimes happens, a woman as practical and conscientious as Sally Tillier decides that her mastectomy deformity is quite livable, doable, the prostheses just fine. With her new bra and the soft, malleable prostheses, no one knows her secret. She can walk and travel and even date without anyone knowing. After the cancer, the idea of additional surgery, further hospitalization, and office visits and worry might seem ridiculous.

Robert might get a call or a message from Sally, saying she's changed her mind. Or she might just never call again, the idea of even stepping in the building too much to bear.

Robert taps his pen on the chart, nodding. "I think that's the right decision for you. I do want to do a few additional measurements before you leave."

"Should I tell Dr. Jacobs?"

"I'll let her know," Robert says, thinking of Sally's surgeon,

Cindy Jacobs, her slightly befuddled gaze, her sturdy, competent hands. Sally has the best surgeon she could possibly have, and Robert wonders if Sally knows that. "She's a wonderful surgeon, and we'll talk more extensively after your surgery."

Mia stands up, and Robert's heart begins to speed up, a trill of adrenaline along his sternum.

"I'm going to go to the waiting room," she says, picking up her jacket. "You don't need me for this."

She smiles at her mother and then turns to Robert. Her eyes are—yes, they're amber, caramel, the color of the taste in his mouth.

"Thank you, Dr. Groszmann," she says, and then she opens the door, walks out, and closes it softly behind her.

Sally sits up and unties the front of her gown, turning her head away to look at the wall. "She's a writer, you know."

Robert slides his chair closer to her, pulling his tape measure from his right pocket. "Really? What does she write?"

"Novels. She's in the paper all the time. Once she was on *Good Morning America*." Sally's pulse beats so fast in the hollow of her neck, Robert wants to put his index finger there to calm her. Instead, he focuses on his tape measure, collarbone to nipple, nipple to nipple. Aureole dimension, chest wall, clavicle.

He rolls up his measure and puts it back in his pocket, pushing back toward the sink in his chair and washing his hands. "Can I get your daughter's books at any bookstore?"

Sally pulls her gown tight around her. "Oh yes. Amazon-dot-com. Barnes and Noble. Borders. She lives in Monte Veda and the bookstore there has her on constant display. Hometown girl makes good and all. But her stories are more—well, they might be geared more for women."

So am I, Robert wants to say, but doesn't. He is geared for women, but only temporarily, for short, quick bursts and then he's alone with his cat.

He moves away from the sink and looks at Sally Tillier. "You've thought about the type and stages of reconstruction?"

Sally nods. "What about that TRAM flap thingy?"

Robert shakes his head. "It won't work for you. You're too thin. Not enough material to work with."

Opening her mouth, Sally looks up at him, but then whatever words she had disappear. She shrugs. "Well, maybe by the time we do this, silicone will be back. Those breasts looked a bit more, well, real. I guess they feel more real, too."

"Some people think so."

He stands up and throws the paper towel in the garbage. "Sally, it's been a pleasure. I think you will be very happy with your choice. We will be in touch in a few months. I wish you the best with your surgery and treatment."

Robert takes her hand, shakes it, feeling her nerves and blood tingling in her palm.

"Thank you, Doctor," she says. "You've been very helpful."

Robert smiles and then leaves the office, Sally's chart held tight against his chest. The moment he's out in the hall, Carla comes over to him, notes in her hand, messages from five patients (*Jackie Lagalante already?*), a consult needed in dermatology and the ER, stat, messages from Drs. Jacobs, Sengupta, Cho, Walters. And in no time at all, Sally Tillier and Mia Alden leave his mind, cancer and novels and all.

❧

"Rob, listen. You're not seeing the big picture," Jack Slater says, sitting back in the booth at Primo. Robert has known Jack since their first year of college at Berkeley, back when Jack was skinny and acne prone. Now, thanks to Accutane and Club Sport Athletic Club, he's the joy of all his female patients.

They've finished a very late dinner and are now drinking

brandy. Jack used to work for Inland, where Robert still works, but has since moved on to private practice, seeing patients in a large, royal suite of offices in Alamo, an expensive bedroom community.

"What picture would that be?" Robert is used to Jack's largesse after a huge meal, his expansive discussion, his sweeping comments, his need to try to understand Robert. Jack always wants to talk about big ideas, turning each and every conversation into proof of how Jack has lived his life 100 percent right, and how all Robert has to do is hurry and catch up.

"Our work. It's art. It's the intersection of art and science. How people look reflects how they feel inside. If you change their appearance, you can change their soul."

"Oh, Christ. Jack! Do you hear yourself? If you feel that way, you have a demented God complex. If you want to do art, go get a potter's wheel. What we do is about helping people."

Jack sips his drink, smiling. "Helping them do what? Feel better about themselves?"

"Yeah."

"So if they feel better about themselves, doesn't that affect their psyches, their souls?"

Robert pushes his hair back and shakes his head. "If I reattach someone's finger, don't you think that person will feel better about himself than he did the moment the jigsaw cut it off?"

"Maybe. But he's only had his finger off for, what? An hour tops? A woman with a big nose or huge jaw will have had that since birth. Her whole personality has been formed based on the fact of this defect. She'll have learned to hide it. She'll have endured teasing. Think what's been affected. Her self-esteem, self-love, self-value. She will have found ways to relate to lovers based on it. Rightly or not, her parents may have even treated her differently because of it. So when I do a rhinoplasty, I can take away her need to hide, to fear, to loathe. I lift that dark shroud off her personality. I change her."

"But patients don't seem to know where to stop," Robert says. "And some of us don't, either. The line is so blurred between what is necessary and what is almost a crime. If we aren't working with people who are sick, who truly need us, how can we call ourselves doctors? How can we even talk about what we do when there are those ultimate-makeover shows?"

"The outer and inner are the same," Jack says, smiling broadly, the old conversation having arrived at his favorite curve. "To work on the average or ugly or annoying outer is to help the inner made sick because of it."

Robert's stomach churns. He's heard this argument his whole career, even believed it himself for long stretches before something or someone would rip an enormous hole in it. For months and often years, he would be lulled by the idea that he was helping people, perfecting them, giving them the lives they really wanted. Then, in an instant, as he stood over a patient, sucking out micro bits of fat from her face, he would see that he was perpetuating the shallow, superficial view the entire world seemed to be embracing these days, giving false hope, covering up reality, pandering to an impossible view of beauty.

And then? And then something really awful happened.

"Do we," Robert says, putting down his glass, "always have to talk about work?"

Jack raises his eyebrows, and Robert knows that he shouldn't have tried to change the subject.

"What else is there?" Jacks says. But he's smiling.

"Oh, I don't know. Your family. Tina. The state of the economy. Our new governor. Anything." *Anything but Leslie,* Robert thinks.

Jack sighs. "God, I wish we could smoke in here."

"A cigar might start a riot."

"You're right."

"About what? The riot or the conversation?"

"Both. Listen, what's going on with Leslie? You haven't said a word about her."

Robert shakes his head. "You couldn't help yourself, could you?"

Jack rolls his eyes. "What? You think that you can avoid this conversation? I know we've had it before a few times, but Rob. Shit. Tell me what happened this time."

"You're trying to kill me, aren't you? You want me dead. You want all my patients."

"I don't need your patients. I want your house. And if you don't ever hook up with another woman, I'll be your next of kin. Don't forget to tell your lawyer."

Robert takes his last sip and pushes the glass away. "Leslie and I didn't work out."

"She was a great girl. I see her sometimes at the gym."

For a second, Robert looks around for the waiter, needing another drink. The waiter sees him and pretends not to, turning his back, too close to closing time to offer up another drink. Robert sighs.

"She wanted different things. She—"

Jack snorts. "Don't tell me. She wanted a commitment. You know, a relationship. God forbid, marriage?"

"Not everyone is as lucky as you are. Not every woman can be Tina."

"Even Tina isn't Tina sometimes. No one is perfect, Rob."

"Haven't you said you are?"

Jack thrums the table with his fingers and glares in mock anger at Robert. The waiter walks up and clears away the empty glasses, a spoon, mumbles something, and leaves the check. Jack takes it, and Robert lets him because it's his turn.

"Well, you could give a woman longer than a year. Or give yourself longer. You might actually get used to her."

"I . . ." Robert starts and then stops. Jack stares at him, and Robert looks at the tablecloth flaked with bread crumbs. He wants to finish the sentence, but he knows it will sound corny, especially to Jack.

"You could try to get over this strange year thing you've got going. Push through to thirteen months or so and see what happens. You might just grow accustomed—"

"Don't you dare start singing that song from *My Fair Lady*," Robert says, holding up his hand. During procedures, Jack listens to musicals—*Oklahoma!*, *South Pacific*, *Camelot*—and belts out the tunes he loves best.

"I've grown accustomed . . ." Jack begins.

Robert tosses a sugar cube at Jack. "Knock it off."

"I'll stop when you have someone to grow accustomed to." Jack throws the cube in the middle of the table and then hands the check back to the waiter.

Robert pushes his hair back and spreads a hand on the tabletop, noticing pepper in between his fingers. "I did meet someone interesting this week."

Jack's eyes widen. "Really? Where?"

"A patient's daughter. She even sent me a thank-you card. But—"

"But what? It's not like you'd be dating a patient. She's a patient once removed. No infringement on the Hippocratic oath. No sexual harassment policy broken. No code of conduct infraction."

Robert rubs his forehead. "It won't work. It can't, and I did something not great. I plugged her into Inland's database and looked her up. She's a member. Married. Two kids. A husband. She must have eczema, too. Scripts for Elidel and Valisone."

"You are a little twisted," Jack says, taking the check back from the waiter, signing the slip, and putting his credit card back in his wallet. "Good to see. I didn't know you had it in you. You usually wait for a woman to find you and bang you over the head with a club and drag you back to your cave."

"Funny." Robert stands, taking his jacket off the chair and tucking in his shirt.

"So what else did you find out? What other confidential info did you expose?" Jack gets up, too, and puts his wallet in his pocket. He and Jack put on their coats and walk through the dining area to the door, pushing out into the evening. They stand side by side, facing the street. A valet takes Jack's ticket and disappears.

"So?" Jack asks.

"One of her kids was in the rehab program."

"I hope it worked," Jack says. "Are you sure it wasn't her?"

"It said adolescent program in her file."

"I hope she's older than that. Otherwise, we'll have to have dinner on visiting days at Santa Rita."

The valet drives up with Jack's Porsche Carerra, and Jack hands him a five-dollar bill. "Come on, I'll drive you to your car. I can't believe you still won't pay for a valet."

Robert shakes his head and holds out his hand to shake Jack's. "No, I'm going to walk up to Bonanza Books. I need something to read."

Jack takes Robert's hand and then pulls him to himself, giving Robert a hug. Jack laughs, the familiar, comforting sound in Robert's ear.

"Try to avoid spying on anyone else this month. And stay away from married women."

"Like you ever did." Robert pulls back, pats his friend's arm.

"I know. But in the long run, did any of those women work out?"

"You were lucky to get away with your life after what's-her-name. Maryann," Robert says. "And anyway, who's talking about a long run?"

Jack opens his car door and laughs again. "Oh, yeah. I forgot I was talking to you. See you later, man."

The sound of the Porsche is guttural, thick, the sound of power, and Jack looks out from behind the windshield and winks. Accelerating, he roars off down the road, the engine vibrating, echoing off the buildings.

"Sweet ride," the valet says.

Robert shrugs and walks away, saying "Mia Alden" under his breath.

≋

There is still more than an hour before closing, but Robert is the only one in Bonanza Books, save the young man behind the counter, who looks up when Robert walks in, then nods and goes back to his magazine, one of those with the strange, large-eyed cartoon characters on the cover.

Robert used to like to read, but in recent years, he's been so busy with his work that the only things he reads for pleasure are *JAMA* and *Lancet*. Even when he's on vacation, he's reading papers on the efficacy of radiosurgery on skin lesions, or the new breakthroughs in rhytidoplasty. But back in college and on his summer breaks when he worked in the lab at UCSF, tending the mice on hormone therapies, he would read whatever he could get his hands on. Home decorating magazines, *Reader's Digest,* poetry journals. Once he even read a romance novel a doctor had hidden under her lab coat, something about a woman in a castle and her vampire lover. It didn't matter. Words were words. Words were entertainment. Words kept him from living alone in his brain.

He still doesn't know what he was trying to avoid.

"Do ya need some help?" the young man suddenly asks.

Robert realizes that he's been standing still in front of the sign that reads NEW FICTION.

He turns to the young man, whose frizzy hair is a wildflower of dark curls around his face. One giant pimple beats on his chin.

"I'm looking for the books by a particular author. Mia Alden."

The young man points to shelves that run along the back of the store. "In literature. Under *A*."

Robert wants to roll his eyes, to tell the young man that he's known how to alphabetize since before kindergarten, but he sees the young man is used to questions like this. *Where is the fiction?* In the fiction section. *Where are the children's books?* Over there, in the children's section. *Where are the magazines?* In the magazine rack.

"Thanks," Robert says, walking toward the far left of the shelf, where a large, black handwritten *A* is taped to the wood.

Abbot, Addonizio, and then Alden, Mia, right before Browne, Susan. Robert cocks his head before he reaches for the books, seeing the smooth spines, the titles in the same font. He reaches for one and pulls it off the shelf, the slick cover sliding in his hands. Flipping it up, he looks at the cover and reads the title. *The Daisy Plate Incident.* Already he hates the story because the title is ridiculous. *The Daisy Plate Incident?* But then he remembers the romance novel, turning the book over. Maybe the title is weird, but there are all sorts of accolades on the back, "Riveting," "A thoughtful take on the excruciating joy of childhood," "A must read," and "An author to watch." Famous authors and reviewers have said these things about Mia and her work, and when he looks at the bottom of the back cover, he sees her picture.

She's done something to her hair since this photo was taken, chopped it off, because here, it's long and flowing over her shoulders. She's leaning over, her chin in her hand, and she *looks* happy, pretty, sexy in her recline.

Mia Alden, the bio reads, *is the author of* Sacramento by Train *and* Beat. *A professor of literature at the University of California, Berkeley, she lives in Northern California with her husband and two sons.*

He can't help it, but his body tingles at the thought of her academic job. He's a snob, and he's always known it. Sometimes he can't understand how anyone can live being a pizza-delivery person or a ticket taker or a cashier. He wants to feel that they—just like him—take pride in what they do, wake up knowing that it's possible they will make a difference in something or for someone. But he doesn't believe they do. No matter how he thinks about it, he can feel their despair as they mop floors and collect bedpans and take his two dollars as he crosses the Bay Bridge. Like the poor kid behind the counter, who works here at night and dreams of what? Being a rock star? A famous poet? An astronaut? Robert can feel the kid's impatience and irritation all the way across the bookstore.

But here is what he knows so far: Mia Alden is a professor and a novelist. She's also married and has a drug addict child. Her mother has cancer. Her sister is a pathologist. Her breasts are hers, natural, large, pushing up out of her sweater. Somewhere on her body, her skin itches. Her eyes make him taste caramel. And there was something in her words and ferocious blush that makes him feel weak now, in the knees, just like the clichés he read in that long-ago romance novel.

Robert pulls Mia's two other novels off the shelf and stacks them in his hands, walking toward the young man at the desk. He's going to read tonight, even though he has surgery in the morning. He's going to start with her first novel, the better-titled *Sacramento by Train*. He's going to find out about Mia Alden the only way he honestly can.

☙

Because his parents died in successive years when Robert was in college, he was well-off early, long before he'd finished his residency and begun his practice. In fact, unlike Jack and most of Robert's other colleagues, Robert was able to complete his course work and extra training without worrying about repaying student loans. He had no loans. He was free and clear from the start.

So when he was hired by Inland, he bought this house in Walnut Creek, an old adobe rancher on the historical registry with a ceramic-tile roof. Built in the traditional Mexican style, the house has an expansive courtyard in the middle, filled with ferns and hibiscus, a fountain, and Spanish tile. The adobe bricks are so thick and dense that in the dead heat of summer, his house stays cool; when the winter fog pulses over the hills and fills in the valleys with chill, his house stays warm. He knows that at least four of his former girlfriends didn't want to break up with him because of the house, staying with him despite silent evenings and separate beds.

He'd come home from work to see Margaret smoothing her hand over the granite counters in the kitchen, or Joy sitting in the overstuffed leather chair, reading in the warm yellow light of his Tiffany lamps. Dara would be in the courtyard, planting a princess flower bush, and Leslie—just last week—would be at his large oak desk, surfing the Internet.

"You're late," Leslie would say, her hands on the keyboard, eyes on the screen. "Where were you?"

"I . . ." he'd begin, but then he wouldn't want to explain anything to her, not anymore. And really, now he's not sure she really wanted him to.

Robert sees that he was no more than a means to comfort and stability, an okay man with a great place to hang out. All of them, even Leslie, might not have noticed if he disappeared.

And it is possible Robert didn't take other jobs because of the house. Despite tantalizing calls from heads of departments from other hospitals (Boston, Macon, Phoenix, Chicago), he said no. He said no to Jack's practice, too. He said no to just about everything.

Now he sits up in bed, *Sacramento by Train* open, his cat, Phyllis, curled at his feet. Every page or two, he flips the book in his hands to look at Mia's photo and read her bio, as if either might have changed since the time before. Then he goes back to the first

chapter, which turns into the second and then third. Phyllis un-
curls, stands, stretches, and jumps off the bed. The night slides on.
Robert keeps reading.

❧

In the morning as Robert stands over Dee Swayze, inserting the
breast extender under her skin (amply saved by Cindy Jacobs), he
thinks about what you can find out about someone from reading
what the person wrote. Oh, he knows about literary criticism, and
how you can't assume the writer and the narrator are the same. But
a writer leaves clues.

"Done here," he says, handing the nurse the scalpel.

The nurse, Rachel, rolls her eyes and puts the scalpel down. "I
can see." But then she hands him the suture line, and Robert begins to close the incision.

Here's what he knows. Because Marla, one of the main characters in *Sacramento by Train,* is a lesbian and a good person and almost a hero, Robert knows that Mia is liberal. Open. Most likely
she votes Democrat or Independent or Green Party.

Mia also approves of public transportation. Marla meets the
other main characters, Rafael and Susan, on a commuter train to
Sacramento, the three of their lives twisting together after they
share a table and a cup of coffee. There are paragraphs about the
freeway, the clog of carbon in the air, the sadness of our isolated
lives behind the wheel.

He was sure that he caught of whiff of mother anger, the pain
of not being approved of. Susan isn't beautiful enough for her
mother's taste, is often being told to cut, tint, streak, dye her hair,
or pluck her eyebrows or lose fifteen pounds. Robert can envision
Sally Tillier saying all those things, though for a novel, he assumes
that a lifetime of criticism has been condensed for the story's sake.
But he's not sure what will happen next with Susan and her

mother—on the last pages he reads, Susan finally gets mad, says what she's been trying to say for years, which sends her mother weeping to her bedroom. He doesn't know how Mia will tie up these loose ends before the novel ends.

The next is sex. Marla and Rafael and Susan have a lot of it. Susan even has sex with Marla once, sort of by accident, during a drunken, snowy night in a ski lodge. But Susan isn't upset or concerned about it. When she goes home, she makes love with Rafael and considers the differences of the two bodies she'd just licked and kissed and slid next to, the way both are equally interesting, the parts that rise and fall, the tastes, the textures. Rafael and Susan love each other, but it's a kind of love based on friendship and the past. And their sex is married sex, the kind that has not been tended to. Susan, as far as he can tell, wants to leave her husband not because he can't bring her to orgasm, but because she can't explain to him how big the world feels, how she wants to touch everyone, everything. How she can almost imagine her life arcing wide and out, away from everything she has known before. Rafael is having an affair with his secretary, a secret he imagines he's kept from Susan, but she digs through his dirty laundry, smells his briefs, finds long red hairs on the inside of his button-down shirts.

In one terrible scene where Susan clutches the hair and the shirt, she begs Rafael to go to counseling and he refuses, slams the bedroom door, drives off to his mistress, though only the reader and not Susan knows this.

Robert can't go this far, but he wonders, hopes, really, that Susan is Mia. Mia has just all right married sex and wants more.

"Okay. She's done." He takes off his gloves and mask.

He's not finished with the novel yet, but he feels Mia's themes in his head, even if he doesn't understand them completely. Love cannot be sliced up into tidy pieces or be contained by rules or religion or culture. It flows over the lines, drenches everything. Love is more important than anything, and once you have love, everything is better. The worst mistake a person can make is to deny love, to push it away, to let the feelings float into the air like so much carbon dioxide.

"Amazing work," a new resident says, and Robert shrugs, rinses his hands, thinking of how all his girlfriends finally left his house, one by one, their backs to him as they walked down the front path toward their cars. He never followed them, not one, not ever. He wouldn't know how. He doesn't know how to get what he wants. He's always stayed inside the lines. For everything. Except once.

FOUR

Mia

Mia, her sisters, Katherine and Dahlia, and Ford sit in the Inland waiting room reserved for friends and families of surgical patients. Sally's neighbor Nydia Nuñez has come and gone, leaving a basket of chocolate chip cookies. Kenzie has just left, as well, promising to call later in the day.

Before she stood up, she turned and whispered in Mia's ear, "I've found a source for some pot. For when your mother does chemo. It makes the nausea go away. Just let me know."

Mia laughs, thinking how strange it would be to welcome that resiny plant back into her life when just a short time ago, she spent all her energy trying to keep it away. Where are all those boys that used to come home with Lucien, slightly dazed and clearly—at least in hindsight—high? She could just call one of them, say, "It's Lucien's mom. And look, don't bother lying to me now. I need some smoke."

No, Kenzie is right. Someone else should supply them now.

Her mother, sick as a dog from chemo, will need it, will probably be happy to take anything that will make her feel better. Mia can't believe it's come to this, sitting in another hospital waiting room, stuck in a chair until someone comes to give them all news. Mia knows what she wants to hear, that the surgery has been a

complete success, the cancer is small, contained, a breeze to handle. "I am certain she won't need chemo," Cindy Jacobs says in this
fantasy. "It's a miracle."

Mia knows that doctors never say things like this, don't wander
around shouting, "She's been cured!"

But Sally has to be okay. Mia knows that. She looks at Katherine and Dahlia and sees from their faces that they feel the same
way, too.

Ford stands up and walks to the water fountain, and Mia
watches his tight, slim form under his wool work pants, the muscles in his back under his cotton shirt. From the moment she met
him, Mia always appreciated Ford's body, his smooth, toned muscles, his flat stomach. But in the past two years, he's seemed to
work harder at it, going to the gym every morning before work and
sometimes coming home late smelling like shampoo. Why is he
working out more lately? For her? To stave off middle age? To find
himself in muscles that he was beginning to forget? A basic fear of
death?

"Had to get in a workout," he'll say, dropping his duffel bag in
the hallway. "Time stops for no man."

Katherine catches Mia's gaze on Ford's backside, shakes her
head, and stands up.

"I'm going to go check at the desk." Katherine plops the basket
of cookies in Mia's lap. "I knew I should have scrubbed in."

"Could you really have done that?" Dahlia asks. She puts down
her *Elle* magazine and takes a cookie from Mia's lap.

Katherine shrugs. "I don't have privileges, but I'm sure I could
have forced the issue. I'll be right back."

Katherine stalks out, and Mia looks at Dahlia. "She can force
just about anything she wants."

Dahlia laughs and then takes a big bite of cookie, the crumbs
falling on her magazine.

The scent of the cookies wavers up from the basket, a buttery, sugary waft. Mia shoves them off her lap and onto the chair next to Dahlia. Ever since she began her Internet search about breast cancer, she's learned that overweight women have a higher incidence of breast cancer. Of all cancers. Of just about any disease. In the days prior to Sally's surgery, she's read about the tests and studies and reports, and knows, clearly, that she's at risk. For one, her own mother has cancer. And Mia has a good twenty-five pounds too many on her body. And too much fat equals too much estrogen, which heightens the risk. Mia is a cancer bull's-eye. Even now, something could be growing in her, a mad cell replicating out of control, spinning into a tumor fueled by fat.

Mia's lost two pounds, but as she looks at Ford's rear as he bends over the water fountain, she realizes that's how much her shoes weigh. She forgot to take them off the first time she got on the scale.

Ford stands and turns around. He's left work and has to go back to San Francisco to tie up some last-minute deal with people from the Pay Rite account. Often, Mia has asked him to explain exactly what he does. As he carefully goes over the job that he's had for the past ten years, Mia thinks she understands it on a basic level. He and his partner, Karen, work with companies to manage employees' stock options. But how they deal with the stock options (she knows what stocks are, but the *options* part is still a question) is what Mia doesn't understand.

"So we work with the employees to set up accounts so that they can buy and sell when they need to. Invest, divest," he said, and as he went on explaining to her the services he and Karen offer, Mia felt her mind wander, nodding when she had to and smiling when he was done.

One day, she thinks, she will really listen. She'll take notes. She'll totally understand.

Katherine stomps back in, her black hair a cape behind her. "She's almost through."

"She's okay?" Ford asks, rolling down his sleeves and buttoning them.

"Seems so. The news from the operating room is good."

Ford looks at Mia, and she can see what he's saying with his eyes. He wants to go because it's good news. Mia wants him to stay because she's not sure it will be. But he's adjusting his tie, fixing his collar. He's going to leave unless she throws herself down on the floor and begs him not to, and she won't do that here, not in front of Katherine.

Ford walks over to Mia and bends down to kiss her on the head. "I'm going to head back. My cell phone's on. Call me when she comes out of it. Call me for anything. I'll be back as soon as I can."

Mia sighs, nods, and looks up at him. For more than half her life, he is who she's turned to for comfort, for help, for company. And he won't stay. "Fine. I'll let you know."

He kisses her again, puts a hand on Katherine's shoulder, and waves to Dahlia. Then he's nothing but a sound of footsteps in the hallway.

"He couldn't wait to get out of here." Katherine sits down and crosses her legs.

Mia breathes in sharply and feels a back molar with her tongue. For a second, she imagines she hears Ford's footsteps coming back toward the waiting room.

"He's got better things to do, I guess," Katherine says. "No keeping him away from the office, not even for a sick mother-in-law."

"You're such a joy to be around," Mia says. "Can you really blame him?"

"Cut it out." Dahlia doesn't look up from her *Elle*. "Knock it off."

Mia sits back and thinks of what Dahlia said. *Cut it out.* That's what Mia would like to do, cut this past month out of the year. She can see the big scissors she would use to get rid of the entire month of February. Maybe she'd cut even more, going all the way back to . . . she's not sure. Maybe three, four years, five. That way she could get rid of Sally's cancer, Lucien's addiction, Ford's inattention, her own boredom. But then she'd be getting rid of good things, too. Days of happiness. A novel or two. Quiet family dinners. Okay, but there are weeks she'd like to get rid of, for sure. Whole days. Solid hours. And then *knock it off*. What would she knock off? There's nothing to really hit except Katherine, of course. Katherine and her big mouth.

"I just really hate this," Katherine says.

"You hate not being in control." Mia looks at her sister, seeing, finally, Katherine's worry.

"Maybe."

"No maybe. A big yes."

"Yes, then. Yes."

Dahlia closes her magazine again as Sally's doctor, Cindy Jacobs, walks in the room. Unlike doctors on all the television shows who are covered in blood and gore by the end of the hour-long show, Cindy looks like she just put on her scrubs, the green cotton smooth and fresh. Mia resolves to ask Katherine if doctors change before coming out to see the family, as if to prove that it was all truly a miracle, an operation done by mind control.

Dahlia stands up, rushes forward. Mia can see her arms are covered in gooseflesh.

"Is she okay?" Dahlia asks.

Cindy Jacobs nods, smiles. "The surgery went very well. I'm very pleased. Her blood pressure wasn't an issue, and she had very little bleeding. She's in recovery right now."

Katherine doesn't smile. "Any complications?"

"None. Everything looks great. Of course, we'll have to wait for the lab reports to get the complete picture."

"That's so wonderful," Mia says.

Cindy looks at Mia, smiling. "Your mother gave me your latest novel this morning before the surgery. I'm looking forward to reading it."

Katherine snorts and shakes her head. Mia stands and walks over to Cindy Jacobs.

"I hope you like it. But thank you, Doctor. We really appreciate your hard work." She holds out her hand and takes Cindy's soft, small one in hers. Cindy's skin feels as smooth and overwashed as Dr. Groszmann's did, the slick skin of a surgeon.

"I'll let you know about the lab reports. And the nurse will come and get you when your mother is out of recovery and in her room."

"Thank you," Dahlia says, and Katherine nods. But Mia can see that all sorts of judgments and ideas have filled Katherine's head. Right now, Mia knows, Katherine is trying to figure out how she herself can do the lab tests. She wants the answers now.

Cindy Jacobs leaves the waiting room, her surgical coat billowing behind her, and Katherine plops down in the chair.

"It will be hours, if not days, before we know anything. They should let me in that lab. I wouldn't even charge them."

Mia rubs her eyes. She picked up Sally, Katherine, and Dahlia at five thirty in the morning to get them to the hospital by six. Sally was admitted, prepped, wheeled into surgery, and now, at one in the afternoon, Mia feels the sleepless night before, the quick, stale doughnut and bad coffee she grabbed in the hospital cafeteria, the irritation crawling across her skin at Katherine's bossiness and her sister's total inability to appreciate anything Mia has ever done.

"Why don't you go ask?" Mia says suddenly. "Go see if you can."

Katherine turns to her and doesn't say anything.

"Go find Dr. Jacobs and ask her if you can get in on the lab work. Tell her that you graduated at the top of your class and have a job so much better than hers and are paid three times as much. Tell her that you can diagnose anything, and do so faster than any pathologist who would work at a crappy HMO like Inland. Go on,

Katherine. Go make a really good impression on all the staff here. I'm sure that will make Mom's stay that much more enjoyable. And it will make it so nice for Mom and me when we come back for follow-up visits. You'll have already conveniently left."

As Mia speaks, Katherine's mouth opens slowly, until she is gaping. When Mia finishes, Katherine says, "Fuck you."

"Well, fuck you, too. You march in here and want to control the entire process. If you were that concerned, you could have come about a month ago. Helped us out with all the decisions. Mom and I watched videos and read stuff on the Internet and called references. If you really wanted to help, you should have thought about it when I called to tell you Mom had cancer."

"Stop it!" Dahlia says, picking up her magazine and rolling it in her palms as if she wants to whack both Mia and Katherine. "For God's sake. We'll find out about Mom's test results soon enough. Nothing either of you is doing now will make it better."

Dahlia throws the magazine across the room and begins to cry. Mia closes her eyes. That's what they should all be doing. Crying. Not fighting. She stands up and walks to Dahlia, sits in the chair next to her, and pats her knee.

"Sorry, Dahls. Sorry. Look, we're all exhausted. I'll go get something for us at the cafeteria." Mia leans down and kisses Dahlia's cheek.

Dahlia nods, and Mia can still see her as she was as a child. When Sally and Katherine and Mia fought, yelling or stomping out of a room, Dahlia would huddle somewhere—the end of the couch, the corner of the living room, behind the hallway door— her face pale, her eyes wide, convinced that this argument meant the end of everything.

Mia stands straight and sighs. She's the big sister and should know better, especially all these years later.

"Look," she says to Katherine, "Mom is going to be all right. We studied up. All the doctors saw her. Even her plastic surgeon told us he didn't think there was lymph involvement. We have to be optimistic."

Katherine nods and then picks up a magazine, a tattered travel magazine from the late '90s. Mia watches her sister's face, her pressed lips, tight jaw. All of this is too much, even for Katherine. "Fine," Katherine says, wiping at her eyes quickly.

"Okay. Good. I'll be back." Mia picks up her purse and walks out of the waiting room. She needs to brush her teeth and wash her face. No, what she really wants is a bath. Then sleep. She wants to stay in bed until her mother's chemo is over, emerging to good news and sunny skies.

"Ms. Alden?"

Mia almost jumps and then stops walking. She tries to breathe, but her heart seems to have grown enormous, blocking off her windpipe. *What is it?* she thinks. *What is this person going to tell me? What has happened to my mother?* Her skin pricks, hair stands up at the back of her head. For a second, she imagines she is going to throw up all over the shiny linoleum.

Turning slowly, Mia almost falls. It's only Dr. Groszmann. He wasn't in this surgery. He doesn't know anything. Or does he? She puts her hand against the wall.

"What is it?"

His face shifts, his smile flattens. "Oh, no. I don't have news. I just— I just wanted to say hello."

Mia closes her eyes for a moment. In a rush, she can see her fear flume up and out of her body slowly, and in its place comes the feeling that overtook her in Dr. Groszmann's office. The hideous pulse of adrenaline, the blush over all her skin, the giddy nerves crackling in her bones.

He walks toward her. She can hear the clack of his black cowboy boots on the clean floor. "Are you all right?"

She nods and then opens her eyes. He's still there, closer now. If she wanted, she could reach out and stroke his cheek.

"I'm sorry. I just thought you might be the nurse."

"The surgery is over, isn't it?"

"Yes, it is. Dr. Jacobs just came in to talk to us." Mia runs her hand through her hair. "I don't know why, but I keep expecting bad news. Like it's impossible for it to be okay."

"It was good news from the surgery, right?" He watches her with his pale blue eyes, and Mia has the urge to move even closer to him, slide her cheek against his, press against his skin until she believes it's good news, too.

Instead, she shrugs. "I hope. I was just going to run down to the cafeteria for some coffee and fruit or something. Everyone in the waiting room is going through a blood-sugar low."

"Surgery is very stressful for everyone," he says.

"But maybe I shouldn't leave. She might come out of recovery."

Dr. Groszmann shakes his head. "No, you have forty minutes at least. Probably more. And she's not alone. Nurses are with her constantly until she's moved to her room."

"Okay." Mia wants to believe him, and she looks at his shoulder, wishing she could rest her head there. Just for a minute, enough time to catch her breath before she has to move into her mother's recuperation. He might be lean as a wild cat, but she can imagine how comforting it would feel to lay her cheek on his chest and have him say, "It will be all right. Your mother will be just fine." She would never want to move again, stuck to his good news like desperate glue.

"Let me walk with you," he says, and he's taking her arm, moving her along the hall. For some reason, she looks back, and sees that Katherine has stepped out into the hall and is watching them. Even from here, Mia can feel Katherine's slicing disapproval.

In the cafeteria, Mia buys a cup of coffee, two bottled waters, three bags of pretzels, three Baby Ruth bars, and three oranges. The cashier finds her a brown bag for everything but the coffee, which she begins to sip after she hands the woman her money. Dr. Groszmann waits for her at a table, a cup of coffee before him.

"Can you sit for a minute?" he asks. "I promise not to keep you here for long."

Mia looks at the clock on the wall and tries to ignore what her skin tells her. *Sit,* it whines. *Find a way to touch him. You need him. He's lovely. Just forget about your mother for a teeny, tiny second.*

"Okay," she says. "For a bit." She sits down and puts the bag on a free chair, keeping her eyes low. She has to force herself into looking at him, her eyes heavier than guilt. Dragging her gaze up from the table, she stops at his mouth, then moves higher to his eyes. "Thanks for coming with me, Dr. Groszmann. I'm so distracted, I probably would have gotten lost."

"Robert."

"Okay. Robert. Then no more Ms. Alden. I don't even know who that is. It's Mia."

He smiles, his teeth even and white. But not too white, not lasered, not bleached, just naturally beautiful. "It's better than 'Hey, you.' Or what do the kids say? 'Yo!' "

"That's not it. It's 'Yo, dude!' "

"Of course. How could I forget?"

"But," Mia says, crossing her legs under the table, "no matter what you said to me in the hallway, I probably would have jumped a mile."

"Like I said earlier, it's hard to have someone you love go through surgery. Sometimes I think it's harder on the family."

She smiles, sips her coffee; her heart lurches against her ribs.

"Thanks for the card," he says abruptly.

Mia almost chokes, managing to stifle the sound in her throat. She's forgotten about the thank-you card she sent him after her mother's second appointment, digging around in her desk for stationery appropriate for the occasion. She doesn't even remember what she said, but she remembers that she sent it mostly for herself. *Thank you,* she wrote, *for making my mother feel comfortable.* What she might have said was *Thank you for making me feel something other than fear. Thank you for making me blush. Thank you for blushing along with me.*

She didn't tell her mother she sent it—she didn't even tell Kenzie.

"You— I mean, thank you. You really made my mother feel better."

Robert looks down at his coffee, holds it in both of his hands. "I was wondering . . ." He stops, turns the cup. The coffee stays completely flat, as if its world isn't spinning. "I know this isn't . . . could I talk with you? E-mail you?"

Two things happen. First, she sees Ford, as he was today, by her side, waiting for news about Sally. She flashes to the moment when Lucien graduated from high school, his arms held wide, his gown like long green wings behind him. And then she sees Harper holding on to the doorjamb, his car keys in his hand, walking in the door with a story about school.

The second thing is that she wants to laugh. All Robert has done is ask if he can e-mail her. She remembers a story Kenzie told her once. A man asked her out for lunch, and Kenzie said, "Oh, I couldn't possibly. I have a boyfriend."

The man looked at her, raised his eyebrows, and said, "I didn't ask you to marry me. I just thought you might like a hamburger."

So Mia doesn't laugh. She looks at Robert, tries not to blink too much. He is brave, braver than Mia. As she watches him, he watches her back. He lets go of his coffee cup and pushes an imaginary flyaway hair away from his face.

Mia reaches for her purse. She unsnaps the top flap and digs around in a side pocket, pulling out a business card.

"This looks kind of cheesy. It has my upcoming novel cover on the front. But my e-mail's there. My Web site." She hands it to him and they touch for a second, her skin giving her a quick, hot thank-you of gooseflesh. "Writers have to be salespeople these days if they want to stay writers."

"What do you have to do? How do you sell yourself?" Robert holds the card carefully, as if he expects a sudden wind to carry it off.

"Oh," Mia says. "Go on the circuit. Talk at writers' conferences. Go to bookstores where the audience will be the manager, my mother, and sometimes my husband."

Mia feels the heavy *d* of *husband* on her tongue. She stops talking for a moment so she can breathe, pretend to be interested in her Styrofoam cup.

"I'm married."

Robert nods. "I know."

Something zings in her chest, fear or joy, she can't be sure. "How?"

"I'm reading *Sacramento by Train*. Your bio mentions your husband."

Mia doesn't even try to hide the blood rushing to her face this time. "Did my mother give you the book? She gave one to Dr. Jacobs. Maybe she thinks you'll all be so impressed that you'll cut just a little bit more carefully. She actually does have a stack by her front door. I swear she gives them out like candy."

He smiles, watches her. She imagines he is following the progress of her blush, his gaze slowly sliding over her face.

"No, Sally just told me about your writing. I bought it myself."

He blinks, and Mia realizes her mouth is open.

"Wow. Thanks."

"One more night and I'll know if Susan leaves Rafael."

Mia turns to look out the large bank of windows. Outside, a new storm has pushed over the hills, a dark wall of cloudy water covering Walnut Creek. She wants to tell him that she doesn't even know if Susan ever left Rafael. While writing the last page, she wanted to fling herself into the imaginary future of the story and ask Susan that very question. "Will you leave? Did you leave?" But Susan never answered, and now, three novels later, she no longer speaks to Mia, not even at night.

Mia turns back to Robert. "Maybe so, maybe not. I'm not giving away anything. You'll have to read all the way to the end."

"In college, I used to have the bad habit of reading the last page before even starting a book. That way, I'd know how it would turn out before I got there."

Again she finds her mouth open. "That's cheating. A betrayal. Horrible. Don't you dare do that with my book."

He raises a hand, the smooth, overwashed palm toward her. "I promise. No back-page reading."

For a moment, they both watch each other, and Mia feels some kind of communication going on between them. It's as if they aren't civilized, a doctor and a writer, but are instead cave people, talking through scent and smell and taste. Her skin is singing to his, even though he's covered in the green scrubs and white cotton coat that are everywhere in this cafeteria. His energy comes through his clothes, over the table, bumping at her, lapping at her in waves. His eyes seem to change color, going from pale blue to navy as the clouds outside shift from gray to black. She can smell the soap he uses and uses and uses all day long, can feel what his hands would feel like on her face, can taste the tips of his fingers.

Plates clatter. Someone drops a glass. A couple sitting next to them laughs at a joke she doesn't hear. People walk by; the smell of overcooked Mexican food slides through the air. Rain begins to pound against the windows. Mia wonders if she can move from this moment, knowing that it's important, crucial, and confusing.

Finally, she looks at the bag of food on the chair next to her. "I better get back. My mom should be out of recovery soon."

He nods, pushes his chair back, stands. Mia grabs the bag and begins to move her chair, but then he's helping her, pulling the chair, taking her elbow.

"What does it mean?" he asks.

Mia thinks to ask him what he's talking about, but she knows. And if she could, she'd say that she has no idea what anything means. She breathes in, ready to say something, but Robert fills in the silence.

"I picked up your other books, too. But that third one. It's the strangest title. *The Daisy Plate Incident*."

They start walking toward the exit. She shakes her head. "Say you and my editor and the rest of the world. Trust me. It will all make sense eventually."

"I hope so," Robert says, and they walk out of the cafeteria into the dark hospital hallway.

Robert says good-bye to her at the bank of elevators, his hand on his topcoat pocket where he's put her card. And when she's back in the waiting room, Katherine and Dahlia peeling oranges, the room a swirl of citrus, she realizes she didn't ask him one single thing about himself.

❧

Sally is groggy; her eyes stay shut even as she talks to them. Mia expected Sally's chest to be swathed with a thick bundle of bandages, but it's covered only by a thin bandage and her gown, though tubes and monitors dangle from her body. Underneath the bandage, though, Mia knows there are two scars, the wicked, bloody gashes made by the knife.

Mia is scared to get too close, but Katherine pushes in next to the bed, pulls up the blanket gently, examines the drains by Sally's underarms.

"Mom," Katherine says. "Mom? How do you feel? Can you tell me?"

A nurse adjusting Sally's IV rolls her eyes at Katherine's bedside manner, and Mia wants to laugh. But she doesn't, trying to be nice now, because even though Robert is only going to e-mail her—all they are going to do is talk—she needs the good karma.

"Fine," Sally whispers.

Dahlia pulls the blanket tight over Sally's feet. "The doctor said everything went so well, Mom." She blinks, rubs her nose, which is already red.

"Hmm," Sally mutters.

"Maybe she should sleep," Mia says. "She's been through a lot."

Katherine turns to Mia, her dark eyes a flare of heat. "Of course she's been through a lot. She's had major surgery. But I'm— Oh, never mind."

Katherine sits down and takes Sally's non-IV hand. The nurse leaves the room, and Dahlia sits down, too, so that they surround their mother. For a second, all is calm, until Mia turns her head and notices a large bouquet of flowers on the small, plain bureau.

"Who are those from?" she asks Dahlia, but Dahlia shrugs.

"I thought someone left them behind."

Mia stands and walks to the bouquet, a tight, bright cluster of roses, mums, and irises. She looks at the card, and then, without turning back to her sisters, opens it. *To Sally. Best wishes for a speedy recovery. Dick Brantley and Mitzie.*

"Dick Brantley," she says.

"Who's he?" Dahlia asks.

"In what smart decade did people finally stop calling their boys *Dick*?" Katherine asks, walking over to the bouquet. She plucks a tiny petal off a miniature yellow mum. "Mom's got a gentleman caller."

"I've never heard of him. No, wait a minute. He might be that fellow who walks with her sometimes. She said something about having coffee now and then with a man. Maybe she said his name was Dick. I'm not sure." Mia tucks the card back in the envelope. "He's not one of her bridge friends."

"It's quite possible you don't know everything about Mom," Katherine says. "Maybe she's been keeping secrets. Maybe she has a secret life we know nothing about." All of them turn to look at Sally, who even in her drugged state seems to be smiling.

"Mom?" Harper walks in the room, his two cousins, Mike and Matt, trailing behind him. He's picked them up at Sally's condo and brought them here for a fifteen-minute visit before taking them to Kentucky Fried Chicken and a movie at the cineplex.

"Hi, sweetie. Hi, guys."

So lanky and tall in the room, Harper almost seems to slouch, not wanting to take up too much space. Dahlia stands to hug him, patting his face, squeezing his shoulders. Mia hugs Mike and Matt, who both seem like little boys compared to Harper. Katherine stands, shifts a little uncomfortably, and sort of waves to them all and then sits back down, picking up Sally's hand again.

"How's Grandma, Mom?" Harper walks to the edge of the hospital bed and grabs the rail. "She looks—"

"She looks asleep," Katherine says. "That's all. The surgery went very well."

Mia puts her arm around Harper's shoulder, realizing how high she has to lift her arm to do so. "Was school good?" she asks quietly. He nods.

"Fine. Is she going to be okay?" Her son turns to her, his eyes lightening briefly, almost amber like her own, full of the same worry she's felt all day except for the brief few minutes with Robert in the cafeteria. For a quick second, she thinks that his worry isn't about Sally at all but about something else, that something in his life is terribly wrong, but then a nurse comes in with a plastic pitcher of water and the flare in Harper's eyes dies down, his face suddenly only sixteen.

"I think so. Yes. She's going to be just fine," Mia says.

Katherine shoots her a look, catching her in the slight lie about Sally's state.

"Well, we are waiting for lab reports," Mia says. "But the surgeon says things look good."

Harper sighs. "Where's Dad?"

"He had to go back to work. He'll be here later."

Now something in Harper's body definitely changes, a shift, a tenseness, a flare of feeling. He pulls away from her arm and goes to sit down next to Mike, who is reading a comic book. For a second, she feels that she's falling through something she thought was sturdy: a kitchen floor, a concrete patio, a bank vault.

"So where are you guys headed to?" Dahlia asks, patting Matt's hair.

"Harper is taking us to *Gory Kill Fest II*," Matt says.

Katherine snorts. "How edifying."

"Why don't you take them to a museum, then?" Mia snaps.

Harper looks at the flowers. "Who sent those?"

But before they can again explore the mystery of Dick and Mitzie, another nurse walks in, carrying another plastic bag of fluid to hook onto the IV. Katherine stands up and moves away from Sally, who still seems to be smiling.

Mia pulls some money out of her purse and hands it to Harper. "Thanks for doing this, sweetie. Aunt Dahlia will be back at the condo when you guys get back."

"Will Dad be home later?" Harper asks as he shoves the money in his wallet.

Mia almost flinches. "Of course."

"Okay."

She kisses him quickly on the cheek and he doesn't pull away. "I'll be home later—or I might stay with Grandma. But Dad will be there."

Harper leans against her lips for a second, and Mia remembers him running toward her across the preschool yard, his coat behind him like a cape, his long curls whirling in the breeze. Then he would fling himself into her arms, pressing his cheek against hers, his little-boy smell in her nose: fruit snacks, paint, tan bark, dirt.

Sally moans a little, and Harper jerks away, staring at his grandmother. Matt and Mike move to his side, all of them staring at the bed.

"You guys go," Dahlia says. "Have fun."

"Drive carefully," Mia says, and the boys wave and smile and leave, the younger boys' excited whispers echoing as they walk down the hall.

"He's so grown-up," Dahlia says, as they watch the nurse check the monitors and machines. "It seems like just yesterday that he was Matt's age, bugging you about buying those comic books. What were they? Anyway, he's a man now. You're almost home free."

Katherine pretends not to pay attention to the conversation, but Mia can see a wash of color on her cheeks. Katherine was the one who babysat the most during high school, two or three jobs at least on the weekends, a string of little kids over at the house, splashing in the pool or making chocolate chip cookies at the big round kitchen table or playing hide-and-seek in the backyard. For a brief spell in med school, Katherine debated whether or not to go into pediatrics, deciding against it, finally, because it was so typically female, like women majoring in English. Wanting to buck the trend was more important at the time, so she decided on pathology, a horrifying specialty Mia thinks no gender would want to dominate.

And in the years since, no woman or man has managed to convince Katherine to settle down, to marry, or to cohabitate, and Katherine never mentions having children. But she's forty now, Mia realizes—not much time left for a family if she wants it.

The nurse fiddles with a line connected to a gadget on Sally's finger and then looks at the sisters lined up at the foot of the bed.

"She's really going to sleep for a while. This might be a good time to go home or eat or whatever. We have your phone numbers."

The nurse turns and leaves the room. Mia feels her sisters' bodies, the warmth of their arms, breathes in their known smells, skin as familiar to her as her children's or her husband's or her mother's.

"Ford's going to come back," Mia says. "I'll stay. You two take the car and go get something to eat."

For a second, it looks to Mia like Katherine will insist that she's the one who should stay, take charge, read the chart after every nurse or doctor interaction, but then her shoulders fall.

"Okay. Dahls?" Katherine says.

Dahlia nods. "Just for a little while, though. The boys and I leave the day after tomorrow, so I really want to be here for Mom."

Then move home, Mia thinks but doesn't say.

Her sisters grab their purses and sweaters. Dahlia puts a hand on Mia's arm and then they leave. Mia slowly walks to the chair at the head of the bed and sits, watching the slight up-and-down movement of her mother's swaddled chest. The machines click and beep and whine. Underneath the bed, bags collect fluid. Underneath the bandages, Sally's wounds try to heal.

"Mom," Mia whispers. "Tell me what to do. Tell me what's going on."

Sally lies still, no words for any of Mia's commands. Mia brings her hand to her blouse and puts it over her own left breast and feels her skin, squeezes her flesh, the living memory of a part of her that grew her children, nourished them.

Out in the hall, the fluorescent lights glint like a migraine aura. Carts clack by. An announcement calls for Dr. Browne. Sally sleeps.

FIVE

Robert

The night after he sat in the cafeteria with Mia, he finishes *Sacramento by Train*. After reading the last paragraph, he wants to throw the book on the floor. His stomach roils. Susan doesn't leave Rafael. No, not even after she sleeps with Marla and then falls in love with John, a colleague. Not after she finds out about Rafael and his secretary. Not even after Rafael finds out about Marla and the drunken escapade at the cabin. There they sit on the deck outside their back door, the sunset a dull orange slice on the horizon. They drink wine; Rafael reaches over and touches Susan's arm. The novel ends.

"Fuck," he says, tossing the book off the bed. He looks up at his ceiling and then reaches down to grab the novel, turning it in his hands to the back cover so he can look at Mia again.

"Why?" he says to her. But she keeps smiling at him, as if she hadn't been in front of him today, exhausted, sad, excited. He loves looking at her face because she hides nothing. Color washes over her cheeks when she is embarrassed, lines form at the corner of her eyes when she smiles, her mouth hangs open when she is surprised. Unlike so many women he knows, she doesn't cover herself with makeup or turn away from him to hide a feeling.

Robert pushes away his blankets, still holding the book, and gets out of bed. He leaves his bedroom and walks to his office, turning on the light and then the computer. As the computer boots up, he sits down on his chair and puts the novel on the desk. *But,* he thinks, *but*. All these words are hers. Things maybe she hasn't said in the context of her real life. He knows that if she didn't believe them in some way, she wouldn't have written them. Robert knows that Rafael and Susan sitting together on the deck was a thought, a desire for wholeness, peace, love, even when it seems impossible, a moment of hope even when it seems wrong.

With a few clicks, Robert is connected to his DSL, and he signs on to his e-mail server. He opens his top desk drawer and takes out her card. Mia Alden. As he rubs his thumb on the thick, solid paper, he wonders what her middle name is. He wants to know what shampoo she uses and what she smells like under her clothes. Is it soap or perfume? Or just her skin? He wonders what she would look like sitting before him naked. He's held so many breasts in his life, felt the weight women carry around with them every day. He wants to hold Mia that way, but differently, not to find disease or recommend augmentation or reduction or reconstruction. Robert wants to take both her breasts—large, lovely breasts, he can tell—in his hands and lean toward her, kissing the skin above her aureole, then letting his tongue find her nipple, large and erect.

Robert shakes his head, trying to ignore the pulse of blood in his groin, his own erection. He taps the card on his desk and then types in her address to a new e-mail message. For a second he stops typing, wondering if anyone else will read this e-mail. Her husband. One of her sons. He looks at the card and realizes that this must be her work e-mail, the one at the university.

He can write her there. It's safe. He wouldn't otherwise. She's a woman who believes in wholeness, peace, and love, and he doesn't want to break her heart before he even has a chance to understand it.

He begins typing again.

```
Dear Mia,
```

he begins, and then he backspaces through to the beginning of
the line.

```
Mia. Dear Mia.
```

He erases the last two words and goes on.

```
It was so nice to see you today. I talked
with Cindy Jacobs later in the afternoon,
and she was very pleased with the outcome
of the surgery. She was able to save quite
a bit of skin, and your mother's recon-
struction should go just as well.
```

Robert stops typing and sighs, pushing back his hair. He
sounds like a doctor. A slightly intrusive doctor, but a doctor all
the same. He thinks to erase everything he's typed, but then he
doesn't. What he's said won't scare her. She won't see his erection
in these words.

```
I finished Sacramento by Train, and I
want to know why it ended the way it did.
Why did you leave us hanging there, forced
```

He erases *forced* and changes it to *sitting*

```
sitting on the deck with Susan and Rafael?
What happens to their marriage? Who com-
promises? Who feels okay? If you know, I
wish you'd tell me. It was a good book. A
good story. Despite the title, I'll start
The Daisy Plate Incident tomorrow.

Robert
```

He sits back in his chair and then hits SEND. In a flash, the e-mail is gone. It's too late to take it back.

❧

When he wakes up, Robert pushes out of bed and walks to his office. It is five a.m., dark still, cold, and he has a seven thirty a.m. surgery. A reconstruction, just like he will do for Sally Tillier. He's left his computer on, and *Sacramento by Train* lies open and upside down on his desk, a book butterfly.

He sits down, rubs his face, stares at the screen. He has nine messages, most of which, he knows, are spam. Robert clicks on his e-mail and scans for what he wants. For a second, his lungs seem to flatten, pressing the air he needs from his body, his heart beating fast to try to bring him oxygen. But wait. There she is. MAlden. He stares at her e-mail address, noting that she wrote this e-mail at two in the morning. His finger hovers over the touch pad, wanting and not wanting to read the e-mail, knowing he should savor the seconds of her that he has. This message may be the last, telling him that she has changed her mind. Or this e-mail might be the first, the beginning of a relationship. He often forgets to pay attention to beginnings, focusing on the ends, the outcomes, which with relationships have usually been bad. But what is he thinking? A relationship! Robert closes his eyes. When he opens them, he clicks on her message and her words open to him.

Hi, Robert. I managed to plug my computer into the hospital-room phone. I'm hiding it from the nurses, though, because I know it must be breaking some kind of rule. My mom's sleeping, and the sleeper chair they brought in for me doesn't look too inviting. My sisters went back to the condo, so I thought I'd check my e-mail, and here you are.

About the book. Well, I don't like stories that end up all pretty and tidy. It doesn't seem real to me. Nothing in my life has ever folded itself into a neat package. So with Susan and Rafael—well, they are going to have to figure it out for themselves. I think they both learned a lot. Figured out what they need, and maybe it isn't each other. But that's not my story. I just wanted them to know.

Have you ever been married? Are you married?

I didn't ask you a thing about yourself today in the cafeteria. I felt selfish when I realized that. You have my books and asked me all the questions, and I have no information about you at all. Except that you're a plastic surgeon. You graduated from UCSF. I saw that on the office wall, and you have all the right credentials, it looks like. But tell me something, Robert. Tell me a story.

Mia

He reads the e-mail again and then again and then again, starving for her, greedy, as if he's eating an orange, pulling the last sweet juice from the sour rind. Mia's a river, awash with words and voice, the beginning of her message pulling him to the end. He felt that when he began to read her book, and then now, with her real self turned into real words for him alone, he knows that she moves. She rocks him with her questions.

Leaning back, he wonders if this short-breathed adrenaline high is always there for him in the beginning. Is this what he's always felt? Was he this excited when he met Leslie? He closes his eyes, brings Leslie forth, her short summer skirt even in autumn, her soft laugh, the way she tucked her brown hair behind her ear when she spoke. Yes, he thinks. Yes. He's felt this excitement before.

Robert sits up, stares again at her message. He doesn't need this. He should delete her message and log off. He'll promise himself to never write to her again. How can he do this with a woman who is married, when it's no different from with Leslie? That's it. He has to call it all off. When he sees her after her mother's surgery, he will be sincere and distant, concerned but stiff. He'll walk away from her just like Margaret, Joy, Dara, and Leslie have walked away from him.

The potential mess he has started with Mia Alden can be avoided. Now. She's so busy with her mother, her writing, her family, she might not even notice if he doesn't write back.

Robert pushes his hair away from his face and then looks at his watch. Five fifteen. In a few minutes, he needs to put on his sweats so he can get a run in before the surgery. He needs to stop at Starbucks for a latte. He has to go over his patient's chart and confer with Kathy Fuji about anesthesia. But there's time to delete or time to write back.

He stares at his hands. He wants to touch Mia. He knows that. And he wants to know her. He can't promise himself more than that. He couldn't promise Mia more if she asked. But this want is real. It may not be more than that, but something in his body tells him that it is. That maybe this time, it's different.

The pulse and glow of the computer screen fills the room with grayish light. He blinks, looks at her message, and then breathes in deeply.

```
Dear Mia,

I have no story.
```

He erases the first sentence because he knows that every life has a story or at least a narrative. A beginning, middle, and, at least for him, a not-yet end.

```
I'm not married. I have never been mar-
ried. I've lived with women, though. And I
have no children. Do you know that commer-
cial where the man gets such a great rate
on a mortgage that he's inspired to always
tell the truth? So he ends up on a date and
says, "I live with my mother and have never
had a relationship longer than three
months." I'm not that bad off, but I'm
telling you what is true. My relationships
have lasted a year or two. And sadly, my
mother is dead.
```

Robert stops and reads what he's written and begins to laugh. Phyllis, who has followed him into the office, stares at him with her copper eyes and then yawns her cat yawn. What woman in the world could read this e-mail and still want to know him? But he feels like the man in the commercial. He wants to tell the truth. He's caught in Mia's current.

```
Here's one story. When I was a resident
at UCSF, I actually forgot to go home and
sleep. I was on call for thirty-six hours,
and when it was over, I went back into an-
other day of work without realizing that
my shift was over. It wasn't until twelve
hours later that the head resident looked
```

at the board and thought to tell me to go home. But the weird part was that I had a memory of driving home, eating some food, and sleeping. I must have fallen asleep for a few minutes somewhere along the line and dreamed it all.

The good news is that I didn't kill anyone that day.

I have to go to work. I'm glad that your mother is recovering well. Maybe I'll have time to come check in on her—you—today.

Robert

⋱

The morning and then afternoon pass in a blur. He performs his first surgery and then his next, everything so clear in the moment. His life, as it often is, is reduced to his hands, the way they move under someone's skin, the angle of his scalpel, the tension in his suture line. All his world seems to be in the moment of his vision and only that vision. He used to go days like that in school and his residency. That's why he could work for two shifts and not realize that he'd forgotten to go home.

His mother used to say "You're driving at night with tiny headlights" when he'd trip over a large piece of furniture or forget to take a shower or stay up all night studying for a trigonometry exam.

Maybe it's why he's never thought too much about his relationships ending so soon, because for the time they lasted, the relationship he was in was all he saw, time compounded by focus.

"Peripheral vision!" Jack says, when Robert doesn't notice a good-looking woman or get excited about a job opportunity at another hospital. "Look around, man!"

But usually, Robert has been so monofocused on whatever is before him, by the time he turns to look around, the woman and the job are gone.

One day as he was driving home, he passed a man and a woman, the man pushing a stroller. The man was about thirty, maybe thirty-two, East Indian, his wife Asian, a little younger. Robert couldn't see the baby, but he saw how the father looked down into the stroller, smiling, his teeth white against his dark skin.

Something deep inside that man made him find a wife, and something in both the man and woman needed that baby, made them make it. It's what people did, driven by an ancient clock that biology set for them, ideas of romance and true love getting mucked up in there in the need to procreate. As he watched them in the crosswalk, laughing, talking gibberish to the baby, Robert wondered what was broken inside him. He's never had those same urges. The nesting. The reproducing. He is missing not only peripheral vision but something very basic, very human.

❧

It's not until after a staff meeting with his colleagues and two patient appointments that Robert remembers Mia. He's remembered her in tiny bits throughout the day, of course. Little bits of dialogue from *Sacramento by Train* have riffed through his mind. Like when Susan cries out "What do you want?" to Rafael.

And he answers, "Does anyone ever know how to answer that question?"

Robert agrees with Rafael, because he's never known the answer himself, at least in the big, existential way. He's wanted food and love and sex and a home and a job, but the bigger want? The ultimate want? Peace? Health? Satisfaction? Joy? He doesn't know. He hasn't bothered to find out.

It's not until four in the afternoon—after the meeting and the appointments—that Robert has time to go up to Sally Tillier's room. He doesn't want to run into Cindy Jacobs, knowing she'll wonder why he's checking up on Sally when she's really Cindy's patient. Not his. Not yet.

So he's glad when he sees Cindy walking down a hall and going through the door to the surgery clinic. He buttons his white coat and heads down the long connecting hall to the hospital building, and then takes the elevator to the third floor.

Pushing his hair back, he walks down the middle of the hallway, nodding at a resident, a nurse, a respitory therapist. Then he slows, angles toward Sally's door, but then stops before walking into the room. There is a man sitting on the edge of Sally's bed, holding her hand. In the second that Robert hovers at the door, he hears the man's low, deep voice, can feel the reassurance in his words. The man is muscled and darkly handsome, his hair black, thick, and full. He must be Mia's husband, Ford. In a fictional universe, he's Rafael.

Robert moves closer.

"You look wonderful," Ford says to Sally.

Sally murmurs something back, her voice sounding a little girlish, a bit flirty.

"Now, don't you start. I'm sure your girls will spoil you. You'll be the queen of the manor for weeks." Ford laughs.

Robert moves closer, his hand on the door, and looks into the room.

A similarly dark, handsome boy—a teenager—sits at the back of the room in a chair, slumped over a comic book. For a quick second, he looks up and sees Robert, blinking as Robert watches the scene on the bed.

Mia has done what he has been unable to do—create a family. Here is the product, a flesh-and-blood boy, a boy who looks exactly like his father.

Robert can suddenly feel all his bones, the slightness of his own body, the worthlessness of everything he's ever done. Backing away from the room and the boy's gaze, he almost falls over a clerk wheeling a stack of charts down the hall. Apologizing, he turns away from Sally, Mia's husband, and Mia's son, and walks back to the elevators, pushing his hair away from his face, trying to find his breath in the thinness of his lungs.

Back in his office, he dictates a chart entry, his face full of heat and blood. He erases what he's said and tries again, knowing he must get everything right. Slowly, he details the outcome of the TRAM flap procedure he performed on Valerie O'Connor. At her final follow-up appointment, there was no evidence of abdominal weakness or hernia. Her lab tests show no recurrence of the cancer; her sonogram clear. He recommends that she continue the exercises shown to her by the physical therapist and come in for all scheduled follow-up exams.

Robert clicks off the recorder and then turns to his computer, clicking on to his e-mail server. He's going to write to Mia now and tell her he's sorry. He can't do this. Won't. Jack would be amazed, because for the first time in a long month of Sundays, he's suddenly had peripheral vision. He can finally see what was to the left and right as well as in front and back. He saw what he didn't want to—Mia's husband. Mia's husband and Sally's reaction to him. A kind man, a good man.

The e-mail program makes the sound that alerts him to mail, and there she is again, MAlden.

```
Dear Robert,

Have you ever killed anyone?

Mia
```

Robert stares at her words and then bends down over his keyboard, wanting to hug his desk, press his heart back into his body.

She's asked the right question, the one he's always wanted an answer to.

≈

He's had one last, late appointment, consulted with an ER doc over a long, jagged wound on a little girl's cheek, and finished his charts. Mia Alden's e-mail is still on his screen, and since he's been in his office, more e-mail has arrived that he doesn't dare look at. Maybe they are all from Mia; Mia with more questions. *Have you ever been in love? Can you be in love? What is your main, true problem? If you could list your top ten faults, what would they be?*

Robert stares at the screen, his desk clock clicking quietly, the noise in the hall only an echo. It's seven thirty, and his medical assistant, Carla, and most of the doctors have gone home.

Robert pushes his hair back and stares at her eight words on the screen and then closes the e-mail. He looks at the list of other e-mail—some from colleagues, a few spam messages that have slipped through the firewall, and then MAlden again.

Dear Robert,

I'm sorry I asked that question. That was really inappropriate. I know that people die in hospitals all the time. No one can make all the right decisions at just the right moment. I can think of all my teaching blunders where I'm sure I forced someone on the wrong path or said an incredibly wrong thing that destroyed the student's confidence or joy or hope. Doctors work with lives, and there's no metaphor there. It's literal, and of course people make mistakes. And then, of course, people die because they die.

So I just wanted to say that. I'm sorry. I'm tired. I wrote that after having had only two hours of sleep last night. Please forgive me.

Mia

Robert rubs his forehead but keeps his eyes on her words. The fluorescent lights hum above him. Outside, the crowded Walnut Creek street roars past his window, the beep of the crosswalk, the pulse of engines and wail of sirens headed toward the ER.

But it's so quiet inside his body, he can feel his pulse, his blood, his hip bones slick in their sockets. He doesn't blink for a long time, and then he does, forcing his eyes away from the screen. Then Robert turns off the program, the computer, and leaves his office, flicking off the overhead light as he goes.

❧

Robert has always loved a hospital at night. The tension and drama are usually reserved for the ICU and the ER; orderlies and senior volunteers aren't wheeling patients to and from radiology or X-ray; visitors who aren't staying over have gone home; lab techs don't whisk open curtains and knock on doors, their vials and syringes and tubes clattering in their baskets. The nurses seem more subdued, quieted by the darkness outside, safe under the lights, calmed by the lack of doctors wanting things. Doctors are reading charts, tidying up, ready to hand over information to attendings, who will drink dark, bitter coffee and wait until morning.

He slips down the hall and then looks into Sally's room again, relieved when he sees that Mia's husband is gone. In fact, no one is in the room but Sally.

The television is on and Sally is awake, blinking at the screen. Robert knocks on the door and then steps in.

"Hi, Mrs. Tillier," he says in his doctor voice, the one that is smooth and calm and slightly detached.

She licks her lips and looks at him as she tries to find her words, the morphine in her blood slowing her reactions.

"Dr. Groszmann," she says. "Hello."

"I thought I'd come by to check on you. See how you're feeling."

Sally shakes her head. "Thank God I didn't have immediate reconstruction. This is bad enough."

Robert walks slowly to a chair, touches the back with his hand, and then pulls it toward him, sitting down. "You're going home tomorrow?"

She nods. "I should have gone home today. But I ran a little fever. It's gone now. Like everything."

Breasts aren't everything, he wants to say to her. He always wants to say this, but he never does. Long ago, he realized he'll never understand how women feel about their breasts. Not in the way society expects them to have them, firm and ripe and on display. His breasts never determined a thing about him. But Sally? She may have known who she was by just looking down at them each day, her nipples pointing her forward, always, since puberty. First, they meant she was a woman, then a lover, then a mother.

"Dr. Jacobs was confident she removed it all," he says instead. "And she was able to save a nice amount of skin for your reconstruction."

"She's a good girl," Sally says, her eyes closing briefly.

There is a noise at the door, and Robert turns to see three women standing there, one of them Mia. He stands up, forces his blush down, and smiles. Mia moves past the other two women, and for a second he imagines she will hug him. But she doesn't.

"Dr. Groszmann," she says. "Hello."

He can't look at her long because he wants to travel her face with his eyes, so he looks at the other two women, who, he can tell, are Sally's other daughters. Both have her face and eyes, and the beginnings of her white hair.

"I thought I'd check on your mom," he says, turning back to Sally, who is now looking at him. "She seems to be doing very well."

One of the daughters walks to him, her hand outstretched. "Katherine Tillier."

She must be the pathologist, he thinks, recognizing that she has never had to learn to modulate her voice, to skirt the truth, because she works with tissue samples and the dead.

"The pathologist," he says, letting go of her tight grip and stepping back.

"The lab reports haven't come back. How long do they take here? Is this delay normal?"

Robert begins to answer, but Mia moves in between them. "Can I talk with you in the hall for a moment?" she asks.

He nods and turns back to Sally. "I'm glad the surgery went well. We'll talk later."

Sally nods, tries to lift her hand, and then lets it relax on the bed. Something about her response makes him uneasy. She seems lethargic, depressed—and not just from the drugs and the effects of the surgery. He'll have to keep track somehow, ask Mia later.

He pushes back his hair and then turns to Mia and her sisters.

"Nice to meet you," he says to Katherine. She smiles a flat, irritated smile, and as he walks by the other sister—who must be the youngest—he stops.

"Robert Groszmann." He holds out his hand.

"Dahlia Regezi."

Of the two sisters, she looks more like Mia, something about the shape of her eyes and the way her lips are raised at the corners. But unlike Mia and Katherine, at least outwardly, she's scared, worried, her eyes already dark with mother loss.

"A pleasure." He smiles again and then follows Mia out into the hall, his heart pounding.

As they walk, he notices how Mia's shirt is wrinkled where she's leaned against the chair in Sally's room. Her hair is messy in the back, blond spikes going in every direction.

At the water fountain, she stops, turns, rubs her cheek, swallows.

"I just wanted to apologize," she says, her eyes glazed with exhaustion. "I can't believe I wrote that. Did you get my e-mail?"

He nods. "Don't—"

"It was a ridiculous question."

"I started it," he says. "I wrote the part before about not killing anyone that day. It follows."

She shrugs. "It's not even what I want to know."

At the nursing station, a nurse looks up over the desk at them and then turns away. Down the hall, someone drops something metal, the *clack* and *ping* echoing. All around them are the sounds of machines, whizzes and beeps and whines.

"What do you want to know?" he asks.

Mia looks up, and he allows himself the pleasure of watching her. In the darkened light of the hall, her eyes are black. Her skin is flushed—as it always seems to be when they talk—her lips full, red, and slightly dry. For a second, he looks at her neck, smooth and solid, and then her breasts, round under her sweater. He forces his gaze back to her face, waiting.

"I want to know what's happening. With us."

He bites the inside of his cheek. He doesn't know what's going on. He hasn't since he opened the examination room door and saw her sitting in the chair. He hasn't read a novel in years, but now he's read one and will soon start another. Her novels. He wishes she had more than three. Even more, he wishes he could be in her thoughts and let her think out stories for him. He wants to know everything.

"Why don't you wear a wedding ring?"

She looks down at her left ring finger, holding up her hand that is small and thick, her fingers round and short.

"We were too poor when we got married. Couldn't afford them."

"Like Susan and Rafael."

"Like Susan and Rafael," she agrees.

"You could afford one now."

Mia takes in a deep breath, her shoulders rising. She looks at him, thinks things he wishes he could hear. Then she nods. "Yes."

"I'm drawn to you," he says without having realized it's what he would say. "From the beginning."

"Me, too."

Katherine sticks her head out of the room, sees them, and then goes back inside.

"How is your mother?" Robert says. "She didn't strike me as someone so . . ."

Mia looks back toward the room, shrugs. "I think my mother's depressed," she says. "I think she's, well, giving up on some-thing. . . . I better go."

Robert moves closer to her. "It could be the pain medication. It slows people down. Thought processes. Feelings. Give her some time. But if it goes on, let me know. I can prescribe something. Have it sent over to the house."

Mia listens, a tear clinging to an eyelash. He reaches out, pinches it gently from her eyelashes, rubbing the moisture between his thumb and finger. Then he touches her arm. Under his hand and her sweater, he feels her heat. Without looking at the nurses' station or back at her mother's door, she leans toward him and kisses his cheek. Robert closes his eyes as she does, taking in her smell—hospital, cotton, early morning soap, tears.

"I'll e-mail you," he says, almost in a whisper.

She bites her lip, looks down, and without looking at him again, walks toward her mother's room.

It's nine when Robert finally gets home, the house dark because he forgot to turn on the outside lights when he left in the morning. Phyllis is at the front door when he opens it, but turns from him the moment he walks in, her tail raised behind her in irritation.

"Sorry, Phyl," he says, turning on the hall light and putting down his briefcase and jacket. "A long day."

Phyllis keeps walking, sashaying toward her food dish in the kitchen. Robert follows her, flicking on lights as he walks down the hall and into the kitchen. The cat has plopped herself in front of her dish, but she won't look at him, not even as he scoops out a cupful of Iams and walks toward her dish.

"You miss Leslie," he says as he pours the kibble. "She kept you company while I worked late, didn't she?"

For a second, he wonders if he's projecting all over poor Phyllis, who is really just hungry and/or bored, if, in fact, cats can be bored. He stands up and watches Phyllis ignore him as she starts to eat. Does he miss Leslie? Does he miss any of his girlfriends? He misses their bodies, he knows that. He misses their company, the meals together, the date nights at the movies. He misses the idea that this woman might be the one. He misses the hope.

He puts away the scoop and listens to Phyllis crunch through her food. But really, who does he miss? His parents, of course. He misses Jack at work, his ironic eyes over his mask, his jokes, his patient way of listening when Robert is angry. And right now, he misses Mia, even though he doesn't know her. Even though she doesn't know him. In a way, Robert knows he's been lonely his whole life, waiting for someone, like some sad, lovelorn sap who believes in parted twins, soul mates, eternal lovers. He wants that slap of the surprise of the perfect someone put right there in front of you. Another part of him knows that love is a choice. You just choose it. You allow yourself to be with that person in front of you, or you choose to be with another. A book he read once convinced him that the most important relationship you ever have is with yourself, and it is that important relationship that is the basis for every relationship a person ever has.

If that's true, he knew then and he knows now, it's no mystery that he's been alone. He can barely stand himself sometimes.

Robert opens the refrigerator, looks in, and then closes it. Leslie and her Mediterranean meals are gone. He grabs the orange juice and carries the entire container with him to his office. He walks in without turning on the light. On his desk, his message machine is blinking, and he presses the button.

"Robert, it's Leslie. I've been meaning to call. I just— Well, I saw Jack today at the gym, and I asked him how you're doing. He didn't say much, and that makes me wonder. I know I shouldn't really care anymore, but I just wanted to talk to you. Just call me sometime. Say hi to Phyllis."

Robert turns off the machine and stands still. If he called, she would come back. All he'd have to do is call. In no time, she'd be sitting at the desk when he came home from work, ignoring him. Phyllis would have someone to pet her late at night, and there'd be food in the refrigerator. He'd sleep in a warm bed next to her warm body. They'd go to parties together. He wouldn't be as lonely. Neither would she, both of them getting some of what they need.

And it wouldn't be wrong. Leslie isn't married. Leslie is free.

He left his computer on this morning, and the light flickers in the dark room. Robert watches it for a moment, blinking, and then he sits down, drinking the juice from the container, a tiny thread spilling down his chin that he wipes away with the back of his hand.

Mia kissed him, and he can still feel her soft, slightly dry lips on his cheek. He closes his eyes and breathes in what he remembers of her smells, her skin, her slightly salty, too-long-in-the-hospital sweat, some perfume or soap or lotion underneath it all. And again, like the night before, he hardens. The eyes of his imagination take off her sweater, her bra, hold her breasts, press her flesh to him, to his lips. And then . . . and then . . .

Putting down the container, he shakes his head. It's like he's surfing the Net for porno, sitting at his desk with a hard-on. But instead, he's getting hard from words and memories of a woman whose body he's never even seen, barely touched, hardly smelled.

Robert clicks on his e-mail icon, and then his mail pops up. Nothing new from MAlden, but then, why would there be? She's right now in the room with her mother and sisters, Dahlia and Katherine, the pathologist, who is probably watching Mia as much as she is watching Sally. In the instant of meeting Katherine, he didn't like her, finding something angry and split about her conversation and questions. If she were his colleague, he would stare at her from across a meeting table, wanting to argue with everything she said. And she, undoubtedly, would fire back alternatives, facts, answers, solutions. He can imagine the fights the Tillier girls had as children, Sally trying to yell them all into silence. Though the youngest one, Dahlia, was probably always an observer, watching the war of her sisters from corners of rooms.

He opens a blank mail page and begins to write.

Dear Mia,

I want to see you when your mother is better, stable, at home. I want to sit down with you and answer all the questions that you have. And I want to ask you things, too. I want to know—I want to know everything, even things that will make me upset. About your marriage. About why you are drawn to me even though you are married. I want to know how this feels. I want to know about your husband.

I went by your mother's room twice today. The first time, your husband was there. I'm assuming it was your husband because he reminded me of Rafael. Tall and dark and handsome. Classic. He was holding Sally's hand and speaking softly to her. At that moment, I had so many questions, questions with answers that might make you not see me anymore once you heard them. Like why would you want to be with me if you had a man like that? What is inside your marriage that I can't see from here? What is missing inside you? The both of you?

And I want to tell you things that might make you not want to see me. About the way I am. About the way I can't be. About how I might not be the person you are looking for at all. I want you to know. If we are going to do whatever this is we are doing, I want the truth to be there right away. Not some terrible surprise.

Robert stops writing and puts his face in his hands, trying not to cry. Phyllis—done eating now and in a state of cat grace—winds her way around his ankles, and Robert concentrates on her steady purr, following the rocking, bumpy cadence of her sound. Finally, after a long moment, he swallows, wipes his eyes, and realizes he's never wanted the truth more than he wants it with Mia Alden.

And the answer to your question is yes, I have killed someone.

Robert

SIX

Sally

When Mia thinks that Sally is asleep, she leaves the room and Sally starts to weep, the kind of weeping she does since the operation, heavy, pulled up from her chest, soundless. Mia found her weeping a couple of times and said, "Mom, Mom. It's okay. It's just the anesthesia. Give yourself some time. You've only been home for two days."

Or Mia said, "It's natural. You've been through major surgery. Something huge happened to you. Of course you are sad, Mom. Just let it out."

That was too much. So now Sally waits until the coast is clear before letting it out. And she knows it's not the anesthesia. It's more. Sometimes it's her body, the way it feels now, shorn and wrong and empty. Other times it's David—how he's not here where he should be, comforting her, helping her, tending to her. Or it's her girls, how things haven't gone the way Sally thought they would. How Katherine has no children. How Dahlia's so far away. How Mia seems so sad. Over and over it goes, until Sally hears Mia walking up the stairs to her bedroom, and she blots her tears and pretends to sleep again.

Wiping her eyes, Sally feels this jag slow, quiet, stop. But she doesn't feel any better. Downstairs, she can hear Mia clattering around in the kitchen, banging pots on the range, slamming the refrigerator door, whapping shut the cupboard doors. Sally pushes herself up to sitting and stares at the television Mia left on. But Sally can't see it, the noise of the messy, soap opera dialogue not even hitting her ears.

She wants to get up and leave. She's had it with the pain and the flipping bandages and the strict no-shower policy. Then there are the drains. Sally's disgusted that Mia must help her drain fluid off the wounds and that her daughter must siphon the blood and pus into tiny measuring cups and chart the fluids that come out of Sally's body.

And besides, Mia is driving her crazy, sitting in Sally's bedroom all day, reading books and magazines or working on her laptop computer. Yesterday, Sally said, "Why don't you go home? I'm fine."

Then Mia started to cry, so Sally stopped talking and pretended to fall asleep. Kids.

Now Sally's just angry. Irritable. Uncomfortable.

She pulls away the blanket and looks down at her chest. If she could have it her way, she'd rip off the bandages and stare at what she feels on her chest, the diagonal scars where her breasts used to be. She wants to walk around her condo naked. She wants to pass by all her mirrors and stare at herself, taking in each reflection so she can memorize her new body. Then she wants to try on all her clothes to see what she should throw out or what seems to suddenly work better than it did before.

She wants to see if she has enough to wear to go on.

And the most important part is she wants to be alone. For a few days. If Mia would go home and Katherine and Dahlia would stop calling and Nydia Nuñez would stop ringing the doorbell, Sally would be able to figure it all out. Over breakfast and lunch and dinner, she could conjure her no-breast life. Sally with No Breasts Tillier. But everyone is distracting her or giving her pain pills so she forgets everything.

"Here's some dinner," Mia says, walking in the room, carrying a tray.

Sally sighs and looks at her daughter. Mia looks terrible, as if she's the one who had her breasts cut off. Her hair sticks up on her head and her face is pale, distracted, blotchy. And though she looks like she's lost weight—praise God—her droopy pants make her look more middle-aged than she is. "No-ass women" Sally's bridge friend, Gloria, calls them, the ones with stomachs but no butts. And there it is again, that something else, some kind of sadness that doesn't have anything to do with Sally's lost flesh, and that makes Sally angry, not wanting anything else in her bedroom but her own grief.

Get out, she wants to scream. *Take your droopy ass and your problems home to Ford.*

But she doesn't say a word. She lets Mia settle the tray over her lap and thighs and sighs again.

"Thanks, dear. Looks good." But it doesn't look good. The pork chop is dead flesh, like a dead breast. As she cuts a piece of meat, she thinks about where they threw her breasts when they were done with them. Is there a garbage can for body parts, a toss of arms and legs and spleens?

"Mom?" Mia asks.

Sally stops cutting. "What?"

"Are you okay?"

"Of course not." Sally puts down her knife and picks up her fork, spearing the tough chop.

"Do you think I should call Dr. Jacobs? Tell her you have pain?"

Sally chews and looks out the window, the sky gun barrel gray. There is nothing Cindy Jacobs can do for her pain. It will take years to excavate it from her insides, grief and loneliness twined with every vein and artery and nerve. No surgeon can begin to attempt that.

Sally swallows, holds back tears, and picks up her knife. "No. I'm fine."

"You just said you weren't."

She puts down her cutlery and looks at Mia. "My God, Mia. How would you feel? I've had my breasts cut off before . . ."

Mia leans in closer. "Before what?"

Sally feels like her mouth is full of sand that has started to trickle down her throat. Breathing hurts, swallowing impossible, but she manages to say, "Before I could use them again."

Mia sits back, her mouth open, a slight gasp pushing out between her lips. "Oh."

Picking up her fork, Sally pierces a green bean, stabbing at it again and again.

"Mom," Mia says.

"Don't." Sally puts up a hand. "It's just what I feel, and I don't want to talk about it. I don't want to talk about anything."

Outside, Sally's neighbor pulls a trash can to the curb, the plastic wheels scratching against the asphalt. Mia stands up and closes the window all the way, the sound dying away. She walks the perimeter of the room, picking up books and photos as she does, saying nothing.

When David was first diagnosed, Sally rushed home from the hospital one day when he was in a deep sleep. Running upstairs, she dug under his winter sweaters and found the handgun he'd bought three years before. She took the gun, the bullets, her grandfather's bowie knife, the steak and carving knives, her sleeping pills, and all the cough medicine, aspirin, and muscle relaxants and brought them over to Doris Armsby next door. Back inside, she found her measuring tape, packing twine, yarn, David's belts, her bathrobe tie, and hid everything in a trunk in the basement. She knew he'd be too weak to walk into the garage and hook up a hose to the back of the car, but from that day onward, she parked both the cars out front.

Thinking about it now, she wants to weep over her pork chop. If he felt like she does—and he knew he was going to die—she should have arranged all his options before him, laying out Seconal and shiny bullets and sharpened knives. It would have been a kindness. She would have been thinking of him, not herself. At the end, when he could barely sit up, when he was in so much pain it hurt to breathe, when he could barely smile, she would have been graciousness and love itself to have brought in the gun and pulled the trigger on her own.

But she hadn't been able to let him go. Even that last day when he didn't know who she was, she wanted him alive. Knowing that blood was moving in his veins was enough to keep her raging sorrow deep and hidden. But the surprise was that the sorrow never came. She was too busy for it then, but now her old friend sorrow is back, waiting for her to embrace it as she never had before, clinging on her arms, whispering in her ear.

"Mom," Mia says, standing at the foot of the bed. "Tell me what to do. I'll do it. I'll call anyone."

Sally wonders who she could call to fix what is wrong inside her. It's not outside. It's not her breasts. Instead, she has something dark blooming inside her like a rotten flower.

She wants to tell her daughter to give her the gun, to cock it, to hold it to her temple and pull the trigger, but then the doorbell rings.

"It's just Nydia," Sally says hurriedly, wanting to tell Mia about the gun. "Just let her stand there."

"Let me go see," Mia says. "I'll be back."

"Hurry," Sally says, knowing what she'll say to Mia when she comes back upstairs.

Mia walks downstairs, and then Sally hears the door open. After a moment, she hears voices, a man's voice and a *yap-yap,* the bark of a tiny dog.

Sally strains to hear the conversation, but it sounds like hellos and brief introductory comments—something about the weather, or maybe it was about the sycamore out front. Then after a second, there are footsteps on the stairs, Mia's and the man's. Outside on the porch, Mitzie yaps away, already lonely for Dick.

"Hey, there," Dick says, peeking his head in the room and then pulling his body inside. He stands by her, his hands on his hips. "How's the patient?"

Mia comes into the room, her face arranged in hopeful lines, as if a visitor is what Sally has been asking for all along.

Maybe Mia's right. Maybe Dick is just what Sally needs. He's lost a wife—first her mind and body to stroke and then all of her to cancer—and knows the terror of the sickroom. He probably has a gun somewhere, stashed under winter sweaters. And Dick likes her, would be willing to help. So Sally smiles her best social smile, wondering how long it will take to convince him that she's better off dead.

❧

The next day, Mia helps Sally walk down the stairs, holding her arm, making sure not to bump against the incisions. Earlier, Mia helped her take a bath in about two inches of water, soaping her back with a loofah, and now Sally wears an outfit she ordered from Coldwater Creek before the surgery, aqua-colored cotton pants and a loose blouse that hangs over her wounds and the tubes, billowy and tentlike, hiding her flatness.

Downstairs, Mia's opened the front door, and a triangle of light brightens the carpet, and Dick Brantley sits on the couch, Mitzie on the porch, her nose touching the screen door.

"My goodness, a day has done wonders," Dick says, standing up and taking her arm.

Mia steps back and says, "Anyone for a soda?"

Dick shakes his head. "Off the stuff. High-fructose corn syrup will kill you. How about a seltzer?"

Sally wonders if she could ingest enough high-fructose corn syrup to kill herself. "Nothing for me," she says.

Dick and she sit down on the couch, and for a moment Sally tries to think of things to say. She could talk about the improving weather, Mitzie and her small cocker loyalty, the surgery itself, Mia's novels, Katherine's work, Dahlia's children. But she can't. Her mouth is tired. More than that, she feels as though there are strings at the corners of her lips, strings that tiny little men are pulling each time she tries to talk. The little men want her to cry, but she won't now that she has formulated a plan. She'll act, she'll do something, before she cries again.

Mia brings in a glass of water for Dick, who takes it with thanks. Then she excuses herself, saying, "I'm going to do some work on the computer," and goes upstairs, leaving Sally alone with Dick Brantley.

"So, how are you feeling?" he asks.

The tiny men tug, but she forces her lips to move. "Better. Mia's been such a help."

Dick nods and sips his water. Sally imagines his gun, the one under his sweaters. The phone rings, but Mia answers it before it can ring again. Sally waits, hoping it's for her, but Mia doesn't clomp down the stairs with the phone.

"You're lucky to have your girls," Dick says. "I've got the boys, but they're across the country with their own families. You know that old saying. What is it? A daughter's a daughter all her life, but a son's a son until he takes a wife. I think it's meant for mothers, but it's true all the same for me."

Sally thinks of Katherine and Dahlia so far away and so infrequently here, their visit for this surgery almost a dream because of all the medication she was on just after the surgery. *Mia's been a Mia all her life,* she thinks. *Mine.* But Mia would never do what Sally wanted her to, much like Sally wouldn't do for David what he needed. Mia would never bring a gun downstairs and hand it to Sally.

And what was it that someone said to her once? Maybe it was

Nydia relating something she heard on a talk show. "Parents are in love with their children. Children just love their parents."

Whatever it was, no one loved anyone enough. Not enough to do what needs to be done.

"Mia's my main support." Sally says this loudly, knowing she's never said it aloud before. But then she continues, quietly, "My other girls have their own lives, like your boys."

"They grow up," Dick says. "What else can they do?"

"They don't— They're not in love with us," Sally blurts.

"In love?" he says. "Well, that's probably a good thing. You can get arrested for that."

Sally shakes her head. "What I mean is they don't need us."

Dick runs a hand through his thick white hair. "That may well be true. But would you want those grown kids coming round here, needing to be taken care of again? It's our turn now. Your turn to be taken care of. The way it goes."

"It's horrible," Sally says. "I can take care of myself."

"That I have no doubt of. This is a minor blip. Pretty soon, you'll be leading the race around the block, laughing at me, just dust in your tracks."

For a second, she looks at Dick, wondering how someone can be this balanced, kind, whole. It doesn't make sense. The world is a horrible place, full of things like cancer and war, and here he is, giving her a happy ending.

She sighs, picks a piece of lint off the couch. "Well, kids."

"Indeed. They do keep me jumping."

"My middle girl. I think she's hiding things from me."

"Like what?"

"I think she's a lesbian." As Sally says the word, she hears another truth she's never let out into the air.

Dick puts down his glass of water and shrugs. "She can get married now, at least in San Francisco, until the courts shut it down."

Sally feels her mouth move upward and then feels a smile pulse in her face. "She's never told me for sure."

"Some things are hard to tell," Dick says. "Especially when you think the person listening won't like it."

Sally feels her mouth relax, as if the little men have taken a break. Her throat fills with what? Gratitude to Dick for saying what she's never been able to about her own daughter? Sally has never moved into that discussion, and maybe that's why Katherine is so far away, covering up her life with the busyness of her work and ideas.

"I just didn't know what to say. How to ask."

"Maybe she can't see that. Maybe you can show her how you feel, and she'll just tell you."

"Maybe," Sally says, suddenly tired. Did Katherine think Sally wouldn't love her because of whom she loved? Maybe once upon a time, Sally would have had a flutter of some kind of ancient moral indignation or embarrassment. Certainly, she wouldn't have brought it up at the bridge table. But Sally knows that if Katherine brought another woman to the house, Sally would welcome them. She would get to know this new woman, make friends, ask her to find a gun. Someone has to help Sally because she can tell Dick isn't going to. He wants her to live, too, like Mia. Even if he has a gun, it will stay unloaded and at home.

"But she could have tried to tell me," she begins. "She could have at least tried."

On the front porch, Mitzie pushes out a little growl, and Dick and Sally turn to see the mailman walk up the front path. Dick stands and opens the screen door, Mitzie bolting in and hiding behind his legs.

"I have an overnight for Mia Alden," the mailman says, eyeing Mitzie and her pointy bottom teeth. Mitzie growls again, her fur standing up on her back.

Mia walks to the landing and then seeing the mailman, runs

down the stairs. "Thank you," she says, taking the gray plastic envelope. The mailman turns to leave, looking back once to make sure Mitzie isn't following him.

"What is it?" Sally asks.

"Some medication for you. They forgot to give it to us during the discharge."

Sally hopes it's something that she can take a lot of. But Mia keeps the pain pills in the guest room next to her bed so she can dole them out. Maybe later. Maybe when Mia goes home, she can swallow them all. She leans back, resting her head on the couch. Maybe this will be it.

Dick takes a last sip of his water and puts the glass back on its coaster. "I think I've worn you out. Mitzie and I are going to finish our walk. So good to see you're doing better, Sal Gal."

Sally starts. Pricks of feeling stab hot under her cheeks and in her eyes. David called her My Gal Sal.

"Thanks for dropping by," Mia says. "Anytime. Please feel welcome. You know where we are."

Mia bends down to pet Mitzie, and then Dick and his dog leave, Mitzie's tags jangling as they walk away. Mia closes the front door and then takes the envelope into the kitchen, where Sally can hear her cutting at it with the kitchen shears. Then there is the tinkle of pills in a plastic bottle and the rush of tap water.

Mia walks back into the living room and puts a little blue oblong pill in Sally's palm and gives her the glass of water.

"There you go." Mia stands over her, her hands on her hips.

"What is it?" Sally asks, but she doesn't wait, putting the pill on her tongue and swallowing it down.

Pushing her hair away from her forehead, Mia cocks her head and holds Sally's gaze. This is what Mia has always done before she lies, the very move she's made since she could talk and make up stories. Maybe this is what she has to do when she writes, the crooked way she looks on the world.

"It's for pain. It will make you feel better."

Sally sighs and hands Mia the glass. Mia walks toward the kitchen, and in the instant, a slash of sun rounds the house and hits Sally's neck, warming her skin. At its pulsing, light touch, Sally wants to weep, loving how the heat and light bathe her firmly, gently, not letting her go. Back in the kitchen, Mia suddenly begins to hum, the melody a song Sally recognizes as her own, a made-up song her mother sang to her.

Sally closes her eyes. She'll give it, this, all of it, two more days. If she doesn't feel better, she'll find the gun, the knife, the hose. It's possible that all those long, loose things she hid from David are still in the trunk she brought from the old house. But with whatever she can find, Sally will end it all. And for now? She closes her eyes, lets the sun tell its daily story on her skin, listens to the highs and lows of the familiar lullaby her oldest daughter pushes out into the air, and falls asleep.

❧

Later that afternoon, she doesn't argue when Mia helps her up the stairs, and she doesn't cry again, though she waits for her tears even as she falls asleep. The next day, she even finds herself smiling when Mia drives them over to her house and Harper tells them the story of how a cop once pulled him over because his girlfriend was sitting in the backseat.

"Looked weird," the cop said.

"I'm pretending he's my chauffuer," Harper's then girlfriend, Lizette, told him. "Keeps him in line. Reminds him who's really the boss."

When this happened, Mia told Sally what Harper omits, the part about the cop finding Harper driving with only one pant leg on. Harper only told Mia the truth when she threatened to call the cops and find out why they were pestering the youth of Monte Veda.

"I think the cops are a form of birth control," Mia said. "I'm just going to let them do what they do."

Later during the visit, Sally holds the phone when Lucien calls from college to talk about his philosophy class, and tells her that no one has free will. "It's a grid. It's all planned. You can't stop it."

"Who?" she asks her grandson. "Who plans it?"

"That's the big question," Lucien says, now done with his theory of life. "How are you, Grandma? Are you doing okay?"

If she is, she wants to tell him, it's not because of her will. Someone planned it. Someone is making her feel better.

"I'm okay," she says, not knowing if she means it.

"I'm not coming home for spring break," Lucien says. "But when I come home for summer, we'll go to the movies."

And somehow—Sally's not sure why or how or when, exactly—two days pass, and then three, and at some point, something begins to close in Sally's body, and it's not her incisions. Something that was wide open and gaping and full of sadness has shut, at least partially. The jagged, harsh tear of grief that made her want to grab Dick Brantley by the shirt collar and beg him for relief has lessened, as if sadness was a radio station she just turned down. By the following morning after that, she manages to switch the station off for most of the day, the morning the hardest part. But after Mia helps her shower and then they go down to eat breakfast, she feels lighter.

Sally looks at the little dish of pills Mia set out on the table, knowing that something in the mix of blue and white and yellow is helping her. Of course, whatever is making her feel better is something here on earth and not a square in Lucien's God grid. Besides, Sally knows that she's not evolved enough to fix herself on her own. She's known that since David died.

By the time of her follow-up appointment, a little over a week after the surgery, Sally sits straight on the examination table, her shoulders held back.

"Are you getting around at home okay?" Dr. Jacobs asks.

Sally nods. "Mia's been there with me since the operation."

Mia looks at the doctor and smiles, and Dr. Jacobs reaches over and pats Mia's knee. "I bet you feel like running away from home about now."

Though Sally feels a tiny ripple of loss run through her body, she barks out a laugh, the sound harsh and different and almost scary. Both the doctor and Mia look at her and then smile, seeing that the sound—though unexpected—is happy.

"She left at seventeen, and I know she didn't plan on coming back," Sally says. "But I don't know what I would have done without her."

Dr. Jacobs nods, and Sally wonders if she can tell her about the gun. Maybe this is a normal reaction, women all over the world craving steel and power and forgetfulness just after the surgery that takes their breasts. Perhaps this is information for a medical journal, and the very idea seems distant to Sally, as if it wasn't just a week ago that she wanted to splatter her brains over a wall. *Maybe I'll tell Mia later,* she thinks. *Maybe one day she will write about it.*

Doctor Jacobs places her fingers gently on Sally's neck and upper chest, feeling for what? Sally can't remember now what she should be scared about. Something about her lymph nodes? Swelling? Watching the wall as the doctor's hands move patiently along her body, Sally knows that she is done. Finished. It's time to start fresh.

"I've changed my mind," Sally blurts out.

"About what?"

"About reconstruction. I don't want it. Not now, not ever."

Mia uncrosses her legs and leans her elbows on her knees. "Mom? When did you decide this?"

"Today. I don't want to go through that. All that stretching and filling of saline and the like."

Sally looks down at Dr. Jacobs, who blinks, bites her lip, nods. "I did a skin-saving mastectomy."

"I know."

"You will most likely want me to go in eventually and reduce the amount of skin. Smooth out your chest."

Sally feels the doctor's words rush along her bare arms. But she knows she's already lost the most important parts, and a little skin removal is nothing. Not one thing. Maybe she won't even have it removed. But if she does, she'll be as smooth and free as an eight-year-old girl.

"Of course. After the chemo, right?"

Dr. Jacobs writes in the chart. "Right. I'll confer with your oncologist, Dr. Gupta. And I'll let Dr. Groszmann know, as well."

Sally plucks at the ties on her gown and then smoothes the fabric over her thighs. "Thank you, Doctor. I'm sorry I waited so long to decide."

Dr. Jacobs stands and smiles, setting down the chart and putting on a pair of latex gloves. "Better you decided now than after you got the implants. So, let's see how your incisions are doing."

Sally opens her gown, noticing as she does that Mia isn't looking at her but at the diagram on the wall with the woman with one breast, her mastectomy scar like a wicked wink, a one-sided smile, a half-kiss on her perfect chest.

"Mia?" Sally says, and Mia looks up, her face not that of the forty-four-year-old woman she is, but that of the girl Sally remembers at David's funeral, the one begging, "What will happen next, Mom? What are we going to do?"

Then as now, Sally has no answer. No information that would have prepared them for the lives they've all led since then, Mia, Katherine, Dahlia, and Sally. No words could have foretold any of it.

We have to live through it, she wants to say now, understanding, finally, that these words are true. But she has no voice for them, can feel nothing but Dr. Jacobs's stethoscope on her chest, the cold metal against her wounded skin.

SEVEN

Mia

For the first day in more than a week and a half, Mia is alone. Sally is at home, Nydia Nuñez sitting with her until three, when Dick Brantley will come over with Mitzie. He promised Mia that he would make Sally walk down her front path and then up and down the street once, maybe twice.

The strange thing is that Sally agreed to the arrangement, not arguing as Mia expected she would.

"Sure," she said. "Dick and Mitzie and I will tear up the street. I've just got to remember not to swing my arms."

Since Dr. Jacobs removed the drainage tubes, Sally has felt a little sore, tender at her incisions, scared to move too fast for too long. But she wanted the walk, wanted Nydia and Dick, wanted Mia to go home.

"I'll come over at six with dinner," Mia promised.

"I don't need a thing," Sally said.

"Mom, I'll be there later." And then she left Sally's condo, feeling as though she could breathe for the first time in weeks.

Now she sits at her desk at home, her computer screen open to her latest novel, a story she doesn't know how to write anymore. Before Sally's diagnosis, Mia had loved this plot, one about two sisters who basically raise themselves after their father's death. It's set in the seventies, and Mia researched all the music and clothes and movies, laughing as she remembered all their terrible haircuts and huge bell-bottom pants.

But since Sally's call, her "I have some bad news," Mia hasn't known how to be in the seventies anymore. She doesn't want to be there at all, close to the time when David died. Even though the story is not about her and Katherine and Dahlia, she doesn't want to remember what it was like in that house. What she wants is here, now, in the new millennium.

After the night she kissed Robert Groszmann on the cheek, she went home and lay down in bed next to Ford, watching his smooth back all night. He breathed slowly, up and down, his rhythm, all his rhythms, so familiar, so known, so calming. She pressed up next to him and promised him silently that she would never talk with Robert Groszmann again. She wouldn't look for him or e-mail him or talk to him. She would forget how he looked at her as they sat across from each other at the cafeteria table. She would ignore the way her body wanted his. It was over, over, over. It was over before she had more to feel guilty about.

She softly stroked Ford's shoulder and vowed to ask him again to go to counseling, even if he would get angry like before and say, "We don't need it. We're fine."

She'd ask again, bring up the sex, knowing that he'd say, "It's not my fault."

That night she promised to do all these things, and she's kept most of the promises. She asked Ford to pick up Sally and bring her back to the condo, telling him she needed to set up the sick-room. Instead of calling Robert and asking him to prescribe an anti-depressant, she called Dr. Jacobs, who arranged for the drugs to be delivered to Sally's house.

Mia's avoided her e-mail entirely, even though she knows that she is probably missing messages from her agent, editors, colleagues, and friends. But she doesn't care. If it's important enough, they will call. Later, after a long while, she will open her e-mail and delete all the messages without looking at them, never knowing if he wrote back or not. And because Sally has decided not to have reconstruction, there will never be any excuse to have to see Robert Groszmann again. Not one. Not ever.

And tonight? Tonight, she'll bring up the counseling. Tonight, she'll do it.

But now she can't write. She turns to look outside her window and watches the goldfinches fighting over their positioning on the thistle-seed bag she bought at Orchard Nursery. Birds seem to fight constantly, each seed a victory. She's been staring at the bag for so long, she can recognize the finch that usually wins the fight, a scruffy female, her olive-colored wings a bit ruffled from scuffles. But there she is, time after time, right in the middle of the bag on the thickest bulge of seed.

If she's not watching the birds, she's watching the squirrels eat the discarded bits off the ground below. If not the squirrels, it's her cats sitting on the fence. One writer she read about taped his office windows dark with paper and then wore a blindfold while writing, so all he would concentrate on were his words. The idea of that makes Mia want to bolt outside. She needs to see. She needs to breathe.

But she can't breathe anywhere right now. If she tries, she takes in Robert, the smell of his cheek, the taste of his skin on her lips. When she closes her eyes, she sees him pushing his hair back from his forehead, smoothing his perfect long ponytail. As she stares at her month-old words on the screen, she hears his voice, hears him say, "I'm drawn to you."

What would Kenzie do? Mia wonders, wishing she could talk to her best friend about this. She could, really. Of course she could. Kenzie knows more about men than anyone Mia has ever known, telling Mia hundreds of date stories over the years. Sex stories. Penis stories. Sad lonely-night stories. But for some reason, Mia's holding this secret tight. But why? It's over with Robert, isn't it? Hasn't she decided to stop? Didn't she promise everything to Ford's quiet, sleeping body?

Mia stands up and walks to the window. The goldfinches fly away, the thistle bag swinging from their tiny legs pushing off into flight. A squirrel starts, looks around, and then bends back to the seed.

There's so much Mia needs to do. It's enormous. Overwhelming. She has to figure out her marriage. She needs to lose weight, work out more, and take up yoga. And then there's her mother. Where to start with that? How to begin with Sally? But for today, Mia needs to make a batch of chili, clean the bathrooms, and pay some bills. First—first she's going to check her e-mail. She has to. She knows now where Lucien inherited his addictive personality. She can't even go more than a week and a half.

She's going to write to Robert.

ᦂ

When she reads his last words, "I have killed someone," Mia wants to weep. He admitted this, wrote this, said this, typed this, thought this, and she didn't answer him for ten days. Now he must think she read the sentence and decided that he was bad, evil, wrong. He's been walking around for a week feeling judged. He probably wishes he'd never met Mia at all.

And like her, he probably has stopped looking at his e-mail, knowing that it would do no good. Her decision was in. He'd waited long enough. It was over.

Mia swallows, rests her head in her hand for a moment, and then starts to write.

```
Dear Robert,

    I could lie to you and say that I've been
so busy with my mom that I haven't had time
```

to write, but even though I have been busy, I'd still be lying. And because you've been so truthful, I have to be. I was scared. I came home from the hospital that night, and I promised myself that I wouldn't write to you or see you again. And then when my mother decided that she wasn't going to have reconstruction, I knew that it was a sign. We weren't supposed to see each other.

But I think about you. This morning, I thought about you. Last night. The day before. The day before that.

Can we meet? Can we talk about what you wrote in your e-mail? I want to know. I don't want to write any more about this. I want to see you in person.

But I'll understand if you don't want to see me. I must seem indecisive. A flake. It's your decision.

Mia

As she browns the ground beef for the chili, she thinks about Robert, imagining him at his desk, reading the e-mails she sent him. She chops the garlic, onions, and bell pepper and talks to Harper about his geometry homework, thinking of Robert pushing his hair back from his face, thinking how to answer her. She thinks of him writing the story of how he killed someone. Killed someone? All afternoon, Mia is in two places, or there are two Mias. One Mia is in the kitchen; one Mia is floating in Robert's office, imagining him.

How can she be this split person, neither one place nor the other? She should be here, at home, with her family.

"Mom?" Harper asks, holding out a piece of paper.

"What?

"Permission slip? The thing we were just talking about?" Harper stares at her, his eyes dark like Ford's, like Sally's.

Mia puts the lid on the chili pot and takes the slip, reading it. "Where are you going?"

Her son shakes his head and goes back to sit at the table. He sighs, rubs his forehead, just like Ford does. "Monterey. The aquarium. What is going on with you and Dad? Is it Grandma still?"

Mia grabs a pen from the wire mesh basket on the counter and signs her name on the slip and then hands it back to Harper. "What do you mean?"

Harper shoves the slip in his backpack. "You're both on some other planet. Pluto, even if it really isn't technically a planet anymore. Just some giant rock floating around the sun."

Mia puts her hand on her hip, staring at her youngest boy. What is he seeing? Is it just her fatigue from taking care of Sally? Or has her betrayal of his father seeped through her skin like whiskey? But Ford? He's who he's become in their long marriage. Helpful, thoughtful, kind, slightly detached. Mia doesn't know what Harper is talking about. Ford seems fine, happy to help out with Sally, content with being alone all those nights Mia stayed at the condo. Unwilling to go to therapy, but okay with the same day in and day out of their lives.

Mia puts the hot pads back in the drawer, opens the chili pot to look in, and then closes it. "It's been a hard time. Grandma's better now, though, and she'll be able to drive tomorrow. I won't have to keep going over there."

Harper zips his backpack, tightening its straps. "You know that book you wrote?"

"Which one?"

"The first. The train one."

Mia nods. Of all the people in her family, only Lucien has read her novels, talking with her about each one, every character, the covers, the titles. Ford and Harper and Sally and Dahlia are proud—Dahlia as well as Sally buying them in batches—but Mia knows that her family doesn't really read them or they don't read them past the first chapters. When people ask her if she's ever had to worry about using her own life as material, she honestly answers no, clear that only one son would find the real intermixed with fiction.

"And?" she asks Harper. "What about it?"

"You know Rafael?"

"You read the book?" Mia pulls out a chair and sits down at the table, staring at Harper. Even though she knows he has something important to say, she can only think of the boy in second grade who had trouble with *Green Eggs and Ham*. For most of his reports now, he skims books and reads up on what he missed on SparkNotes.com. If he were younger or not trying to be serious, she'd stand up and hug him tight, proud that he had gotten through her whole story.

But then she sighs, knowing that he could only have done so because he was worried.

"Most of it. Anyway, you know Rafael? The guy?"

Mia used to know Rafael. For years, he lived in her fingers and arms and brain and heart. But now, like the rest of the story, she's let him go, off into the death of characters with no sequels to revive them. What he loved and hated and cared about has become exactly what Rafael and *Sacramento by Train* is: an old story.

"Of course. What is it, Harper?"

"You know what he did. With his secretary."

Something pings in her chest. Her breath stops. How can Harper know about her and Robert already? How can she be guilty when she hasn't even had the opportunity to sin? To enjoy the sin. How can she pay for it now without having the joy of the crime?

"Yes. He had an affair," she says, her eyes steady.

"Well," Harper says. "It happens, right? In real life. And then people go on. Like Rafael and Susan."

Mia leans forward, feeling her thighs press against the wooden chair. "What are you saying, Harper?"

Maybe it is the question or her forward movement or the fact that he has only five minutes to get to his math tutor, but whatever the reason, Harper stands up and swings his backpack onto his shoulder. "I'm just talking about it, that's all."

He walks around the table, hesitates, and then kisses her on the forehead. "It was a good book."

She holds his shoulder, feels the hard muscle there, and then puts a hand to his head. He allows her touch and then slowly pulls away.

"Harper." Mia pivots in the chair to watch him walk toward the front door.

"What?" He turns, his eyes narrowed. Then he looks at his watch. "I've got to go."

And then he's gone, the door closing behind him.

Mia turns forward, leans against the table, liking the hard press against her stomach. She was right in the first place. She should never have opened her e-mail, never answered Robert. Her boy already knows the entire story and it hasn't even happened yet.

On the deck out front, a blue jay hops onto the birdbath, dipping his black-soot bill into the water and then raising his head, his throat vibrating as he swallows. On the stove, the chili bubbles, tomato and garlic steam filling the kitchen.

Mia stands up and lowers the heat on the range, staring at the stove dials.

Her boy knows. He can see that she wants something else, needs it. He's read into her words, her complacent smiles, her acceptance that this is her life. Maybe he's read an e-mail. Maybe he somehow saw her with Robert in the hospital. But how?

She picks up the spoon, hits it gently against the counter. She's making things up, she knows that. But even Harper's seeing inside her doesn't make her stop craving Robert. Even now, she's thinking about him.

The chili rumbles into a simmer. Mia breathes in and then turns away, walks down the hall into her office, and sits at her desk.

❦

Instead of looking at her e-mail, though, she calls Kenzie, who is on BART, headed to her acupuncture appointment in San Francisco.

"I can barely hear you," Kenzie says. "Wait."

Some loud noise in the background slowly disappears, and then Kenzie is back on the line.

"Kids and music. Christ. What's up? How's your mom?"

"I have to tell you something," Mia says. "It's—it's not good. It's not about my mom or anything. But it's—"

Kenzie laughs, interrupting Mia. "You sound like you've betrayed me. Did you use some of my life in your latest story? Did you promise some other boring professor a date with your best friend?"

"No. I'll never set you up again. I promise. It's not that."

"Are you calling me to tell me I need to lose weight? My ass is finally an embarrassment?"

"Right. If your ass is an embarrassment, then mine is a scandal."

"Well, then, just get over it. What is it?"

Mia rubs her nose and sits back in her desk chair. "I think . . ." she begins, and then stops, listening for the sounds of Harper running up the stairs, desperate to find his math book. But the house is silent except for the occasional slight *ting* of the chili pot. "I think I'm going— I think I'm getting involved with another man."

Kenzie doesn't say anything for a second, the muted roar of the BART train constant in the background. "Rockridge. Rockridge Station," the train operator says over the loudspeaker.

"Who?" Kenzie asks finally.

"The plastic surgeon. The one my mom went to see." With the truth in the air, Mia expects to feel worse, her transgressions validated by sound. But she actually feels—she feels better. She finds a breath deep in her lungs and sucks in air.

"Has anything happened yet?"

"Not really. We've talked. E-mailed. I didn't write to him for a week or so, thinking I would forget about it. As if my attraction for him was really all about being scared about my mom's surgery or something. As if I could make it go away. But I can't. It's just that Harper said something weird. I wonder if he—"

"Are you— Have you?" Kenzie stops talking. The train operator mumbles something, doors open and close, the BART train roars. "Look, we're about to go underground. I'll call you after my appointment. Don't—don't do anything yet, okay? I mean, anything real. Just wait—"

The conversation cuts off, Kenzie somewhere underneath Oakland. Mia hangs up her phone and turns to her computer.

    Dear Mia

Robert has written.

Mia forces her eyes to stay on his words. "Dear." "Mia." She doesn't want to read any further, know anything more. All she knows is that he's written back. He's forgiven her enough to do that. He's calling her "dear."

Mia looks at her clock. It's four. It's a Tuesday. A month ago, she didn't know Robert Groszmann. A month ago, she wasn't really able to look at her marriage. A month from now. A month from now. She breathes in and reads on.

    I'm glad you wrote back. Yes, we can
    meet. Let's meet. When? I can get away for
    lunches on the days I'm not in surgery.

```
Nights are good for me, but I imagine they
aren't for you. Give me a date. Let's fig-
ure it out.

    Robert
```

She reads his e-mail over and then stands up and grabs her calendar off the wall. Mia brings it back to her desk and looks at the March and then April dates. Toward the middle of April, her days are full of black ink—a reading, a conference, a trip to L.A., a trip to New York. A book signing. A lecture.

Flipping back to March, she sees all the empty space. Some, she knows, will be taken up with Sally.

Clicking on REPLY, she writes,

```
    Robert,

I can meet for lunch most of next week
and the next, depending on my mother's ap-
pointments. In April
```

Mia stops writing and stares at the screen. Los Angeles. New York. Bakersfield. Minneapolis. She's going all these places and she's going alone, Ford staying in Monte Veda with Harper. During her first book tour, Ford and Harper and Lucien, who was still at home then and still in rehab, went with her on some of her trips, finding movies to go to during her discussions or lectures or workshops. But lately, Ford talks about all the work he has to do, tells her that Harper can't afford to miss any more school. Mia assumes it's because one more novel isn't such a big deal. They all celebrated her first novel as if it were a new baby, but now she's like the mother who has had children too close together, no one wanting to give her another baby shower.

So now when she has to go to a workshop or lecture, Ford and Harper beg off, eat pizza or go to Chinese food night after night, and rent movies at Blockbuster that Mia would never want in the house. Horror. Murder. Vengeance. Slapstick.

She'll be alone. She puts her fingers on the keyboard.

```
In April, I have a number of trips I'm
taking for my new novel. A couple of days
down south. Overnight in the valley. Four
days in Manhattan. A weekend of freezing
to death in the Northeast.
```

She doesn't know what she's writing or saying. But she doesn't erase it. She wants him to know.

```
So let's meet for lunch. Give me a day.
I'll come to Walnut Creek.

   Mia
```

Mia sends the e-mail and then pushes her chair back, ready to go into the kitchen and check the chili. But before she can, her computer makes the sound it makes when mail comes, a trill of electronic bells. She clicks on the icon, and it's Robert.

```
What about Tuesday? One p.m. Kenitos.
I'll make reservations.
```

Without thinking, she answers.

```
Yes. See you there.
```

And then she sends it. Mia pushes back, shaking her head. Even though she's done nothing more than make herself open, vulnerable, exposed, she's amazed. E-mail makes adultery so convenient. As she thinks this, she bends over and jots it down. A good thought. For a character. But now she's this character, and she stands up, her thighs bumping against her desk, and moves fast out of the room, as if she's trying to pretend she wasn't the one who wrote the e-mail or made a date. Made a date.

☙

Ford is happy tonight, relaxed, pleased, as if he's just gotten a load of good news. She stares at him when he walks in the door and puts his wallet and watch in the bowl on the sideboard. He's humming to himself, his movements happy beats to his song. Mia wants to ask him what has happened, but then she thinks about Harper's question. Because of her betrayal, Mia knows that she doesn't deserve to hear what Ford isn't telling her.

But at least he's in a good mood. She will ask him about the therapy. Maybe it's not too late. Maybe they can fix what's wrong before she does something completely crazy.

Ford came home just as Harper returned from his tutor, and even accompanied Mia to Sally's, talking with Sally as Mia reheated the chili and made corn bread for her mother.

Now, back at home, he sits on the front deck, talking with Harper about a movie that's coming out, something Harper read about in *Premier* magazine.

"We'll go when your mother's out of town." He looks back into the kitchen, where Mia loads the dishwasher. "You know how she hates anything with chain saws and hatchets."

"I heard that," she calls out to them. "Stop making fun of me."

She hears her voice saying the words, but it's as if she's plastered on the kitchen wall, stretched from oven to table. Her chest hurts with a truth she will not tell Ford. She bites down on her teeth, her jaw sore from holding back the words. *I'm going to lunch with another man.*

"But it's true. You jump up and run out of the room when anything scary happens."

Mia laughs, but thinks, *I'm still here. And it's scary now. It's getting worse by the minute.*

She starts the dishwasher and rubs her arms, willing herself to stay in her body. But with any sound—Harper pushing back his chair, opening the screen door, slamming it shut—she tingles, soars out of her cells. She can't swallow, and she wonders how she will explain this to Kenzie. To Ford, when she's caught. To Harper, who seems to already know.

Ford comes inside now, the March breeze pulling fog from the coast. He was home early enough to change into jeans and a T-shirt, and it's not hard for Mia to see him as he was in college; the same lean body, tight, muscular arms, round ass. The man she agreed to stay with her entire life.

"He's gorgeous," Kenzie said when she first met Ford. "Even if he's named for a car."

"He's not named for a car. For a town in Texas where his grand-mother was born," Mia said.

"Oh, forget that. It's the gorgeous part that's important."

"I know," Mia said, wondering even then how long she'd have to know Kenzie before she told her that his long, sexy body and beautiful skin and wet, warm mouth weren't enough for her.

❧

Harper is in his room, his door closed, the muffled sound of ear-phone music slipping slightly under his door. Ford is asleep on the couch, the television on. In the kitchen, the dishwasher is fuming steam, the air sticky and sweet with the smell of soap.

Mia stands in the hallway, looking out toward the living room, the phone in her hand. It doesn't look like she's going to be able to talk with Ford about counseling. If she wakes him, he'll be groggy and then grumpy, waving her off and walking into the bedroom. And she can't talk right now, anyway. Her heart has changed rhythms since this afternoon, the usual *thump thump* turned into a *thump, thumpity-thump, thump*. She tries not to imagine this is a sign, a detail provided her from her own body, a warning to go back to normal. Now. Before it's too late. Before stroke or cardiac arrest. Before death.

As she watches Ford sleep, she presses 2, Kenzie's number on the speed dial. Kenzie answers and without saying hello, she starts talking. She's knows it's Mia because she has caller ID.

"I didn't know if I should call you."

Mia walks into her room and shuts the door, enough to keep sound in and enough to let her hear any movement coming down the hallway. "I'm glad you didn't."

"You didn't do anything, did you?"

Sitting on the bed, Mia crosses her legs. She watches the slit of light coming from under Harper's door. "Tuesday at one."

Kenzie doesn't say anything, and Mia can hear her friend's breathing. "Well, I knew it would happen one day."

"Nothing's happened yet."

"No, that's true." Kenzie pauses. "But, you know, that's not true, either. It has happened. Something's happened. You're on your way to making a terrible mistake."

For a second, Mia fumes with a sudden anger. After all she's told Kenzie over the years, after all the lunches and dinners and drinks where marriage and love and happiness and sex have been the main components of their conversation, she wants Kenzie to wish her well. To laugh, throw her head back as she does, and then say, "You go, girl."

But none of this is happening. Mia wants to hang up, and almost begins to say something when Kenzie sighs.

"Listen, I know why you're doing this, Mia. I know things haven't been, well, what you've wanted with Ford. I know I've told you that you can find what you want out there. But it scares me. I don't want you to get hurt. I don't want you to lose what you have. It's too important. Too hard to find. Sounds stupid and old-fashioned, but that's how I feel."

Mia can't move her mouth for a second, unable to speak. This isn't Kenzie. Mia looks at the floor, touches her lower lip with a finger.

"Look, wait," Kenzie says. "It's what I feel, at least in part. My other part wants you to go and then tell me all about it."

Mia smiles, relieved. And then she thinks again of the line she heard so long ago. "And he didn't ask me to marry him. It's just lunch."

Now Kenzie laughs. "Fine. Okay. You're right. I have you married and living in another state already. You might be disgusted by the way he eats. He might belch or fart or ask you to pay."

"He might have dentures he puts in his water glass."

"He might be addicted to Viagra."

"Then I can send him over to you."

"Don't you dare." Kenzie laughs again. "One man on Viagra in this lifetime is enough."

Mia rubs her cheek and changes the phone to her other ear. Kenzie dated a lawyer in his late fifties whose doctor didn't seem to realize how often the lawyer renewed his prescription. "The man has a perpetual hard-on," Kenzie said. "I know, I know. You'd think I'd be appreciative. But after a while, I told him to turn on the television just so I would have something to do while he finished."

Then there is the silence that Mia likes best, both of them there on the line but not needing to speak.

Kenzie says, "Let me know. Call me afterward."

"I will."

"Be careful," Kenzie says, and Mia knows as she hangs up the phone that Kenzie is talking about her heart.

❧

Later that night, after the house is shut down and even Harper is finally asleep, Ford starts with his hips, pushing them against her leg, her ass, his hand finding her breast. His hand rubs and rubs, soft-moving circles of palm, and then he brings his head up and latches on to a nipple. Sometimes he looks at her as he sucks, but tonight the room is dark and she can't tell if he's staring. What does he think he'll see? Does he want her eyes to be closed, her chin up, her mouth open? Should she be panting with desire? After all these years, does he imagine the sex could change?

Does she? What does she want from him? What does she want from herself and her own body?

Mia watches the wisp of light and shadow on the ceiling, the wind moving branches into the outside light, ghost trees on the plaster.

Then he moves his hand to her stomach and slides it down, touching her so suddenly she wants to flinch. She doesn't know why she is surprised, because this is his move, his fingers casting about for wetness. Tonight, there is some, juice from her e-mails with Robert, her fear turning into heat in her center. As he finds her soft, slick wetness, he stops, unlatches from her nipple, says, "Are you a little turned on tonight?"

"Yes," she says, and she's not lying. Because in between them is Robert's body. He's there just outside of her, watching her naked flesh, seeing her erect nipple, feeling her sluice of desire.

"Mia," he says, not a question but a statement, as if he's reminding himself of who he's with, where he is.

"Yes?" she whispers. He breathes in, almost says a word, something slight and mostly incoherent. What is it? Is there something he needs to tell her? Is there someone else in the bed with them besides Robert's ghost? But then Ford is silent, and instead of speaking, he moves on top of her, and she spreads her legs, letting his so-known penis find its way into her. Then he is moving, sliding over and on top of her, kissing her, touching her breast, pushing, pushing until she feels something like pleasure.

EIGHT

Sally

"I see," Sally says into the phone, but her eyes are closed. She shut them the minute she heard Dr. Gupta's voice on the phone. No matter what people have told her about the changes and advances in chemotherapy, she's scared of her oncologist, scared of the word "oncology" itself. She wishes she could just hang up.

"This is good news, really," Dr. Gupta says. "Stage two is not advanced, you know. The treatment will be very straightforward."

She wants to tell Dr. Gupta that he is wrong. Straightforward would mean that there had been no spread to the lymph nodes. Straightforward would mean that the cancer was at stage one, or even better, not on the scale at all. Was that possible? Sally wanted hers to be the first case of stage minus one.

"I've sent the reports to your daughter. She will likely tell you the same thing, Mrs. Tillier. But we can talk more at your appointment this week."

"Do people decide not to do chemo?" Sally asks. "Is that an option?"

In the background of the phone call, Sally can hear music in Dr. Gupta's office. What is it? Jazz? The blues?

"Of course, you make the choices, Mrs. Tillier. But I would advise you to go through with the protocol."

"Have you ever had chemo?" Sally asks, her face flushing, from the question or a hot flash, she doesn't know.

There is another pause, a saxophone, a drum, a piano in her ear. "No, I have not."

"Okay," Sally says. "I'll see you Tuesday."

"Good afternoon, Mrs. Tillier," Dr. Gupta says, and then he and the music are gone.

Sally puts down the phone and scratches her head by her left ear. As she lowers her arm, she feels again how her breast is gone. She moves her right arm and feels how that one is gone, too. As she walks into the living room, she remembers being five or six and running across the grass at school, her arms swinging, nothing impeding her movements. No ache from breasts sore before a period, no flesh weighing her down, no embarrassment from the jiggle-jiggle of her up-and-down movements.

She pushes off hard from her next step, leaning forward for a second, about to run, but then she stops. She's not at the playground; she's not five or six. Right now, she should have her breasts, her nipples, the fat under the skin, the milk ducts. As she stands in the living room, Sally cups the empty space on her chest, trying to remember her breasts' size and feel and form. She tries to conjure up how the heaviness of her flesh felt in David's hands all those years ago, before the cancer made him too weak to even lean forward and kiss her good night on the cheek. Sally closes her eyes, imagines her body, the early breasts pushing out of the plane of childhood, the mother breasts full of milk, the middle-aged sag and drift of skin and tissue, the nipples large and prominent. But she clutches nothing but air.

She shakes her head and then looks out the window, surprised at how happy she is to see Dick walking up the front path, Mitzie a wag of excited dog body behind him. Sally goes to the front door and pulls it open, her face flushed. She watches as Dick bends down and talks to his dog, encouraging her with quick, soft, "Calm down, now. That a girl," and "Who's my girl?"

Sally can imagine him talking to his children that way. To Ellen, his poor wife. To her.

Mitzie yaps more loudly and follows him as he stands straight and continues toward Sally.

"Let's go on a drive," she says, the words out before she really even thinks them. "Then let's go get a milk shake. A chocolate milk shake. At Hubcaps."

"Great," says Dick. He smiles at her from under his golfing hat. "We'll have to take Mitzie home first."

"We'll get the shakes to go," Sally says. "We'll drink them as we walk down Main Street. Mitzie can come with us."

Dick stands straighter; Mitzie wags her tail. Sally grabs her sweater and purse from the table by the door.

"Sounds good, right, Mitzie?" Dick says, and Sally pulls the door closed, locking it behind them.

❧

Now that the drainage tubes are out, Sally is glad to be walking down the street, a milk shake cup in her hand, feeling almost happy. The tubes hurt and chafed, cutting into her skin, keeping her on her back all night. During the day, she'd worn the white camisole with pockets the nurse coordinator at Inland had given her. The pockets held the collection receptacles, little plastic bottles the tubes were connected to. She'd felt as if she were one of those people with an artificial heart, carrying around an important organ on the outside, not really all alive inside. Or maybe it was more like someone who had to cart around oxygen. Actually, Sally knew that it was more like someone with a colostomy, a bag hidden under a loose pair of pants. But she felt trapped, controlled, and the minute Dr. Jacobs took the tubes out and bandaged the incisions, she felt free. Now she can swing her arms. She doesn't have to wear the camisole, her incisions pressed against the cotton shell under her blouse.

"Damn fine shake," Dick says, putting his cup in a trash can. Mitzie yaps, wags her tail, as if she expects the cup to fly out again and back into Dick's hand. Sally smiles to herself, wonders when she started thinking about a dog's hopes.

"My favorite," Sally says, still sipping her shake. They pass a bedding store, a wine bar, an Italian restaurant. No one stares at Sally. No one can see through her blouse. No one knows that underneath all her clothes, she's a child.

Dick clears his throat, takes her elbow as they cross the street. They step up onto the curb and stand in front of the bookstore. Automatically, Sally scans for Mia's books in the window. But her daughter's new novel doesn't come out for two weeks. If it's not in the window then, Sally knows she will walk in the bookstore and talk with the owner, Norman. She does this at all the local stores. And when she goes into any bookstore, she sneaks to the shelves and turns Mia's books to face front, the covers a good advertisement. Sometimes she sneaks a stack to the front table, even though Mia has looked at Sally in horror when Sally tells her what she has done.

"Mom! The publishers have to pay for that," Mia said. "You just can't move the books around."

"Who cares? Even if they stay there for a day, you might get a sale or two. Someone will put them back."

Mia shook her head, and now Sally feels the urge to do something that doesn't remind her of cancer. She wants to walk into the store and take all of Mia's backlist and put it out front, where everyone can see.

But Dick walks on, up toward the bank. "Lovely spring. Not too warm, not too chill."

"Are you taking any trips this year? Last spring you went to Greece." Sally remembers the quick conversations about trips and weather they'd had before, most of them on the sidewalk in front of her condo, Mitzie jumping onto Sally's pant leg.

"I had thought about taking a cruise through the Panama Canal. Then the boat takes you up to Costa Rica. The rain forests and such. Apparently, you take little trips in to see the local tribes. But I don't know. My oldest son's been after me to spend my money. 'Buy a new car,' he says. 'Take a trip,' he says. 'Spend it all, Dad. I don't want it.'" Dick shakes his head. "He doesn't really need the money, it's true. But it seems . . ."

Dick trails off, pulls gently on Mitzie's leash. They all stop walking and wait for the light to change.

"It's not how we were raised." Sally thinks of her mother and father, wealthy enough, but they'd earned it all. Her father had finished medical school at the beginning of the Depression, completed his residency, married his fiancée, and started his practice by the end of it. Those lean years carried into the fuller ones, Sally's mother a stickler about finishing what was on the dinner plate (even canned peas) and wearing clothes out until they were beyond the help of a needle and thread. There were new cars every two years and vacations to Minnesota, but no fancy camps and trips and computer games and clothes and more clothes. She and David, and then Sally on her own, didn't raise Mia, Katherine, and Dahlia to think that the world was their oyster. There was the Del Mar Hotel in Santa Barbara for a week in the summer and a winter trip to Yosemite or Tahoe, but not much more than that.

"No, indeed," Dick says, taking her elbow again, and the light changes and the little walking man flashes green.

"You *should* go," Sally says.

"Well," Dick says, waving his hand. Sally stares at his hand and wrist, the skin smooth despite age spots and a bulging blue vein or two.

"I think your son is right. In fact, I've decided that I'm going to spend my money. My kids are fine. I worry a little about Dahlia, of course. If Steve and she split up, I'm not sure how they would divide their business. But I really don't think that will happen. They're a good couple. It's just mother worry. And really, I don't think I could get through all the money I have. My husband made some good investments before he died, and it's all done very well."

Dick turns to her and smiles, his dark brown eyes intense against his fair skin. "Who knows? We could try to spend it all. What about a trip around the world?"

"I've always wanted to go to Bangladesh." As Sally says the name, she realizes it's true. But why? Why Bangladesh? "And Tokyo and Budapest and—and Edinburgh."

Dick rubs his forehead, moves aside as a woman carrying four large shopping bags passes him. They stop at the next corner and press the button to cross the street.

"I'm not sure about India. Or Japan. Or even Hungary. But Scotland. I'd love to go to Scotland. Sort of a romantic idea. All that green. The highlands. Red-haired women, men playing bagpipes. The whole fairy tale. Maybe I'd even buy a kilt to wear at the senior center to scare the ladies."

In the middle of the crosswalk, Sally grabs Dick's arm. "Let's go, Dick. Let's go to Scotland."

They stop and stare at each other. Sally realizes she's never said anything this wild to anyone on the planet. A vacation? With a man she's only really known for a few months? As she stares at him, his face happy as he mulls over the idea, Sally is hit with the truth that she's never really gone anywhere without someone she's related to, either by blood or marriage. But the idea is out there, floating in the middle of Main Street.

A car honks, and Dick pulls Sally and Mitzie across the street. They start walking back to the car. Sally tosses her milk shake cup into a trash can, but this time, Mitzie ignores the experience.

Dick stops again, this time with his hand on Sally's shoulder, only six inches from her incisions.

"You're joking with me, right?" he asks, blinking.

"No, I don't think so," Sally says.

"What will your daughters say?"

"I don't know," Sally says, though she can hear Katherine perfectly.

"He could be a murderer," Katherine will say. "He might be a gold digger. You don't even know him very well. And what do you need a man for? Go on a trip by yourself. A woman needs a man like a fish needs a bicycle."

Dahlia will say, "Okay, Mom. Sounds good."

Mia won't say anything, nodding, listening to Sally talk. Then, after a long pause, she'll ask, "Are you sure about this?"

Sally can imagine Mia wanting to take notes: a long-widowed mother off on a far-flung vacation with a tall, dark—okay, not dark, very gray, actually—man. She can hear Mia ask, "How do you think it's going to turn out?"

Right now, Sally can see Mia's eyes watching her.

"Bring me postcards," Mia will say once the story has taken hold. "Take lots of pictures."

Dick squeezes her a little, all of his fingers pressing on her gently. She likes his touch, his warm fingers. "Do you think you should talk to them about this?"

One finger at a time, he lets go of her shoulder, and they begin walking again. Suddenly and without warning, Sally is tired, wishing they were already back at the car. Her incisions pulse. Her throat feels itchy. But more than anything, she wants to go to Scotland. She wants to see Loch Ness. She wants to listen to Scottish people talk, their accents lulling her into exactly what Dick said—a fairy tale.

She wants to see Dick Brantley in a kilt at the senior center, chatting up Evelyn Hagen, his long legs on display.

And since the cancer diagnosis, Sally has talked about every single detail with her daughters. Talk, talk, talk. All this talk after years of not really talking about anything important. Truthfully, she's tired of the truth and disclosing her feelings, exposing her body to everyone's gaze. She wants to leave her surgery and all that her surgery means far behind.

"I'll tell them," Sally says, glad to see Dick's solid Lincoln Town Car a block away. "But I'll tell them after we've made the arrangements. We'll plan to go after my chemo is through, Dick. Four or five months. I'm not certain how it will go yet. I have an appointment on Tuesday. But then we'll go to Scotland."

Dick reaches into his pocket and pulls out his keys. As they near the car, he presses a button and all the doors unlock. Mitzie barks and jumps up on the door, scratching lightly with her tiny claws. Dick opens the car door for Sally and smiles at her.

"Scotland," he says.

"Yes," Sally says, sitting down. She leans against the smooth leather seats and breathes in the whiff of new-car smell. *Scotland,* she thinks.

❧

"If I were the oncologist," Katherine says into the phone, "I'd recommend just tamoxifen. With your path report, it's indicated."

"Katherine," Sally says, "you're a pathologist. Dr. Gupta is an oncologist. A specialist. And anyway, I haven't even seen him in person yet."

Sally takes off her sweater and puts it on the couch. She leans forward and sees the Lincoln Town Car disappear around the corner, thinks about the kiss Dick gave her on the cheek as he said good-bye on her doorstep. Sally liked it, the feel of his man's face against her skin, his slightly chocolaty breath.

Sighing, she sits on the couch and listens to Katherine go on and on and on about new chemo protocols and hormonal treatments. Katherine has a terrible habit of talking without asking a question for minutes. Occasionally, Sally has wanted to tell her to join a debate club or go into teaching, the only places other than court where people can talk so long and get away with it. Maybe because Katherine has worked with so many dead people, she feels it's entirely appropriate to talk in huge, clunky paragraphs. None of her patients yawn, shift uncomfortably in chairs, or interrupt. Sally looks around her living room and then closes her eyes, leaning back against the couch.

What will Scotland feel like? she wonders. In her dreams, the Scottish air is soft and almost green. That doesn't make sense, but even more than she does with Ireland, Sally thinks of Scotland as green, despite her knowledge of its big cities and overcast skies. Green hills. Green golf courses. Sea green, olive, moss, loden, celadon, cypress, jade.

"Mother!" Katherine says. "Are you asleep?"

"Not yet, dear. But listen, I will certainly call you after I've seen Dr. Gupta. Nydia Nuñez is going to take me to my appointment on Tuesday, and I'll call you right after I get back."

"Why isn't Mia taking you?" Katherine says with a snort. "She's on sabbatical, for God's sake."

Sally opens her mouth, about to tell Katherine how when Sally found out about the appointment, she did indeed call Mia, but something in Mia's voice was strange, different. Sally knew Mia had a lunch date or a shopping trip with Kenzie or something else she had to push aside and rearrange for yet another Inland visit with Sally. In the instant of Mia's hesitation, Sally pulled the conversation to a stop and then turned it around, maneuvering Nydia into it. Sally could hear Mia's relief and thanks.

And now Sally wants to tell Katherine how many hours Mia has stayed with her, feeding her, cleaning her, helping her through the days when Sally wanted a gun more than she wanted water. But she still hasn't told anyone about how she wanted to die, and she certainly can't bear to hear anything else Katherine has to say right now. So she simply replies, "She had something to do with Harper."

"Oh," Katherine says, instantly defused with the insertion of parental duties, something she cannot malign because she knows she has no right. "Well, call me right away. Or what about a speakerphone? Does Dr. Gupta have a speakerphone? I could be there at the appointment with you."

"I don't know, Katherine," Sally says. "I'll let you know."

"You promise?"

Sally yawns. "Of course. I'll talk with you later, dear." And before Katherine can say anything more than good-bye, Sally hangs up, puts the phone down on the floor, and rests her head on the arm of the couch, falling into a quick, deep sleep.

❧

"It is my feeling, Mrs. Tillier," Dr. Gupta says, "that because the pathology report indicated that there may have been a slight chance of cancerous cells in the right nodes, you would do well with a course of both Cytoxin and then Adriamycin, and then begin tamoxifen thereafter."

Sally sits on the other side of Dr. Gupta's desk, glad to be finally talking to a doctor while wearing all of her own clothes. Earlier in the attached exam room, she shucked off her top once again, and like Dr. Groszmann and Dr. Jacobs, Dr. Gupta examined her, put his fingers into her armpits, skimmed the lines of her incisions softly with his fingertips. He even made her lie down on the table and undo her pants, palpating her abdomen. She was too scared to ask what he was looking for, suddenly afraid that breast cancer could move into the belly, a rare, little-known side effect of surgery. Then he lifted her arms and inspected the drain incisions, clucking at her bruises.

But now Sally almost feels civilized. She crosses her legs and leans forward.

"My daughter, who is a doctor," she begins, feeling guilty about how she cut off Katherine before she could really get going on this subject, "seems to think that tamoxifen alone would be, well, enough."

Dr. Gupta nods and then pushes his glasses back against the bridge of his nose. "Yes, this is often the case with a stage one or stage two diagnosis. But you see, Mrs. Tillier, when Dr. Jacobs shot the dye into your system to find suspect nodes, rather a lot of blue nodes turned up. This does not mean they are cancerous, of course, but sometimes—well, to hedge our bets, a course of chemo can reduce the chance of anything sneaking through. Preventative, more or less. And because your cancer is receptive to hormones, the tamoxifen will repress any further stimulation."

"So you say it won't come back if I do all of this?"

Dr. Gupta rubs the smooth brown skin under his nose with a long finger. "With no treatment, the percentage of reccurrence in ten years is nineteen percent. With tamoxifen alone, it's fifteen percent. With tamoxifen and chemotherapy treatment, your odds are thirteen percent. You are not an old woman, Mrs. Tillier. That two percent can mean seeing more of those grandchildren you have told me about."

Sally watches him, sees how even if he is wrong, he means well. He believes what he says. She knows he would never put anyone through chemo unless he thought it was the right choice. Dr. Gupta, she knows, would prescribe it for his mother. His wife. His sister. His own daughter, if he had to.

"But of course, it is your choice. And you are free to talk with any of my colleagues about this type of treatment."

Sally sits back. This is not what she wanted. Now she will go bald and throw up and lose weight. Her rear will be as flat as her chest. She'll travel to Scotland like a bag of bones. A bagpipe of bones.

"How long will this chemo go on? When will it be over?"

Dr. Gupta looks at the calendar on his desk, flipping through the months into summer. "Let us see. . . . We won't start for a week or more. And then you will have six treatments, three weeks apart. So let's say by the end of July, give or take a week or two."

"Fine," Sally says, and then blurts, "and then I'm going to Scotland."

"Scotland," he says.

"I'm going no matter what. I am going."

"Aye, lassie," Dr. Gupta says, smiling. "I dinna said you couldn't."

Nydia Nuñez drives like a teenager, swerving in and out of traffic. Thankfully, they are now stopped at the intersection of South Main and Mount Diablo Boulevard, which is a very long light. Over the window, Sally clutches what Katherine always calls the Jesus handle.

"I think that's what Barb down the street did. You know, the chemo and the tamoxi stuff. And look at her? Seven years later!"

Sally nods, watching the corner full of pedestrians. If she were with Mia, she would ask her daughter to stop off at Nordstrom so Sally could look for loose blouses with pockets over the breasts. Or where the breasts were. Camp shirts, her mother used to call them. But she wants something nice for her walks with Dick. And Sally knows she will need hats. And scarves. But no wig. There's something about a wig that is always wrong, the color too even, the style a little too big or too straight or too perfect. She's always thought men (most not as lucky as Dick, with a full head of hair) look better bald than with a comb-over or a toupee, both looking ridiculous and somehow tragic. So she will not pretend. She will only cover.

"And her kids have had six kids since then. So she's been a grandmother all those times over. Look what the drugs gave her!" Nydia beats a little rhythm on the steering wheel with her palm. "It's really very good news."

"Yes," Sally says, and then she starts, leans toward the window, blinking. There's Mia, walking down from the parking garage. For a second, Sally wonders if she's conjuring up her daughter as a cure to Nydia's constant ramble, but no. Sally would know her daughter anywhere, the roll of her large hips, her confident gait, the way her arms swing away from her body as she walks.

Sally almost says something, but then presses her lips together. If she says one word, Nydia will honk, blast through the intersection at the first sign of green. Then she will pull over and ask Mia a hundred questions while traffic backs up behind them.

So Mia rounds the block, heading down toward a row of restaurants. Sally rubs her forehead.

"Tired?" Nydia asks.

"Very," Sally lies.

"Well, just close your eyes for a bit. Take a little snooze. I'll have you home in no time."

The light changes, and Nydia accelerates. Sally turns her head slightly to look for any sign of Mia, but her daughter is gone, having disappeared into one building or another. Nydia turns on the radio and begins to hum along to a song so loud and annoying that Sally thinks that probably Harper and Lucien know it.

"I love this song," Nydia says as she picks up more speed. "It's my new favorite."

NINE

Robert

It takes hours before Robert realizes what is wrong with him. All morning as he saw patients, he felt pressure under his throat. For a minute, he imagined his carotids were suddenly clogged, stroke imminent. Then his mind began to float up and out of the exam room, hovering somewhere in downtown Walnut Creek. As he nodded and listened to Mrs. Morales and Ms. Hoffman and Ms. Liu, he realized he was looking for a parking place near Kenitos; he was walking down the sidewalk toward the restaurant; he was sitting across from Mia, smiling; he was saying brilliant, funny things; he was holding her hand; he was in the parking garage, kissing her.

He's not sure any of this will even happen. It's possible this first lunch will be the last, but he can't stop imagining, his heart beating wild as he does.

But it wasn't until he noticed his real, nonimaginary hands that he knew he was so nervous. Beyond nervous. Intensely scared. Almost frozen with fear.

But now it's too late. He's sitting in Kenitos, facing the front window. He's arrived fifteen minutes early, and now it's one minute to one. He's already finished his water and a piece of bread. He wants to throw up; he wants to leave. He wants to cancel all his appointments, quit his job, and leave the country. He wants to call Jack and arrange to meet him at the Golden Lion for an ill-advised afternoon drink and perhaps a syringe of morphine.

Yet as he thinks to push his chair back, he sees Mia enter the space framed by the window, her arms swinging as she walks, her short hair ruffling in the wind. She squints into the glare of the window but doesn't slow. And then she pulls open the thick wooden door, walks into the restaurant, stands in front of the maitre d', who turns to Robert. Mia sees Robert, moves forward. There is nothing Robert can do now to stop anything.

They smile at each other as the maitre d' takes over the conversation, seating Mia, handing her a menu, telling her that their waiter will be with them shortly. Mia takes some time scooting her chair in, arranging her sweater, and setting her purse on the floor. Robert wants to grab her arms and pull her to him, but instead he sips at his water, which is now simply a few melting ice cubes. When she is settled, he puts down the glass.

"You're here," he says, feeling instantly stupid. "I mean, you made it."

Mia sits back and then leans forward. She folds her arms and rests her elbows on the table. "I made it."

Robert wants to laugh, feeling ridiculous. What he really wants to say is that he needs to hold her and sleep with her and then get to know her and sleep with her some more. He wants to ask her questions about her life and he wants to tell her things that he doesn't even understand how to say yet.

"Do you eat here often?" Mia asks, her face pale.

"Never. I always liked the name, though." Robert looks at the menu. "The maitre d' said the roasted chicken special is wonderful."

"This is weird, isn't it?" Mia says. She puts the menu on one of the empty chairs. "I mean, we don't really want to talk about chicken, do we?"

Robert relaxes, his shoulders loosening, his hands unclenching. "No. But I was thinking there's not really a set dialogue for this kind of lunch, is there?"

"Not really. I've never seen a book on it. You know, *Rules for Dating Those You Shouldn't.* Maybe it could be my next one. I'll end up on *Dr. Phil* or *Oprah,* my career finally made."

The waiter comes over and tells them about the chicken, which they both order. Along with glasses of wine. They hand him the menus and then look at each other. Robert clears his throat.

"Okay, let's just say what we need to say. Get it over with. Forget all the small stuff about the weather and work and whatnot."

Mia laughs. "How long is your lunch? We might be here for days."

Robert doesn't say anything, wanting her to begin. To start it. To start everything.

She cocks her head, bites her lower lip. "Okay. Here's this. I've always thought that people who cheat are weak. I think, *Go ahead and be unhappy, but leave first.* Be brave. Talk about it with your spouse. Be honest. Be real. Do the hard work. And then find someone else."

Robert sits back, stares at Mia, wondering what to say. She's right; he knows that. He agrees with her, but he wants to argue, to change her mind and his own.

"But," he starts, but then the waiter is at their table with the wine and a couple of comments. The busboy fills their water glasses. Mia looks down at her hands.

"But," Robert begins once they are alone, "what if you meet that person while you are in the relationship? What if you haven't had the presence of mind to figure out what's wrong and then you find something that's, well, right?"

Mia nods. "True, but—but in my enlightened and unforgiving scenario, I should have talked to my husband before I even e-mailed you. Before going out to lunch. Before anything."

"We haven't done anything, Mia. We're having lunch."

"You're smarter than that, Robert. We've done more than that." Mia sips her wine, her pale face now flushed.

"I know. But not technically. It depends on how you define adultery." He picks up his glass and holds it up, looking at Mia through the pale yellow of the Rombauer Chardonnay. "Is it words or thoughts or deeds?"

"You sound like Clinton."

"I'm starting to understand him now."

"You didn't before? You're not a Republican, are you?"

Robert laughs and puts down his wineglass. "Never. East Coast Jew. Democrat to the core."

They look at each other. Mia's eyes are dark in the restaurant's hushed light. He tries not to, but he lets his eyes slide along her neck. For a second, he wonders if she's thinking about his body. He sighs.

"What else?" he asks.

"Really?"

"Yes."

Mia brings a hand to her cheek and breathes in, her breasts rising as she does. "Okay. Why me? Does this happen a lot? Do you find yourself attracted to many patients, or daughters or sisters or mothers of patients?"

For a second, Robert is angry and wishes he'd never asked her to say what she needed to. What does she think he is? A Casanova? A total greaseball, smarmy doctor, waiting in his office for someone with the perfect body? But as his anger and his thoughts die down, he knows he wants to ask her the same thing, only backward.

He sips his wine, licks his lips. Sits back again. "No, this hasn't happened before. I've never dated a patient or a family member of a patient. You were . . ." He tries to find the words, but there aren't words because what Mia was that day when he walked into the room was a feeling. "I felt—this sounds so sophomoric—like we were talking with our skins. I had a reaction to you."

"Like the hives?" Mia laughs at her own words. "Nausea? Gastrointestinal upset? Eczema?"

Robert almost asks her about her own skin, wondering where it bothers her, where she has an itch. But he knows that she wouldn't appreciate his spying on her records. Not now, maybe not ever.

"It affected my brain," he says. "I could barely concentrate on your mother."

The restaurant is filling and emptying in waves, the maitre d' passing by their table as he leads people to their tables. A wave of smells—cooked onions, garlic, and olive oil—flows into the dining area. Robert looks up and sees that Mia is watching him.

"Well, that's what happened to me, too," she says. "But I blushed. I think I blushed everywhere, all over. I couldn't stop it. I couldn't even look at you for a while because I was scared that you'd notice and think I was ridiculous."

"I noticed that you weren't looking at me. I thought I was boring you."

"It's kind of hard to be bored when your mother has cancer." She looks down at her bread plate.

"You seemed to handle her illness all right," he says.

"Clearly. And now here I am at a restaurant with you," she says, looking at him, smiling. "Maybe that's an indication. I'm flipped out by death, and now I'm embarking on a wild adventure." Mia stops talking for a moment, tilts her head, and looks at him. "But no. I wasn't bored. I was trying to act the way I should have been acting. Concerned for my mother. Normal."

"I know I wasn't thinking straight." Robert takes a piece of bread from the basket and then drops it on his bread plate. He knows he can't eat, but he wants to be doing something.

"Once I could look at you, I thought you were handsome," Mia says. She doesn't turn from him when he catches her gaze. "I liked your ponytail. Your cowboy boots. I thought you were sexy. I wondered what it would be like to be next to your body. And then I thought how stupid I was for thinking that way, when I'm, well, me."

"What does that mean?"

"Please," she begins, but then the waiter comes over with their meals, placing the plates carefully in front of them. Robert and Mia turn down the offer of freshly ground pepper, and then look at each other again.

"What do you mean?" he asks again.

"I'm not exactly perfect," she says, shrugging. "You make people perfect. That's your job. All those breasts and butts you see every day. Unlined faces."

Robert bites down on his back teeth, his jaw hard. This is what he always hears. He thought better of Mia. Thought she knew more. He picks up his fork and knife, slices a piece of his chicken.

"That's not my job."

"What?"

"It's not my job to make people perfect. Sometimes I'm just trying to help them feel okay."

And when he says this, Mia gets it. He can tell by the way her face stills, her eyes focus. Jack always told him there were two kinds of people on the planet. "It's like this, Robert. There's those who get it and those who don't. For everything."

Mia is one who gets it quickly, just like that.

She takes a bite of her chicken and then puts down her fork. "I'm sorry. What you were going to do for my mom. That was to make her feel normal. The rest, well, that's just my inherent low self-esteem talking. Comes from being raised among thin women."

"I think," Robert says, hoping he can manage these words without sounding like an ass. "I think you are beautiful."

Mia laughs, the sound deep and throaty and real. She shakes her head. "I will go as far as attractive. But I'll balk at pretty. I can't even go to beautiful."

"But it doesn't matter what you think about yourself. I'm looking at you," Robert says. "I'm the one seeing you."

"Fine," she says, moving a green bean with her fork. "What else? What other big stuff is there?"

At first, Robert thinks his pager is buzzing against his waist, but then he realizes the vibrations in his body are nerves. He pushes his hair back, looking at Mia. "Your marriage?"

She looks up and then back at her plate, the green beans arranged in a geometrical design. The busboy refills Robert's glass and walks away. Mia breathes in through her nose, her whole chest lifting at the inhale. She seems to swallow the air before she speaks.

"I've known Ford for twenty-two years. We married early. Had kids. Made money as we were going along." She stops. "But that's not the story, is it?"

Robert presses a bread crumb on his plate with his thumb. "I don't know what the story is. It sounds like Susan and Rafael's a little, though."

"It is," she says. "You know what they say: 'Write what you know.' "

"So?"

"So the truth is— I mean, that's what we're doing here, right?" When she looks at him, he knows that she wants him to tell her to lie, to make up another story, one that won't hurt to say. But he can't.

"Yes. The truth."

"The truth is we've grown apart. Or we were never really connected in a way I wanted to be connected."

"What way is that, exactly?" he asks.

"I don't really know. Maybe I'm just making it all up, what I want." She shrugs, her eyes watering. She looks away from him, flicks at her eyes with her hand. He wants to reach out and touch under her eyes with his fingertips, wipe away her sadness. But he just waits.

"I'm sorry," she says after a moment. "I just don't talk about this except with my friend Kenzie. I must need a great deal of therapy."

"We all need therapy," he says. "And don't be sorry. I'm sorry. Go on. Tell me."

She nods. "Well, we had the kids so early, though, that there wasn't time to worry about what I wanted, to realize that we didn't have anything keeping us together but the past. The past and the kids."

Mia scratches her hand absently, little red lines blooming on her skin.

"And I've never been attracted to him. In that way you're supposed to be. Or in the way I wanted to be attracted to him. Something that pushes from the inside out. And it's not just about sex, though, of course, that's part of it. It's about a feeling of wanting that is deeper than that." She flushes and sits back. Robert leans closer and then stops. He pushes his plate away from him.

"You weren't even attracted to him when you first met?"

"No."

"Why did you marry him, then?"

"Good reasons. Safety. Trust. Hope. And a basic, real love."

Robert nods, knowing that that's why he stayed with some of his girlfriends after the fires burned out. Sometimes comfort is more important than passion. He can see Mia staying for that alone. The children would have made it even harder for her to leave.

"Have you," he begins, not wanting to ask this question at all. "Have you worked on it? Counseling?"

"Ford—it's not his way. We went to counseling years ago, but when it got to the part, well, the sex and how I feel, he didn't want to go anymore. Said we could work on it ourselves. But the thing is, if that core attraction isn't there, I don't know if it can be worked on."

Robert feels the question coming out of him before he can stop it. "Are you attracted to me that way?"

Mia has teared up again, a smudge of mascara at the corner of her right eye. "Yes. Yes, I am."

≼

They walk out of the restaurant together, Robert holding open the door, Mia passing by him, the smell of her in his nose. He needs to be back at the hospital at three, and it's two forty-two and thirty seconds. He can take five minutes to walk her to her car, jump into his, and get back before his next patient. Five minutes. Five more Mia minutes.

"I'm sorry about that back there," Mia says. "I didn't mean to cry."

Slowly, Robert puts his hand on the small of her back, and he feels her flesh start, surge, heat under his palm. She doesn't pull away.

"That's okay. It's not a topic I bet you want to talk about all the time."

She shakes her head. "Only with Kenzie."

"You can trust her?"

Mia pauses and then nods. "Yes."

"What about your sister Katherine?" he says, smiling. "I bet she'd understand. She seemed like the kind of woman who appreciates the subtleties of marriage."

Mia turns to him, the sun striking her eyes so that they look liquid. "Oh, she'd love to hear me tell it. She'd tell me I should be with a woman."

"She's a lesbian?"

"Only half of the time," Mia says. "Bisexual. She says that it gives her better odds for finding a Friday-night date."

"She's probably right," Robert says.

They turn the corner and then stop in front of a Volvo station wagon. Seeing it, Robert remembers Mia's two children, her life as a mother, as a wife. He can still feel her boy's gaze on him as he stood outside Sally Tillier's hospital room door.

Robert's throat tightens, and he takes his hand from her back. "When can I see you again?"

"When *can* you see me again?" she says. "I'm the one on sabbatical."

"Thursday?" he asks. "Same time?"

Mia pulls her keys out of her purse. "Let's go somewhere else."

He knows where he wants to take her, but he's not sure that she's ready. But before he can say anything, she nods and says, "Your house. After what you told me, I want to see it."

He closes his eyes, swallows, and nods back. He forces himself to open his eyes and look at her. "My house." Then without knowing how to stop himself, he leans over and kisses her. She smells like Altoids—but he doesn't know if he's smelling his own breath, because she gave him a mint, too. When she opens her lips to him, he tastes not only the peppermint but sliced oranges drizzled with balsamic vinegar, a background of dark coffee. Her lips make him want to sink against her; her tongue makes him want to pull something out of her that he can take home with him. Her voice, her thoughts, her laugh. For a moment, her breasts are pressed against him and her hand smoothes up behind his neck, her fingers touching his ponytail. Then she pulls her chest from his, her mouth from his. Slowly, her tongue leaves his, her lips leave his, her breath leaves his.

Her eyes are still closed, and he can see how fast her chest goes up and down. As fast as his.

"E-mail me," she says finally, opening her eyes. "Tell me how to get to your house."

Robert nods. "I will."

Mia clicks her door open and then turns to him. "We did it again."

"What?" he asks, putting his hands in his pockets, hoping she can't see his erection.

"We didn't talk about you. We didn't talk about—"

"I know," Robert says. "We will."

Mia stares at him and then bites her lip. "Okay, Robert Grosz-mann, M.D. I'll see you Thursday."

He forces himself to stay put. He needs to be back in the hospital in twelve minutes. If he moves forward, he will kiss her again, despite all his patients who might be roaming the streets, despite all her students or fans spying out of the linen shop behind them. Despite the patient who is probably already sitting in his exam room, freezing in her gown.

Mia gets in her car, starts the engine, and then waves, pulling out into the street. He turns, follows the Volvo until she makes a left-hand turn and is gone.

◆

Once, Jack said, "You know, people forget how many mistakes *they* make a day. Running a red light. Pushing the wine stopper in instead of pulling it out. Slicing a finger while cutting an onion. Typos. Spilling paint. Tripping over the dog. And why, then, does anyone think we don't make mistakes? Why are doctors supposed to be above that? Like we know something everyone else doesn't?"

Jack had been drunk at the time, but even so, Robert agreed with him. If the average person could follow a doctor—maybe a surgeon like him—around for a day and if the doctor was honest, it would be clear in about an hour that doctors weren't better than anyone else. But instead of spilled paint, it was a sloppily written prescription that resulted in the wrong drug in the right bottle. It was a misread of a slide that sent a sick man home with a cancer that would have time to multiply even further. Or it was just boredom or fatigue or anger or an incessant pager that kept the doctor from paying attention, making him miss a key point, the telling symptom, the worry in a patient's face.

Now, after his lunch with Mia, Robert forces himself out of the memory of her, of their kiss. He pushes himself into the moment with Mrs. Millar, his gloved hand under her armpit, feeling her lymph nodes. As he always does with patients, he does not look at her face while he does this exam, even though they are just inches apart. He keeps this distance so he can help Mrs. Millar forget they are so close, and he does this because he doesn't want anything on his face to show if he feels something he doesn't like. And at this moment, he doesn't like the way her nodes feel; they are hard and swollen under her armpit, and he is certain that the surgery will not reveal the best news.

As he moves his fingers slowly, Robert realizes he will not perform the delayed reconstruction on Mrs. Millar for a long time, maybe never. She will come out of her surgery with a stage-three or -four diagnosis, and spend the next months of her life trying to live. Certainly, they will talk further about all her options after he finishes this exam, peeling off his gloves and washing his hands. He will make another appointment with her to confirm that she does, indeed, want a delayed reconstruction. But sometime—either before her surgery or after—she will decide she needs to focus on living. Mrs. Millar is only fifty-six, and the chemo will be long and painful. Maybe later, maybe after the drugs and the hats and wigs and weight loss and despair, she will decide to come back to him, her body scoured and purged by chemo, her immune system regrown cell by cell. But Robert doesn't think so. He thinks Mrs. Millar will have had enough.

Robert slides back in his chair and looks at her. He takes off his gloves and throws them away. She nods, sighs, and begins to cry.

"It's bad, isn't it," she says rather than asks.

He wants to lie, to tell Mrs. Millar it will be all right. Maybe before, he would have extolled the virtues of chemo and radiation, and brought up the wonders of tamoxifen and Herceptin, a new, improved weapon for the war on cancer. He might have told her what a wonderful surgeon Cindy Jacobs is; accurate; steady, clever, thorough. But now Robert just takes her hand, lets her cry, and only later, when Mrs. Millar has left his office, clutching the slip noting her second appointment, does he realize that he managed to forget Mia and her lunchtime tears.

ᴥ

At home, Phyllis is ignoring him, as usual, her tail whooshing back and forth behind her as she faces her empty dish. The floorboards creak under him as he walks to the kitchen to find, again, that he's forgotten to go shopping. There is so much he can't seem to supply himself with, food being the most obvious.

"Shit," he says, putting down his briefcase. Now he wishes he'd taken home the chicken that neither he nor Mia could really finish. He thinks it was good, but he's not sure, as all his senses were focused on Mia, her words, her face, her body.

Robert is about to pick up the phone and call DiGrassi's Pizza for a delivery, when the phone rings.

"I'm down here by myself," Jack says before Robert can say anything more than hello, "imagining what my best friend is doing without me. I'm hoping he's got a girlfriend, a replacement for the beautiful Leslie. Finally, I think, he's found someone to settle down with."

"Shit," Robert says again. He's not only forgotten to shop, he's forgotten his standing date with Jack.

"Rob, get your ass over here or we're finished."

He knows he has to go meet Jack, but his body is weary, all his appointments and his lunch with Mia heavy inside him. But there's food at Basso's, and maybe he can talk to Jack about Mia.

"All right. I'll be there in ten minutes."

"Make it seven, or I'm finding a new boyfriend."

Robert hangs up the phone. He wants to go in and check his

e-mail, but if he does that, he knows he'll never make it to the restaurant. So he fills Phyllis's dish, turns off the kitchen lights, and leaves.

Jack is on his second beer, an empty bread basket in front of him. He has a tan from a weekend trip to Palm Springs; his tie lies in a loose pile on the tabletop.

"I'm crushed," he says, as Robert sits down. "I'm mortally wounded. Stood up."

"I've redeemed myself, haven't I?" Robert waves the waiter over and orders a beer, taking the menu, feeling the repetitive motions from his lunch today. *Maybe,* he thinks, *I should only eat in restaurants, never shopping, never cooking.* All he has to do is sit and order and wait and then eat. But then it wouldn't be much different from the way he eats at home.

"Not yet. You need to tell me a good story."

"What about you tell me about Palm Springs? How was the golf?"

Jack holds up a hand. "I'm the one who's been waiting."

Robert nods, reading the menu. The waiter comes back, takes their orders, and then Robert sits back, his hand on the beer the waiter brought him. Robert knows he's already told Jack about Mia and how he read her medical file. But as he opens his mouth to talk about Mia, he suddenly feels protective of her, of them. Or is he scared? As if by breathing the words into the air, he'll jinx the whole thing. And he can't do that before Thursday, before she comes to his house.

"What are you thinking?" Jack stares at him, no longer ready to joke. "Something up with a patient?"

Robert rubs his forehead, closes his eyes.

"Man, what is going on? Nothing happened like . . ."

Robert shakes his head. "No. Nothing at work." He doesn't know how to say what he has to, but if he can't talk with Jack, who can he talk with? Jack is his best, oldest friend. The one person who knows everything. "It's the patient's daughter."

Jack sips his beer, sits back, thinks. Then he says, "The one with the medical file? With the kid in rehab?"

"Yeah. We went out to lunch today."

"One lunch did this to you? That's it? Nothing more than a meal?"

Putting the beer on the table, Jack folds his arms, staring across at Robert. Finally, he laughs. "You're gone."

"What?"

"You're gone, Rob. I haven't seen you like this since—since, Christ, I don't know. You've got that weird, spacey thing going on, kind of like you used to have during finals."

The waiter brings over their salads, and Robert stares at the arrangement of greens and vegetables. He does feel like it's finals, needing to learn all the important things before the big test, the one that could make or break him. All these days, all the e-mails, the meeting in the cafeteria, their lunch today, Mia's swift kiss in the hospital corridor, the deeper kiss by the car—all of this is leading to something he can't really see but knows is crucial.

He picks up his fork, spears a tomato. "Yeah, I'm gone."

"What's she like?

"She's . . . I don't know. Smart. Talented. Pretty."

"Sounds like most of the women you've dated. And this one's married. Kind of a drawback."

Robert sighs. "Yeah. But I feel— I feel something different when I'm with her. I can't really explain."

"Well," Jack says. "Be careful. This one is complicated."

"I know."

"It's not perfect, Rob. It's not easy. But it's good." Jack laughs, sits back, wipes his hands on his napkin. "It's about fucking time."

❧

This time when Robert comes home, he doesn't go into the kitchen. Instead, he walks into the living room and turns on the lights. He stands in the middle of the room and turns around slowly, looking at his leather furniture, his full bookshelves, the potted dracaena and palm, dark wool rugs. He pretends he's Mia, seeing his house for the first time. He imagines he's Mia trying to figure him out by looking at what's here in this room. He's pulling clues from objects, from the ceiling beams, from the oak-plank floor, from the windows looking out to the courtyard.

After a few minutes, he knows he wants Mia to see him as she sees his house. Attractive. Good-looking. Comfortable. Sturdy and solid and clear.

Turning off the lights, he leaves the living room and walks to his study. He clicks on the e-mail program, his hands shaking. He wishes she were here now. Right now. And before he reads any of his e-mail from friends and colleagues, he writes to Mia. He writes to her and tells her how to get to his house.

TEN

Mia

In the long night after her lunch with Robert, Mia lies awake in her bed, Ford next to her, snoring softly. Her body is pressed up to his, her breast against his back, her stomach against his naked ass, her arm holding him, her hand on his chest. Harper is still awake, his music in the hallway, and outside an owl trills a spring song over the bay laurels and oaks.

Ford made love to her again, the second time this week. Again as he held her body, his hands and arms seemed to be filled with an explanation of some kind. He was slower, tentative, just plain different, needing to tell her something important. But even as they moved together, she didn't ask what he needed to say, and now Mia wonders if like Harper, Ford knows about Robert, too. It's as if she is giving off radio waves or signals or pheromones that relay a message of betrayal that everyone can hear or see or smell.

But after all the kissing and sucking and penetration, the rocking and Ford's moans, the caresses and sighs, he's said nothing, and now he is asleep and Mia holds him and her guilt.

Mia moves her hand on his chest, her fingers traveling through the scant hair. When they met, he had exactly three hairs growing in the bone valley between his pectorals, and now, with time and age, his chest is full of black, springy hair. She feels she knows every hair follicle. She knows everything about his body: the feel of his skin, his smooth shoulders, his strong arms, his wonderfully long fingers. She knows his smells, the way hard alcohol comes out of his pores at night, the tang of his morning breath, the whiff of his underarms and crotch. She's held him while he's thrown up—she's comforted him in fever and through cold. She's cut his toenails; she's bathed him and washed his hair after his bunion surgery. Every single thing she's done for her children, she's done for Ford, except, really, to wipe him after he's gone to the bathroom. But she would if he needed her to. She would without flinching.

And he's known her in this exact way, through all the growing and then aging of their flesh, through childbirth, through illness, through the sex they've had for years, all kinds, the experimental and the comforting. He's watched her gain and lose and gain weight. He doesn't leave the bed when she passes gas at night; he laughs, makes a joke, keeps watching the news. He stays in the bathroom when she changes a tampon. They know each other in a way Mia realizes she doesn't literally have the time or strength to get to know another human being. She will never know Robert's body in this way, and then she wonders why if she's been graced to know another person the way she knows Ford, why does she want something else? Isn't this enough? She can hear Sally's voice in her head, saying words Sally hasn't really uttered.

"You shouldn't give up something so many people will never have. Someone who loves you. Someone who takes care of you. Don't you realize that on this planet there are millions of lonely people? Be grateful for what's in front of you. You're imagining a kind of love that doesn't really exist. That doesn't last for long. For heaven's sake, Mia, be a good girl. Snap out of this!"

Mia sighs, moves in closer to Ford's strong body. Sally's right. There is something terribly wrong with her if Ford and his solid love aren't enough.

And she wants Robert so much, even though she would be

cheating. "Cheating." What a terrible word. Is what she's doing with Robert cheating? Or is she cheating herself by staying with Ford when she doesn't feel connected, attracted, engaged? Is she cheating Ford out of a love he might find with someone else? Is she cheating Harper out of his family by not insisting on counseling? She should wake Ford up right now and demand it. Not let him go back to sleep until he cries out *yes*.

Mia traces Ford's shoulder, stares at his skin, dark in the night bedroom. She doesn't wake him; doesn't shake him out of his dream. She can't. She doesn't suddenly have the language to tell him what she hasn't before. Would she use the word "cheating"? Why do they use the word "cheating" at all? Why not just call it living? All of them are trying to find something, right?

She presses her face to Ford's neck, breathing him in. He stirs, presses back against her, brings a hand to her hip, squeezes, sighs, goes back to sleep.

Falling to her back, she looks up at the ceiling. They know each other like animals, like cave people, creatures who sniff and scratch at each other, the body of a loved one the same as their own. But she knows that Ford doesn't understand all of her, and if that is true, she must not understand all of him. His body, like hers, must be missing that same elemental connection. There are thoughts she's withheld, ideas, wishes, hopes. Desires. He doesn't read much of her writing these days, though he is proud. And what about her? She doesn't ask enough questions about his work, his meetings, his business trips. She doesn't know the specifics of his days or the fine details of his trade, though she spends his money as well as her own. Mia doesn't know his business partner, Karen, very well at all—having shared nothing more than a few brief conversations with her when she called Ford at the office—and she doesn't really feel the need to.

Mia and Ford have parented two children, but those children are older now, far past the age when she and Ford traded off diaper changes, traded off reading to the boys in bed, traded off doing dishes. They no longer fight about who gets to go away for a weekend trip alone with friends, because they both can go anywhere without any child coming to harm.

Mia wipes her eyes. Aside from this physical connection of known flesh, there isn't anything else but history—the past that is half of her entire life—holding them together. Just that. Just half her life.

☙

Mia looks over at Kenzie, who pumps furiously on the elliptical machine, her curly red hair, breasts, and ass bobbing in a nice way, nice enough for the men walking past their two machines to smile. But Kenzie doesn't notice the men because she is looking at Mia, who is moving much more slowly than her friend.

"So it was good?" Kenzie says in an unaccustomed whisper. "You're going to see him when? Tomorrow?"

"It was good." Mia picks up her water bottle and takes a sip. "And I'm going over to his house."

"Where does he live?" Kenzie sounds normal, trying to ask her normal kinds of questions, but her eyes roam Mia's face, as if she expects Mia's hiding something behind her eyes or ears or in her mouth.

"Walnut Creek. He has an adobe. It's a historical-preservation house. With a plaque, even." Mia puts down her water bottle and tries to move faster. She should do this every single day, not just the three or four times a week when Kenzie has time to work out with her.

"Oh," Kenzie says. She turns to look at the television, so Mia does, too. On the screen, Meredith Vieira is asking the question: "A glossectomy is an operation that removes which body part?" The answers are nose, tongue, kneecap, navel.

"Tongue," Mia whispers.

"What?"

"Tongue." Mia shrugs, points at the television, and then drops her hand when Kenzie continues to stare at her. "Listen, are you mad at me?"

Kenzie shakes her head, but then she stops moving. "No. I'm not mad at you. I just don't understand. I mean—"

Kenzie lowers her voice, rubs sweat off her cheek. "Adultery is only okay—it's only okay if you end up together."

Mia snorts, rears back, stops the movement of the machine, the whir of the motor wheezing silent. "What planet are you from, Kenz? Where is this coming from? What about all your—" She stops, whispers, "Adventures."

Mia stands still, confused. All the stories, the married men, the single men, the men in relationships. She's listened to all that Kenzie has told her, and now when she finally has something to say, Kenzie won't hear her out?

"I don't understand what you're saying," Mia says.

Kenzie doesn't say anything as the two men walk by again, and this time she sees their glances. She shakes her head. "I don't know. But I just don't get it. I just don't know why you are . . . No, that's not true. I do know why."

Mia starts moving again slowly, her heart pounding not from exercise but from the look on Kenzie's face. "What don't you know?"

"You're not going to leave Ford, are you?" Kenzie whispers. Mia breathes in, and they both start to move again, treading miles to nowhere.

"I'm going over to Robert's house. That's not leaving Ford."

"Are you going to sleep with Robert?"

Mia's body knows the answer before she does, a plumb line of heat moving from her throat to groin. "Yes."

"And what else?"

"What else is there?" Mia whispers, her voice so low that Kenzie leans toward her.

"Living with him. Actually loving him. And then leaving Ford and Harper and Lucien."

"Kenzie," Mia says, stopping again. "Lucien is grown. Harper is in high school. And sleeping with someone else is not living and loving and leaving."

"You need to tell Ford first." Kenzie moves faster, her legs pushing hard on the machine. "At the very least, you need to tell him and then offer to go to therapy. You owe him that, Mia. That's the very least that you owe him."

Mia feels stuck, something hard pressing against her throat. She turns and looks in front of her, her legs moving faster. "You know what happened when I asked him to go to therapy before. You know how upset he got when I brought up the sex stuff."

Kenzie turns toward Mia, but Mia keeps staring ahead.

"That was before—before you were going to do something like this. Like maybe leave him. I think he might feel differently now."

"Maybe," she says, knowing that, of course, Kenzie is right. "I've wanted to tell him."

"Christ, Mia. You've got no choice. This is coming out of left field!"

Mia swallows finally, instant tears in her eyes. "It's not like this should surprise you, Kenzie. I've told you how I feel a hundred times."

Kenzie stops and almost jumps off her machine. "But this is real. This is . . . Let's go outside. I think I'm going to have a heart attack."

Before Mia can even slow down her machine, Kenzie is walking toward the doors that lead to the pool. Mia watches her throw her towel down on the wooden table and then slump into a chair. Slowly, Mia steps off the pedals, finds her balance, and follows Kenzie, pushing out into the air.

"Tell me what is going on with you," Mia says, sitting down and pulling her chair close. "If I can't talk about it with you, who can I tell?"

Kenzie shakes her head and then looks at Mia. "I don't like it."

Mia shakes her head. What was to like? And why, suddenly, was Kenzie putting a restriction on what they talked about? Why was she judging Mia on what she'd known about Mia all along?

"I'm not asking you to like it." Mia sniffs, wipes her eyes, wonders who she'll be able to talk with now that Kenzie won't help her.

Three small children run by, their towels wrapped around their cold bodies. In the pool, a submerged swim instructor waves them toward the pool.

Kenzie rubs her cheek, sighs. "It scares me. And pisses me off."

"It scares me, too," Mia says. "I know I'm doing something incredibly stupid. I could be ruining everything. But it's like I've come to a point where I either jump or head back and forget about it."

"What's *it?*" Kenzie says.

"Love."

"Oh, for Christ's sake, Mia!" Kenzie raises her hands as she speaks and then lets them hang in the air. A swimmer in the pool stares up at them, adjusts his goggles and pushes off the wall for another lap. "Love. It doesn't always last. Don't you know what it's like out there? What if Robert doesn't work out? Where will you be then?"

Mia is silent, shame and heat and tears everywhere in her body at once. "You don't think Robert really wants to be with me?"

"No!" Kenzie says just as loud. "No, I don't mean that."

She shakes her hands as if they show what *that* is. "What I mean is Ford is a good man. A solid, wonderful, fucking sexy man. Wait." As Mia shakes her head, Kenzie raises her hands, palms out. "Let me talk. Just wait. And you've had your problems, and I know he doesn't seem to really understand you all the time or do it for you in bed. But, Mia, like I said, you need to go to counseling first. You owe it to Ford to tell him how you're feeling. You don't just decide one day that you're ready and find another man who turns you on."

Mia sits back and crosses her arms. "I didn't find him. He

opened the door and was there. I didn't want to find him, Kenzie. You know that."

Leaning forward, Kenzie looks at Mia, her green eyes slit against the light reflected off the pool and deck. Then her shoulders sag, her tense face relaxes. "I know you didn't, Mia."

"Then why are you so angry? Why can't you feel the way you did when you said, 'No one person can meet all our needs'? Right now, you sound just like my mother."

Kenzie rolls her eyes and then closes them. "Because no matter what I ever said, I want to believe in you and Ford. I want to believe that there's a man for me. Like Ford. Like Robert. I want to believe that Robert and Ford are the same person. That all that time and commitment and desire come in one person. And . . ." She stops and rubs her forehead. "And it's my turn. I've been like this for years. You don't know what it's like, and if you do this, you might end up just like me. Picking men from their photos on Date.com."

Kenzie wipes her eyes with her towel and then scrunches up her face, pretending to carefully study the swimmer thrashing across the pool. After an early marriage in her twenties, Kenzie has been single, dating, having her adventures, once living with a man—Liam—for a year. That year was filled with dinners at the Aldens', Mia and Ford and Kenzie and Liam sitting out on the deck eating and drinking wine; the four of them going to plays in the city; all of them flying down to L.A. to visit the Getty Museum when it opened. But then Liam was transferred back to Dublin, and Kenzie stayed home. Since then, there have been dates and monthlong relationships, but no Ford or no Robert for her.

As Mia watches her best friend, she is hit with waves of sorrow and regret that rip up her chest and flow into her throat. She shakes her head, unable to believe that this is Kenzie's reaction, unable to believe how much it hurts. If Kenzie—the person who truly knows Mia the best—thinks her plans with Robert are unwise, how can Mia go forward? How can she want what must be ridiculous and stupid? How can this biggest thing, what she wants most, be wrong?

Kenzie wipes her eyes again, shakes her head. Mia nods, pretending to understand the silence between them, but inside, her bones ache. Why did she think Kenzie would really understand? All along, Mia's whining and moaning about married love was tolerable when it was only theoretical. When it didn't hurt Kenzie. When it was safe. But now Kenzie must think Mia is throwing away the very thing Kenzie has always wanted.

"I'm sorry," Mia says, not knowing what she is sorry for. For telling Kenzie at all? For loving Robert? For not appreciating Ford the way Kenzie wants her to? For Kenzie and her love life—for Liam and all the wrong men she ever dated?

But Kenzie seems to understand, this "sorry" the right sorry. "I know."

"I'm not leaving Ford," Mia says quietly.

"I know."

"I'm just—"

"I know," Kenzie says, putting her hand on Mia's arm. "I'm sorry, too. I am. I want to know what you are feeling. I want to be there for you. Really."

Mia puts her hand on top of Kenzie's and sits back. She wants to believe Kenzie, but Mia knows she has to stop talking about Robert. For the first time in two decades, Mia sees a subject that Kenzie can't relate to, won't relate to. Refuses to. Mia knows she can't tell Kenzie anything else about Ford or Robert or sex or meetings in adobe houses. She is going to have to do this alone.

❧

"Hel-lo?" Lucien says on the phone, the way he always says it, as if he's an unknown son calling a strange family. He uses his low voice, a kidding voice, the voice he's borrowed from Ford, one of the voices Ford used when he read to the boys: the voice of monsters and gremlins and trolls and dwarves from all the fairy tales.

Mia is in the kitchen, holding a hot pad and a meat thermometer. The chicken seems to still be frozen in the middle, the temperature inside barely 140, which means pink. Outside, the fowl looks like a burn victim, a tragedy, a horror. They'll have to go for Chinese food downtown.

"Hmm," Mia begins, looking at the chicken through the oven door. "Hi, Lucien."

"What's going on?"

"I'm killing dinner. What's up with you?" Mia puts down the thermometer and hot pad and leans against the counter. In the living room, Harper watches *The History of the Gun,* a show Mia describes as the program about the evolution of death.

"I forgot about the utilities," Lucien begins. "My roommates are hounding me, and I spent what I had already."

"Yes," she says, waiting. Every month since he moved into a rental house with three other guys, he's been unable to handle a budget.

"I forgot. Really."

"Uh-huh. So, what are you reading?" Mia asks, ignoring the fact that her oldest son is again asking for more money, his addictions gone but his impulsiveness still evident. On whims, he's driven home from Olympia without telling anyone, barreling straight down Highway 5 for ten hours, getting two tickets and busting the radiator of his used Infiniti G20. He's decided to hitchhike across the country, calling Mia and Ford from South Falls, the home of Mia's uncle Ralph, her father's older brother. He and one of his roommates, Jay, decided to explore homelessness, and slept on the streets of Seattle one night, finding an old mattress in an alley, huddling next to each other. But unlike the other homeless people they met that weekend, they stopped for a big breakfast at Pig 'n' Pancake on the way home.

Lucien began writing short stories when he was ten, finding Mia's old portable typewriter in the garage and arranging a writing station for himself. Somehow he learned to type, avoiding the typing manuals and all those lines of *j ; j ; j ;* and *a f a f a f* that Mia labored through in high school.

Now he stays up all night and writes. He eats Froot Loops in mixing bowls. She knows he will be a better writer than she is. He amazes her.

"The Story of O," he says. "Pretty tame."

"Not back then."

"A simultaneous orgasm was revolutionary in the twenties. Now it's in those romance books at Safeway. . . ." And Lucien is off, comparing D. H. Lawrence to Erica Jong to Pauline Réage to Henry Miller to MTV to daytime soaps. His class this semester is "Sex, Gender, and Sexuality: The Multimedia Mirror."

"How much?" Mia asks after their discussion.

"Fifty."

"Are you okay?" "Okay" is the key word, the easy word, the word that conveys everything.

"Great. Okay."

"I'll put it in the bank tomorrow on my way to—when I do some errands."

"Thanks."

"Try to stop smoking so much. What do they cost a pack now?"

"Yeah, yeah."

"I mean it, Luc."

"How's everything there?" Lucien asks, and she wishes he were older, that he'd already finished his class, that he was married. That he had arced far enough out of childhood and away from her so that she could tell him the story. Because she can really talk to Lucien, and he would understand. But he's her son, will always be her son, and he would never understand this thing that has to do with his father.

"Okay," she says. She tells Lucien she loves him, and they hang up.

⁊

Just as Ford, Harper, and Mia are leaving for the Chinese restaurant downtown, Dick Brantley pulls up in his giant Lincoln and the passenger's-side window rolls down. Sally puts her arm out and waves. Mia stops on the walkway, staring at her mother, who is smiling, her face full of light and heat, her eyes wide. Dick leans down and waves, too.

"Where are you going?" Sally asks. Ford walks up to the car and puts his hand on the door.

"Chinese downtown. There was a massacre in the kitchen," Ford says, looking back at Mia, who crosses her arms.

"Oh, we'll join you, okay? I love their Mongolian beef. That sounds good, doesn't it, Dick?"

Dick nods, and Ford pats the door. "Okay, we'll see you down there."

The Lincoln slides away, and Mia, Harper, and Ford get into Ford's BMW.

"Grandma looked high," Harper said. Mia is about to argue with him, but then she knows that Harper saw Lucien high enough times to know what high looks like. And he's right. Her eyes were bright and glossy and full of pleasure, and that's not a look Mia has ever seen on her mother's face before. Not that she can remember. And Dick looked a bit goofy, too, smiling, almost stunned.

Everything in Mia stills, and she knows that her mother has gained something from losing her breasts. But what? What's taken their place? Is it the Zoloft that Mia had Dr. Jacobs prescribe? Or is it being with this man, Dick Brantley? Or is it something else, some kind of strange freedom that the surgery has given her? Some way of connecting with the world in a way Sally's never done before? There's more of Sally than ever.

"She's just feeling better," Ford says. "She's free of the cancer. The pain from the surgery is gone. Anyone would look like that."

Mia nods and gazes out the window. Fog is rolling over the hills, the last of the sunlight glinting gold off the waves of white. She keeps nodding and then stops because it's not just that her mother has lost something or that she is free of pain. There's something else, something in Sally's eyes that reminds Mia of escape. Of freedom. Of release.

Somehow Sally has found what Mia wants.

❦

"Don't you adore this place?" Sally says once they are all seated at a large round table at the restaurant. In the middle, a lazy Susan rumbles in a circle as everyone takes a teacup.

Sally whispers, "They try to be chic, but there's all those little ceramic creatures on the windowsill. See?"

She points, but only Harper and Dick look. Ford studies the menu, and Mia watches her mother. As she does, Mia finds herself pulled toward Ford, her thigh against his, their knees touching. If she were on the couch in the living room with him, she'd slip her hand around his back and rub his side. Suddenly, she wants to take him home and make love with him, though nothing in her body is telling her to do this. Not her vagina. Not her breasts. Not her stomach, the pulse she found there when she first saw Robert. It's her mind that wants to, and she wonders why the two aren't connected.

Maybe she's just afraid of being without Ford. Like Kenzie says, she doesn't know what it's like out there.

"Well?" Sally looks at Mia. "Honey, where are you?"

"Oh, sorry. What?" Mia sees the waitress is looking at her, so she closes her menu. "What about kung pao chicken?"

"Love that dish," Dick says, and they all hand the waitress their menus.

"Once when I was here," Sally says, "a man got angry because there was no butter for his rice. Can you imagine? Butter on rice in a Chinese restaurant!"

Ford presses his knee hard against Mia's, their recognition of silly Sally talk. Mia presses back, and something opens in her chest. She swallows, hoping it will fill up before she starts to think about tomorrow.

Mia sips her water and then puts the glass down. She wipes her mouth and sees that Harper is staring at Ford, watching his father talk to Dick Brantley about the workers' compensation crisis in California. Harper's eyes have the veil of boredom he uses when he wants to hear something but not be detected, the look his fourth-grade teacher said he wore just to make her angry. He's always received good grades, though, despite it.

"How was school today?" Mia asks, and when Harper flicks his eyes at her, the veil is gone.

"Fine," he says, and then the workers' compensation discussion is over, and Sally and Dick are asking Harper questions about high school. What classes is he taking? Does he have a new girlfriend? What does he want to study in college? Who is his favorite teacher?

Harper sits back, slightly flushed, and answers each question until the soup comes.

"There," Sally says, looking into the bowl the waitress places in front of her. "Isn't that wonderful?"

Mia stares at the spinach and rice and chicken floating in the steaming broth. Is it wonderful? Is soup wonderful when there are hacked-off breasts and adultery and drug addiction and loss and pain and need and suffering everywhere?

"Yes," Dick says. "It's all absolutely wonderful."

Mia holds the directions to Robert's house in one hand as she drives, looking at the street signs, the paper, the road. She could kill someone right now, run over a jogger, a toddler, an old person on one of those three-wheeled bicycles, and not even realize it. She shouldn't be driving anyway; her stomach is somewhere in her head, and her brain in her crotch. She feels like she weighs nothing and she feels stuck to the steering wheel, her hands lead.

Finally, having managed not to hit person or object, Mia pulls up in front of an adobe house. A Jeep is parked in the driveway. Turning off the Volvo's engine, she notices the way the house looks solid, sitting firmly on its large plot. The roof is tiled, the bright spring light making it glow like a terra-cotta sun. The window frames are wood; the windows are paned with old glass, the reflections warbley. Robert has landscaped from front door to street, wild, bunchy grasses and dark stones and perennials Mia could never plant under all her oak trees. In the backyard, a huge madrone branches up and over the house.

As she takes her hands from the wheel, Mia looks at them, all her fingers trembling. She clenches them together, staring out the window. What will she do? How can she get out of the car? Maybe Robert will find her here hours later, stuck in this position.

For a moment, she just sits still, unable to breathe right, unable to swallow. But somehow Mia manages to fold up the directions and grab her purse. Then she stops, opens her purse, and finds her Altoids, popping one in her mouth. She sucks on it for a moment, and then spits it into a Kleenex.

She gets out of the car, and little lights spread in her vision, translucent white orbs that flutter at the edges of her sight like moths. She isn't breathing, so she closes her eyes and finds a way to pull air into her lungs, one breath, two breaths, three, and then she opens her eyes and the lights are gone.

Smoothing her hair, she walks up the steps, her eyes focused on the small doorbell, but before she can stick her finger out to push it or before she can turn and run back to her car and drive off, Robert opens the front door. He smiles, pushes back his hair, opens the door wide. And Mia knows it's too late. For everything. Her stomach pulses, her eyes prick with tears. Ford's face opens and then closes in her mind. She sees him sitting in the living room, laughing at something on the television; she feels him sitting next to her at a meeting at Lucien's rehab; she hears him whisper to her at night, saying, "Turn over."

Mia stares at Robert. How can she do this? What is going to happen is horrifying and terrible. It's cruel and wrong and bad. But it's other things, too. It's absolutely wonderful.

❧

"I love it," she says, turning around in the middle of the living room. "It's just amazing. I wouldn't leave the house. I'd stay here all day long."

"Thank you," he says, and as she watches him, she knows he wants to say something else. So does she. But this is what they must do first. She must tour the house. She must see everything.

"I love that pond. Do you spend a lot of time out in the courtyard?" She walks to the doors that lead to the open middle of the house. Light pours onto the wide leaves of exotic-looking plants that Mia has no names for.

"If I didn't work so much, I would."

"Too bad you don't work at home. I would park myself out there and wri—" She stops, feeling like she's jumped into the end of a story before working out the middle. The end of a story that she might never finish.

Robert walks to her, takes her hand. The house tour is over.

He leans to her, kisses her cheek, her nose, her mouth. Mia puts her arms around him, pressing his tight body to hers. This kiss starts like the one they had on the sidewalk, but then it turns into more, their mouths unable to get as close as they need, even their tongues not long enough to make it real. Even though she can feel his thighs on hers, his erection against her stomach, it's not enough. Robert slowly brings his hands up her sides and moves them toward her middle, up onto her breasts. Mia pulls her mouth away from his because she can't handle all this feeling.

"Come with me," Robert says, and he takes her hand.

"Is this the end of the tour?" Mia asks.

"No. I hope it's just the beginning."

She wants to laugh, but it's not funny. They head down a long, Spanish-tiled hall. A cat sits in the corner, its tail wrapped carefully around its legs.

Robert pushes open a door, and they walk into a bedroom, his bedroom. He turns and kisses her again, this time his hands pulling her blouse free from her pants. Mia brings her hands to her buttons, but her fingers don't seem to be working right, the small pieces of plastic almost slippery and much too thin to push through material. Robert moves away and unbuttons his shirt. They watch each other, the yellow room light hugging them. Mia wants to close her eyes and feel the strong current in her body, electricity she feels everywhere. But she can't take her eyes off him, his slim, muscled chest, his long, lean arms.

Here is the body of a man, a new body Mia has never touched, the first body in more than twenty years she won't recognize by touch. She wonders if all the things she knows about sex will transfer to what she does with Robert.

Mia feels like a person coming back to a country she left long ago, wondering if the language is still the same.

Pulling off her blouse, Mia stands in front of him in the bra she bought the day before at Nordstrom.

"Oh," he says, stepping back, watching her. "Oh."

If she blushed when she first saw Robert that day in the exam room, she's on fire now, her face pulsing with feeling. He isn't looking at her face, though; his eyes on her throat, neck, breasts. He reaches out and takes her arm and pulls her to him. When their skins touch, she closes her eyes, leans against his shoulder as he gently unhooks her bra.

The bra falls to the ground, and then her nipples are against him. She can't bear how good he feels. She should leave before she feels one more millimeter of his lovely body. But he's kissing her again, moving his lips down her face, her neck, his hands under her breasts. He has a breast in each hand, his mouth on one nipple, sucking so deeply she moans.

She opens her eyes and looks down at his head moving at her chest. Seeing the black band that holds his hair in a ponytail, Mia reaches down, pulls his hair free of the elastic, and watches it flow dark over his shoulders. She moves her fingers through it, so fine and soft, and he stands straight. She looks down, his erection a bulge against his jeans.

He breathes in deeply and smiles. "Can we take off the rest of our clothes?"

Mia nods, and he unbuttons his pants. She unbuttons hers and then slides down the zipper, wishing she could present him with her younger body. Even though he's already told her he doesn't believe in perfection, she knows *she* still does; she can't help it. And as he undresses, she watches him, and he is perfect. His thighs and legs are firm and strong, and his penis juts dark and thick through the opening in his boxers.

Her mother's voice sails forth into Mia's mind. *If you weren't so wide in the beam. What about the grapefruit diet? If you lost just fifteen pounds . . .* Mia cuts Sally off because she knows it doesn't matter now. Robert wants her. At least it's very clear his body does. Her body wants his, too; the underwear she is taking off is wet where it hugged her tight.

"You're beautiful, Mia," Robert says, kicking away the clothes on the floor between them.

"I am?" she blurts, almost moaning again when she feels his penis on her bare skin. She reaches down to put her hand around him, and closes her eyes.

Before he can answer, she says, "So are you."

They are kissing again, his skin on hers, his hands on her body. She feels a slight slick of wetness on the head of his penis, and she almost sinks to the floor, knowing that she wants him, needs the passion that Sally and Kenzie say doesn't exist. But here it is, here in the form of this beautiful, erect man who is holding her, whom she holds back.

"Come here," Robert murmurs, and then they are on his bed, on top of the covers, and Mia stops thinking, stops hearing Sally or Kenzie or even her own mind, stops her own guilt, and she is body and mind all at once, together.

❧

Though Mia has written about adultery in her novels, it has been a lifetime since she herself lay in a bed after sex with a man other than Ford. Or before sex. Or just lay in a bed with another man at all, clothed or unclothed. The very idea of where she is at this moment is completely unbelievable. Yet it's true. She is naked in Robert's bed, on her side, his chest against hers, his arm wrapped around her waist, his leg holding her close. Her heart is beating so slowly, Mia wonders if the orgasm she had with him has so surprised her system, it's deciding to shut down, quit while it's ahead. She doesn't know if her mind can handle the overload, either. Poor Robert will be left with a comatose woman and a lot of explaining to do.

"What are you thinking?" he says, and then laughs. "That's a cliché, right?"

His breath smells like green tea, and she lifts her lips to kiss him softly, just his top lip. His hand presses on her upper back, pulling her closer. Between them, his penis is slick and soft on her belly.

"Well," she says, "maybe. A cigarette is worse. Overdone."

"Did you ever smoke?" he asks.

"A little bit in college. Ford—" She stops, sighs, continues on. "Ford shamed me out of it. I used to have a little hidey spot where I'd go behind a classroom building, and he'd find me. So I quit. The next thing I knew, I was pregnant with Lucien. I guess my body gave the all clear."

Robert is silent, but she can feel his pulse, his heart, against her body.

"What about you?"

"No," he says. "But I smoked a lot of pot my senior year of college, once I was accepted to UCSF medical school. That was the year my father died. The first year of med school, though, convinced me to stop smoking pot. Actually, I thought I had every disease I studied. Lung cancer was my biggest fear. So since then, I just drink a little bit. Nothing else."

Mia rubs her face on his neck, strokes his sides, reaches a hand to his ass, which is small, tight, and rounded.

"Robert," she says.

"Hmm." He kisses her temple, and his penis stirs.

Mia moves on top of him, looking down into his pale blue eyes. His hair fans out on the pillow, and she reaches down to stroke a lock against the smooth cotton. Her body is coming out of its lethargy, her mind spinning with desire and fear.

"This was so nice," she says.

"And?" His face stills, waiting.

Here is the spot, the place. Now. She could do it now. She could tell him that she has to go home and she has to stay home, for good, forever. She needs to say she can't do this to Ford, who deserves her trust, or to Harper, who still needs her full attention.

Mia could insist that there should be no more e-mails or meetings or lunches. What she's done wasn't so bad, right? Only once. She won't tell Kenzie. She'll never write a sex scene like this in any of her novels—no afternoon trysts, warm adobe bedrooms, beautiful doctors with long lunch breaks. She'll just drive home, shower, and then make her family a big dinner. She'll convince Ford that once and for all—no matter what he says—they need to go to a therapist. In a month, a half a year, a year, this afternoon will be like a movie she watched, a whirl of flickering, transient images. She won't even ever write about adultery anymore, period, keeping her characters faithful and happy, committed till death do them part, each novel complete with a tidy, uplifting resolution.

Then when she's eighty, Mia will sit in her rocker and think, *That was a lovely dream. How nice.*

And if she leaves now, if she throws on her clothes and drives home fast, Robert can never break her heart, as she imagines he might. After all, she's married, overweight, confused. She's no prize catch, and eventually, he'll figure that out. Or maybe he already has. He hasn't even told her very much about himself; she's not yet heard the story about how he killed someone. He's let her into his house, that's all.

But he's looking up at her, his eyes wide, his mouth set. This is the man who made her blush so deeply the first time she met him. She can still feel the cell memory of it, the way everything inside her seemed to expand. This is the man who excites her so much, her body and her mind have finally found each other, as she always imagined they could.

As she looks at this man underneath her, she knows she could get sucked down into wanting. Of wanting what she's always wanted. Mia knows she's greedy. To want more is selfish. To want more is to test fate, pulling one final, gaudy thing on board simply to lose the rest of the load she's collected for years. Hasn't she been gifted with her children and her husband and her writing? What about her teaching and mother and sisters and friends? But the need for this thing in her body, this loving with Robert, has always been there. For years, she's been saying good-bye to her want, watching it float away on a life raft to the middle of an uncharted ocean. *Good-bye,* she thought, waving as she sailed on. *Maybe next life.*

She touches Robert's face, kisses his mouth, looks at him and then the clock. "How long is your lunch hour?"

"I don't have to be back until three," he says, almost laughing. He flips her down and brings his mouth to her chest, sliding his face along her body until he reaches a nipple.

Mia opens her legs to him, his penis hard against her thigh. *So there will be more,* she thinks. *I don't have to wave good-bye just yet.*

He lifts his head from her breast and reaches for another condom on his bedside table. His hair falls onto her face, the room streaks of light and dark, the rest just Robert, his smells, his skin, his voice. She presses her lips on his throat and listens to the crinkle of the little foil package.

"Mia," he says, pushing inside her, his body hot for hers, at least for now.

"More," she says. She moves with him, toward him, against him, around him. Mia closes her eyes.

ELEVEN

Sally

Sally sits in the white vinyl recliner in the treatment room at Inland. Unlike many patients on chemo, she has decided against the port-o-cath, the catheter inserted in her chest for an ultimately less painful course of chemo. Instead, she told Dr. Gupta she'd had enough tragedy to her chest, and she didn't care if her arm was poked and pulled every three weeks.

"The last thing I need is another damn tube in there," she said.

"Hmm," Dr. Gupta said, scratching his cheek with his pen. "May I see your right arm, then, Mrs. Tillier?"

She held out her arm, and he examined her skin, her body, laying his slim brown fingers on the soft, thin flesh between her fore- and upper arm. Then he ran his hand down to her hand, peering at the weave of blue at her wrist.

"Your veins look good, Mrs. Tillier, so I will acquiesce. However, if there is trouble at a later date, I will insist on the port-o-cath."

So now her right arm is held out on a little platform on the side of the chair, the Cytoxin hanging above her on an IV stand. Mia sits in a metal chair next to the recliner, her laptop resting on her knees, the electrical cord winding behind Mia's chair and plugged into the wall.

"I thought the point of laptops was being able to bring them anywhere without . . ." Sally waves her left arm. "Attachments."

Mia stops typing, holding back, Sally knows, a sigh. "The batteries only keep it going for about a half an hour. Maybe a little more. It's no big deal to plug it in. The nurse said it was fine—wouldn't interrupt any special machines or anything."

Without warning, Mia smiles at Sally, and Sally pauses. Her whole body pauses. There, in this instant, there is baby Mia looking up at Sally as Sally dries her on her lap after a shallow bath in the big porcelain tub. Mia with her amber eyes, joyful, happy, giggling in her baby roundness. Mia, the baby who, when on Sally's shoulder, patted Sally's back in the same rhythm that Sally patted Mia's.

This same baby, child, girl, woman looks at Sally as the drug feeds into Sally's body, winding into her bloodstream.

"Are you excited about the book?" Sally asks, thinking that this is the reason for Mia's happiness.

"Uh?" Mia looks up from her computer screen. "Oh yes. Of course. I've got all those trips coming up. You've talked to Nydia and Dick, right? About their coming here with you while I'm gone?"

"Dick has special plans for me. He said I'll be the only chemo patient in the world who's had so much fun."

Mia shakes her head. "He really likes you."

"Are you surprised?" Sally asks, knowing that in a way, she herself is.

"Of course not, Mom. It's just that you haven't, well . . . It's not like you've really wanted a . . ."

"Boyfriend."

Mia's eyes widen. "He's your boyfriend?"

Sally waves her hand. "I don't know. Let's call him my gentleman caller. A good, vague term."

"Wow." Mia turns back to her screen but doesn't type.

"But Nydia will help out, too," Sally says. "Dick can't do it all."

Mia nods but doesn't turn to look at Sally, and Sally wonders what Mia is really thinking about.

Finally, Mia closes the computer and puts it on the table next to the bed. "Listen, Mom, Katherine could come out. For a week."

"No, no. It's all covered. Never mind it. It will all work out. But tell me about the book."

"Good reviews so far." Mia bites her lip.

"Then what is it?"

Mia pushes her hair back, her bangs sticking straight up from her forehead. Sally thinks again of what Nydia said, that parents are in love with their children, but children aren't in love with their parents. Would Nydia's theory explain why Sally's heart feels heavy now with love for her child? Mia is here—not in love with Sally but here, anyway, out of duty or obligation or need or fear. But here, anyway.

"Mom," Mia says. "It's nothing. Do you want me to read to you?"

"Do you have your book? With all this going on, I haven't had time to read the copy you gave me."

"No. I'm sick of that story. My story—"

She stops, shaking her head again. She reaches into her bag, pulling out an assortment of paperback novels and holding them out like a fan. "Pick, Mom. Pick your story."

Sally's veins pinch and burn, the crackle of the drug inside her starting to flare into fire. She reaches out her left hand and taps the dullest book cover, something brown and green and indistinct.

"This one. This is the story I want to hear."

Mia laughs. "Strange pick. *A Hole in the Heart.* Can you take it?"

Sally nods, knowing she's had a hole in her heart for a long time, since David died, and all her organs and flesh and muscle and bone have learned to live with it.

Closing her eyes, Sally nods again and then leans back on the recliner. Soon there is the lull of Mia's voice, the story of a girl in her mind, and then only the crackle of drug, the noise of the hospital, and then nothing.

❧

On the way home in the car, Sally turns to Mia. "I'm going to Scotland. In five months."

Mia keeps her eyes on the road but her mouth opens and then shuts. Quickly, she glances at Sally and then focuses on the traffic in front of her. Unlike Nydia, Mia is a careful driver, a safe mother driver, her hands locked at ten and two, the positions Sally remembers screaming about one day in the old Buick Sportwagon after Mia tried to make a U-turn using one loose hand.

"Scotland? On a tour? Who's going with you? Nydia? Marlene from the bridge group?"

"No. I'm going with Dick." Sally stares straight ahead at the traffic but then says, "He's a good man. He—he's encouraging."

Again, Mia's mouth opens and closes, but she doesn't glance at Sally this time. Seconds pass. Outside the car, traffic presses in, flows out, moves along. The sky is the color of new blueberries.

"Good," Mia says finally. "Okay. But are you sure?"

"Yes. It's not as if—you know, I don't really know if he, well, wants to go to another level." Sally feels flushed, her heart beating under her missing breasts. "I'm not sure if he wants me that way. But we get along so well. He's been wonderful during all this."

"He has." Mia turns right and merges into oncoming traffic. "I like him a lot, Mom."

"So," Sally says. "When this is over. When I've had a month off and can eat again and my butt doesn't look like a skillet, Dick and I are going to take a tour. Historic Celtic Sites. Denair Parvati at Triple A set it all up. I've paid my deposit. A month, with a week in Ireland to boot."

"Oh. Wow. Okay." Mia gives her a quick look. "It will be fun."

Sally sits back, suddenly feeling empty. What was she expecting? A fight? Not from Mia, surely. That will come later, with Katherine. Maybe it's that the trip doesn't sound like enough, not yet. It doesn't sound like as much life as Sally wants. A tour to Scotland. So what? People go on tours all the time. She turns her head to look at the group of people on the corner, waiting for the light to change. She really wants to go; she really wants to be with Dick. So what is it that she's looking for? What does she imagine? What does she want?

The crosswalk flashes its green man, and Sally suddenly sees herself lifting her blouse, showing her scars to someone other than Dr. Jacobs, someone other than Dr. Groszmann. She's showing them to Dick, and the look on his face is not what she imagines.

"Well," Sally says loudly. Mia almost flinches. "How about a quick milk shake? You know how I love them. Strike while the iron is hot, while I still feel like eating. The nurse said about day three I will feel ill." *Feel like dying* is what she heard under the nurse's words. Well, Sally has already felt like dying, but she has her blue pill now—the one Mia snuck into her daily regimen that changed things—and she won't give it up.

"Okay," Mia says, making a right onto Main Street. "A milk shake. Even though I shouldn't."

Mia shrugs, and Sally leans over and puts her hand on Mia's warm thigh.

"You're lovely," she says, wanting to add "joyful, giggling, round, as beautiful as a wet warm baby." But "lovely" seems enough. Mia smiles and drives on, taking them toward something sweet.

❧

In the time before the nausea, Sally cleans her house. She digs through the back of the guest room closet, finding old Christmas wrapping paper and warranties for appliances that she's long ago given to Goodwill. When she moved from the Monte Veda house to her condo, she kept some board games, imagining that she'd need to have something to do with Lucien and Harper, as well as Matt and Mike, when they visited. But the boys weren't interested in Scrabble or Monopoly or Life; they asked Sally to go down to the video store instead to rent movies. So now she pulls the games out of the closet and stacks them on top of David's old puzzles.

After Nydia offers and then takes Sally's donations to the Goodwill drop box, Sally goes through her photos. The last year she put any photos in an album was the year after David died. For one year, she pretended, and there are the girls in birthday hats and at swim meets and at Girl Scout meetings. For all the world—the world that would have looked at Sally's albums—the family seems normal, intact, complete. After all, it could have been David behind the camera, clicking away.

Sally drives down to Long's Drugs and buys five large photo albums. For hours, she sorts the pictures by year, trying to construct a chronological narrative, and then, slowly, she slips the photos in the albums, pressing down on the sticky plastic, trapping the images forever.

On the Sunday following her chemo, Sally feels the drug open its fist and grab her stomach. Her head begins to pound; her body feels light, weightless, nothing, like one of the dust bunnies under her bed. She moves only from her bed to the living room couch, slumping against the armrest.

Then she seems to sink, falling into each and every cell, her insides heavy. She wants to lift out of her body before the throbbing, aching dullness gets worse; she needs to get out of her own body. She remembers feeling this need for escape during her labor with Mia, pulling on the nurse's arm and saying, "I need to go home. Now."

There's a yap at her door and then a knock. When she doesn't answer it right away, Dick rings the bell once and then again. Sally pushes herself up and opens the door, knowing that if she doesn't answer, he'll call 911 or Mia. Or worse, Katherine, asking for expert instructions.

Dick steps back when she opens the door, and Sally wonders for a second if her hair has fallen out all at once or if she looks crazed with pain and fear. But then she realizes he moved back only so she could push open the screen door.

"How are you doing?" he says, stepping inside and taking off Mitzie's leash. The dog jumps on the couch and curls up in a tight dog-body circle.

Sally smoothes her hair, adjusts her robe as she stands before him, feeling messy and unkempt. Dick watches her, his eyes wide, waiting for an answer.

"I'm not doing too well today. Maybe I overdid things the past couple of days. I've been cleaning." She motions to the couch, and they both sit down.

"You can't do everything at once. You need to get well first. This is only your first round, Sal Gal."

She shrugs and pushes her robe away from her chest, her body warm and clammy. "I don't think I'm going to do well with chemo."

"It's hard, that I know," he says, and Sally thinks of Ellen. He does know. Dick slaps his knee lightly. "But it can be done, and you've the spark to get through."

"It—this will sound strange."

"What?" He moves a little closer to her.

"Chemotherapy tastes funny."

Dick smiles and then tilts his head back and laughs. Sally can't help but smile, as well, even though there's some kind of metal taste in her mouth. Metal or something cold, hard, unnatural.

"Only you," he says.

Sally shrugs. "I just wish it were over."

"Sally," he says, patting her knee. "Give it time."

"I know my hair will fall out. That seems like the worst indignity."

He nods. "It does happen."

"I've lost my breasts," she reminds him.

"I know." He blushes, drops his gaze, and pats Mitzie's back.

"Have you ever seen what it looks like?" Sally says. Of course he knows what illness looks like, having lived through the years with his wife. But Sally's scars? Her mastectomy deformity? He's probably never seen anything like it.

Dick shakes his head and looks out the window. She can see his pulse beating on the side of his neck.

She is shaking with something like fear, but it feels different, like electricity in her body, an energy that is pushing away the dull throb of ache in her stomach.

"Can I show you?" She knows that Scotland might vanish just like that, a puff of dream snuffed out by truth.

Dick runs his hands over Mitzie's body. Sally expects to see his thighs flex as he stands, pushes away from her couch, her living room, her. She hears what he will say, his "I think that's a crazy thing to ask me. I'm going to go now. I'll show myself out."

The back of Sally's neck tenses, and when she brings her hands to her robe to close up the neck, he looks at her and holds out a hand as if to stop her.

"Yes."

Sally wants to ask him if he's sure, if he really can stand the scars on her chest, if he ever wanted to see her naked in the first place. But if she asks him anything, she won't show him. And in a way, she's never really looked at the scars herself. Of course, she's taken a shower and cleaned herself with soap and water and dried herself off with a towel. Every morning, she puts on her camisole or her cotton shell, pulling fabric over her chest, trying to ignore the two mean, pale eyebrows of scar where her breasts used to be. But she's never *really* looked, in the way that "looking" means "seeing," means "understanding."

She pushes back her robe, letting it fall behind her. Then she slowly unbuttons her nightgown, her fingers shaking as she maneuvers the small white buttons through the holes. One, two, three, four, five, and then there is enough room to push her shoulders through the opening. Shoulders, chest, and then scars. With her eyes closed, she holds her body out to him.

The living room air licks cold on her skin, the prick of chill running along the lines of her just-healed incisions. In her body, her heart has taken over, drowning out all her other organs, the rush and pound of blood in her ears and throat and stomach and groin.

And then something happens, something that has never happened. As she sits, trying to hold herself still, the shaking in her body threatening to spill her to the floor, she feels Dick's quiet fingers touching the diagonal line of puckered flesh where her left breast used to be.

She keeps her eyes closed, unable to believe that what she feels is real. But he runs one finger and then two back along the scar, and then he does the same on her right scar, back and forth, as light as a moth.

Swallowing, Sally slowly opens her eyes and there he is, leaning forward, his eyes on her chest, his face not sad, not disgusted. Interested. Compassionate. Calm.

He looks up at her, nods, carefully places his full palm on the middle of her chest in between her incisions. "It's going to be all right," he says. "You're . . . it's you."

She doesn't believe that her incisions or her operation are her, and she doesn't think that anything will be all right, because it never has been before. But this moment is all right. And maybe, Sally thinks, as she leans against Dick's shoulder and lets him button up her nightgown, she can pretend that the next moment will be all right, and then the next. Maybe if she's lucky, she can fake her way into next week, when this intense chemical sickness and pain will disappear.

❧

The nausea is like nothing she's ever felt before, not when she was pregnant, not when she caught the stomach flu that year Dahlia brought it home from fifth-grade camp. It is worse than food poisoning, except she doesn't have diarrhea. Her whole body feels the need to expel, to purge, to release everything inside her at once. If she could, she'd pull her guts out with a string and leave them on the bathroom floor, ridding herself of the parts that hurt.

She kneels by the toilet, Mia's right hand holding her shoulder, her left hand her forehead.

"Mom, let me bring a basin to your room. You need to be in bed."

Sally shakes her head. The only thing that feels good besides Mia's touch is the cool white tile under her knees. Then she throws up again, but there is nothing to throw up, her gag empty and croaking.

She waits, gags again, and then she slumps back onto Mia. Mia's body is shaking, and Sally realizes that her daughter is crying. She thinks to pat Mia's thigh, but she can't move her hand.

"I thought Dr. Gupta gave you something to stop the nausea," Mia says, her voice full of confusion. "It shouldn't be like this. How can it be like this for four months?"

Mia pulls Sally against herself, and Sally knows how Lucien and Harper must have felt, so much comfort in Mia's body, the exact way a mother should feel—soft belly, strong arms.

They sit on the bathroom floor like this for a while, until Sally knows the nausea has passed, the chemicals so deep into her body now, there is nothing left for her to purge.

"Let me take you to bed," Mia says, pulling Sally up off the floor, and then she's actually picking Sally up. Her baby is picking her up, carrying her to the bed, tucking her in. Sally closes her eyes and hears Mia on the phone, talking to someone, her voice sharp, direct, harsh. Then there is another call, one that is calmer and longer, Mia's voice different, fuller, sadder, light. Then there's a laugh, a giggle. A pause. Another string of quiet questions.

Is it Ford? Sally wonders. *Did Mia ask him to come over?*

But even before Mia hangs up the phone, Sally feels herself fade into a grainy sleep, one that rides just above the itchy burn of the drug killing everything inside her.

❧

The next afternoon, Sally and Dick sit outside on her patio on the new teak chairs Sally bought before the diagnosis. The sun has slanted down toward the hills, shadows creating triangles on the cement. Dick is drinking iced tea, and Sally holds a glass of tap water. Mia spent the night and then drove down to Inland to pick up a drug she must have convinced Dr. Gupta to prescribe, detailing in length Sally's reaction. Now Sally feels better, her stomach tolerating the water and the chicken broth Mia made before leaving just after lunch.

"I told them you're going to need a home nurse if this keeps up," Mia said. "That got him to order up the antinausea drug. He said it will start working quickly. I just hope he knows what he's doing."

"Thank you," Sally said. "He's a good doctor, really. I don't think he knew how I would feel."

Mia shook her head. "Now I know what you meant all these years about the 'crappy HMO.' Nothing seems to be based on patient care. Just cost."

Though the nausea has subsided, the drug makes her feel a little floaty, a little alien. Dick seems to be hovering in an almost imperceptible white fuzz.

He puts down his iced tea and smiles. "The air will do you wonders. When Ellen was in the nursing home, I'd take her out every day. Used to make her smile when nothing else would."

Sally nods. "You were good to her," she says.

"What else can you do?" he says. "How else can you live?"

"You don't have to be so nice to me," she says. "You could just forget to come over, starting now. You could decide to cancel Scotland. You could pack up and move closer to your son."

Dick shakes his head and then looks up, blinking against the light. "Maybe so. But I like you, Sally. Always have. Even back when Ellen was still alive in the home and you'd say nice little things as we passed by each other. Talked to Mitzie. Seemed interested."

She had been interested, hadn't she? Sally thinks so, but maybe she was just being polite to the nice man and his sick wife, acting the way her mother taught her.

"Smile!" Frona said through lightly clenched teeth, as the Sorensens and the Volbergs and the Thomases walked in the door. "Say something pleasant."

But no. That's not true. She liked when Dick stopped by, taking off his golf hat as he spoke to her. She'd felt sorry for Ellen, sloping in her wheelchair seat, but she'd admired something in Ellen's always cheerful face. Sally had even liked the little yipping Mitzie.

And after Ellen died, if Sally is honest with herself now, she knows she timed her walks to Dick's, clear that if she started out at three fifteen heading north, she would catch him at three thirty-five heading south. They would have a nice ten-to-fifteen-minute chat, and Sally would part from him, mulling over the questions she would ask him next time.

And besides, he had his hair. All of it. Not a comb-over. Not a little round patch of skin on top. Sure, it was white, but he had a thick head of wondrous curly hair that Sally wanted to touch.

For a second, she flashes to Dick's hand on her chest, the gentle touch of his fingers.

"I was interested," Sally says quickly. "But it's going to take more than interest to keep you coming back here these days. I'm not going to be in shape for much more than sitting."

"You're going to be fine," Dick says, and Sally wonders how many times he told that to Ellen as she sat slumped, crooked in her wheelchair at the home.

But Sally isn't Ellen, not yet. Hopefully not ever. "You're right," she says, feeling the new drug push calm through her body. "I am."

TWELVE

Robert

Mia's body is like an ocean Robert wants to swim in. So he swims. He pulls and strokes and sucks in her salt. He rides the waves of her orgasms; he slips his hands over the eddies of her hips, the current of her long, solid thigh muscles.

Quiet now in his bed, his left hand cups her right breast, and he wants to tell her things that she probably doesn't want to hear, things she can't hear now. He wants to tell her how her breast in his hand feels different than all the breasts he feels every day. Yes, it is composed of flesh and fat like all women's breasts, but these, this, are hers.

Gently, he squeezes her softness. Robert loves the subtle sag of her breasts as she stands before him, the way they spread to the side when she is underneath him, the way they sway when she is above him. With his fingertips, he follows the whoosh of almost invisible stretch marks from pregnancy and nursing. Her nipples are large, rose colored, thick. Even now, he can feel them on his tongue.

This is their second time at his house, and he knows by the way he's already begun to grow hard again—by how much he needs her—that these stolen Tuesdays and Thursdays will never be enough. They haven't been able to meet for a week because Sally has had a violent reaction to the chemo. When Mia called him from Sally's house one day, he almost blurted, "I'll come over to help," but he knew he couldn't. He's not official. He's a secret, and mostly, that's all right.

Mia turns into his armpit, rubs her face on his side, bringing a hand up on top of his chest, her fingers running along his sternum. "You always smell like tea."

"Must be my cologne. It's called Tea."

Mia pushes herself up. "Are you kidding?"

"Yes." Robert pulls her down, putting both arms around her. "It's not my cologne. It's a soap. I get it at Trader Joe's."

"But why does your breath smell like it? Are you a soap eater?"

"Well, let's think about this. I drink tea. Do you think that's it?"

She pushes at him and then pulls herself on top of him. "Smart-ass."

Mia hovers over Robert, her eyes dark under her bangs. She leans down and kisses him once, pulls back, and then presses her body on his and kisses him again.

Feeling her, all of her, feeling himself respond, everything becomes liquid, water, a swirl of sea foam.

❧

"I start my book stuff tonight," she says later. "A lecture to a fiction group. They love to ask me about my entire life, ask for me to send a book to my agent, want to get something published tomorrow, and then only one person in the back row will buy a book. Writers are the worst. Like vultures. I know from personal experience. I am one."

"I don't have the new book yet," he says, looking quickly at his bedside table. He's almost done with *The Daisy Plate Incident*, but he's having trouble reading it and it's not because of the title. Whenever the main character, Quinn, speaks, he hears Mia, feels her, the reaction in his body too strange to maintain a long read.

"Oh, I think you'll get a free, autographed copy," she says, pulling back the covers and sitting up. "Maybe I'll write something X-rated on the title page."

"You better not. When the historians find it later, there will be dissertations on Mia Alden's secret love affair with a mysterious doctor."

He hears her quick intake of breath, sees her face still. She pushes a hand through her hair and exhales. "Right."

Robert touches her thigh. He shouldn't have said that, shouldn't have reminded her how she's doing something wrong. They both, he understands, know they are.

"So, you're going to Bakersfield this weekend?"

She nods. "You know what they say about Bakersfield."

"No."

"*Sun, Fun, Stay, Play.* City motto. It's also the home of Buck Owens's Crystal Palace. You should see it. Full of country memorabilia and a thousand photographs of Buck Owens with any celebrity he could drag into view."

"How do you know all this?"

"Oh, I'm a tremendous favorite in Bakersfield. The public can't get enough of me. I go every year, and I don't leave until I go to the Crystal Palace."

Robert runs his finger down to her kneecap and then back. "I'd like to see it."

She starts to laugh and then stops. "Really?"

"I could meet you there. Saturday night. Meet you after your reading at the hotel. Then in the morning, we could take in the amazing sights." Robert is talking, but he feels like he's holding his breath, knowing that rejection could come any moment in the look on her face, the movement of her shoulders, the position of her spine.

But Mia doesn't pull away, change, shift. Instead, she places a hand on his belly and says, "Yes."

Because of the time change, it is still dark when Robert starts his run, the sky an eerie slate gray, a luminous streak of white coming up over Mount Diablo. He has a long day today, two surgeries, follow-up appointments with patients, new evaluations, which are the worst, the women still reeling from their diagnoses.

A car spins past, the headlights glowing like moons. Robert quickens his pace, turns up a dead-end street, headed for the open space at the end of the cul-de-sac. Inside the houses, lights flick on. A dog barks from inside a garage. Up in a live oak on the approaching hill, a robin begins to sing.

With every footstep, he's thinking about Mia, but he's also thinking about Ford, this man Mia is married to but doesn't— what? Love. She loves Ford. They spent all these years together, some happy, some quiet, some slightly discontent and anxious. Ford never did anything harsh, violent, mean. Mia told Robert that they simply grew apart, but growing apart means that at one time there was *part*ness. Wholeness. Something to lean away from.

And now, after Robert has slept with his wife, Ford has become a person to Robert, a man he has conversations with as he walks from his office to the hospital building, when he drives to work, when he runs.

"Ford," Robert asks, "do you still love her?"

Ford stares at him.

"Because if you don't, well, I have to say I do. I know it's early, but I do."

Ford kicks at the floor with his shoe, puts his hands in his pockets, listens to Robert.

"She loves you. I know that. But she says she doesn't really connect with you in a lot of ways. She never did, Ford. She told me."

Robert pushes up the hill, swinging his arms. Ford crosses his arms and nods.

"You have Harper at home. That's hard. I know Mia doesn't want to do anything to hurt him. Or Lucien. So I'm asking. Can she leave you? Can I have her?"

Just as he does every time—compliant and kind and silent—Ford nods again, and Robert whisks him out of his mind, concentrating on reaching the ridge, already needing the breath of the downslope.

Mia would not like being asked for, as if she were property. She would not want to be *had*. She would not want Robert to ask Ford's permission for anything related to her. Robert knows this because he's read her novels, knows that her strong female characters—Susan and Quinn—would not tolerate becoming possessions, things belonging to any man.

He doesn't really know how not to want her in this way. He wants her like he wants food. Like he wants sleep. How he needs her is nothing like how he wants his house or job or car or even his friends. Mia, all of her, seems elemental, necessary for his life. Robert knows that he has to have her, not just her body, but her thoughts and ideas and her voice. This has never been true before, not once.

Robert shakes out his arms as he starts down the hill. He can't ask anyone for Mia but Mia, and he can't ask for her yet. He can't say the words. Not now, not for a long time. Not until she wants him as much as he wants her. But what Robert tried not to think about is what he would do with Mia once she has left Ford. After all, what has he done with all his girlfriends? One year tops, and then each relationship was over, the women walking down his front path, either because they were exasperated by him or he asked them to leave. Yes, he wants Mia, but for how long? He feels so differently about Mia, but has he really changed? Do people actually change?

The ground is hard and cold under his shoes and he feels his long strides resonate in his thigh bones. The sky begins to widen into gray, the lightest of blues. Robert makes it to the short flat stretch before the next hill. Here's what he knows. A woman like Mia deserves forever. And Robert doesn't know if he can offer forever to anyone.

What do you say, Ford? Will you take her back? If it doesn't work out, will you not let me ruin her entire life?

He begins to climb the second hill, and the sun slips golden along the horizon, spreading light over the mountains in the distance. Maybe, he thinks, he should stop obsessing about more and later and forever. Maybe he should think about yesterday—Mia warm in his arms—and maybe today, which is all about his job. By tonight, he can allow himself to think about tomorrow, just a bit. He won't think about Bakersfield because that's thinking about Mia in the future.

It's possible that all this time with his various girlfriends, he's been living so far in the future that he's broken up with them or they've left before they'd even had a chance to be together. A year couldn't even measure the amount of time they'd spent together in Robert's head, whole lifetimes, so that by the time they left, he'd already grown old and died.

So as he runs, he makes a deal with himself, a promise. He will not think about Mia except for the real details of time they spend together. But he can have all that he wants of that, lolling in the memories of her in his bed. He will not imagine the future with her, thinking about how she will visit her children or how she will handle the effects of her divorce. He will not mentally place her in his house, watching her move from room to room. He will stop imagining her writing in the courtyard, her laptop on the wooden table, her fingers determined on the keyboard. He will stay in the present and not in some kind of contrived future made up of hopes and desire. No more. And most of all, he thinks—exhaling, inhaling, exhaling, inhaling, his feet moving on the dirt path, the air cool on his shoulders—he will stop talking to Ford.

On Saturday evening at five, Robert pulls into the parking lot of La Quinta Inn, just off Highway 99. As he turns into the hotel, he notices the sign for Buck Owens's Crystal Palace just a bit down the street, and as he turns off the car engine, he wonders if he and Mia will really take a look inside. All he can remember about Buck Owens is the show *Hee Haw,* watching television with his parents when he was a kid. Buck played the guitar and the other guy—sort of round and friendly faced—played the banjo. There was the lady with the hat with a price tag still on it, but that's all the memory Robert has.

Robert gets out of the car and looks around the motel. Mia called him as he was driving down, and told him what room she was in. So now Robert walks to the stairs and heads up to the third floor.

"It's not a fancy place," Mia said. "But the group put me up. What can I say?"

Robert knows he wouldn't care if they were at a Motel 6 or worse. He wouldn't care if they were camping, sleeping outside under a dark, rainy sky. Tonight, he'll get to sleep all night with her. And thinking only hours into the future, tomorrow he will wake up with her.

He starts to knock at Room 313, but after only one quick rap, Mia pulls open the door. Robert stares at her. She's wearing a long, tight black skirt and a dark red low-cut blouse that hugs her waist and clings to her body. Her hair is bigger somehow, perfect, and she wears makeup, lipstick, blush, eyeliner that somehow makes her eyes green. Curving along her neck and down to the valley of her cleavage is a long silver necklace. He blinks, seeing the writer Mia. The professor Mia. The professional Mia. Instead of daughter Mia or lover Mia.

"Robert!" she says, grabbing his wrist and leading him in. "I was getting worried."

He swallows. "They slowed traffic because of some wind thing. Dust."

She closes the door and kisses him. She smells different, like perfume and paper and a big, airless meeting room. He lets his hands slide along her waist, his flesh moving slickly against her silk blouse. He kisses her back and her mouth is the same, filled with peppermint. He pulls away and looks at her again.

"This might not be a fancy place, but you're all fancy," he says.

"I have to look the part periodically," she says, kissing him on the cheek, the nose, the ear.

"I like the way you look," he says, pressing her to him.

"I know. It's a miracle." Mia laughs, her sound rumbling into him.

"Stop it," he says, and he pulls away from her, looking at her from her high heels to her hair. "You are a queen."

"If you don't stop, I'm going to take a shower and wash it all off. The clock will strike midnight, and I'll become the girl covered in cinders."

"Deep down she was always a queen."

"Robert, I'm serious."

He smiles. "A shower sounds like a great idea. Can I join you?"

❧

Later, they are in bed. The motel room hums with noise from the air conditioner and something under the desk. A modem? Below in the parking lot, large trucks are rumbling through, deep bass welts of music throbbing against the asphalt. Robert stands up and pushes back the curtains, watching the shiny, buffed red and blue and silver pickups pull into spaces, the drivers getting out and slapping each other on the back as the freed music curls up and into the darkening sky.

"A convention," he says. "A yahoo festival."

"Robert," Mia says from under the blankets, "they're probably doctors."

He shrugs, closes the curtain, and turns to face Mia. Her nice clothes and his own are on the floor, her hair wild from the way he ran his hands through it as he made love to her. In this second, his heart feels empty and full at the same time, as if he can't decide if loss or love is the truth.

"Come back to bed," she says.

He knows he should leave before it happens. All he needs to do is dress, walk out of the room, pass by the pickups in the parking lot, and get in his car. In minutes, he could be back on Highway 99. In four hours, he could be back in his house, flicking on the lights, watching Phyllis wind her way toward the kitchen and her cat bowl.

Robert watches Mia watch him.

"I need to tell you," he says.

"I know," she says.

◊

"I wasn't paying attention to the signs." Robert has slipped on his boxers and is sitting in the chair next to the bed. Mia wears his shirt and is cross-legged, leaning against the headboard. She doesn't say anything, but her eyes never leave his.

"The first one wasn't my fault. I wasn't even in the room. I was still scrubbing, but I saw it happen. She'd come to me for microsuction on her face—just taking off a little fat under her chin. It wasn't going to be a big deal, but when the anesthesiologist gave her the anesthetic, she went into arrest. Everyone did everything right. She wasn't given too much, and the anesthesiologist had her monitored. She just reacted. She. Her name was Melinda."

Robert shakes his head, bites down on his cheek. "They shocked her back into a rhythm, but it was too late. She never woke up, and died five days later."

He stops talking and in his silence, Mia asks, "You said 'signs.' Why was Melinda a sign?"

"She was trying to tell me something. Not actually, but in what happened. She was trying to tell me to be careful. To pay attention."

Mia leans over and touches his thigh. She blinks, and he can tell she's trying to find something to say. But after a moment, she squeezes him and then sits back.

"Go on," she says.

"A few months later, I had a patient named Joyce Studin. She came for an eyelid tuck. And it wasn't just cosmetic. Her vision was being impacted. I had done this procedure a hundred times, on patients with more visual impaction than Joyce. And she was in great shape."

Robert doesn't want them, not now, but tears heat his eyes. He rubs his face, wiping them away before they show. "But something happened. During the surgery, her heart stopped. Just like Melinda's. And when she went into arrest, I accidentally nicked a cranial nerve. I didn't know it then because we were so focused on keeping her alive, but when she was in the coma, her whole eyelid sagged, hung there in her unconscious face. Every time I checked on her, her family asked me about it, more worried about her eye than the fact that her EEG showed there was little brain activity."

" 'Will you be able to fix it?' her husband asked me every single day for three days, even in the hour just before the family decided she was going to come off life support. 'Will she look all right?' her mother asked. I couldn't stand it. I didn't have the courage to stay with them as she died."

Mia gets out of bed and crouches down next to his knees, leaning her face on his thighs. Robert strokes her hair and lets his tears come. "I decided then that what I did was wrong. That I was in some carnival branch of medicine. I wanted to get out, but I didn't know what else I could do, so I decided to only work with cancer or emergency patients from then on. No one got it. Jack kept telling me to let it go, but I couldn't."

He wipes his eyes. "I hate it."

Mia looks up. "What?"

"Everything."

"Tell me."

Robert thinks, wondering how to say it. There's so much. Not just about being a doctor but about being human. He pushes his hair back, swallows. "I hate being in the position to make such big mistakes."

She stands and then straddles his legs, sitting down and facing him. The shirt she wears is open, and he can see the curve of her breasts. He never wants to hold them in an exam room, telling her where he will cut and how he will insert expanders. He never wants to reconstruct her nipples, trying to play God with needle and ink. He pulls her close, knowing she has to go in immediately and get a mammogram. Right away. The moment she gets home from Bakersfield.

As he holds her, thinking how he will save her from cells he has no control over, he knows he is stuck in the future and the past. Melinda and Joyce are sitting on his shoulders, as they always are every day, but he's also giving Mia a cancer she doesn't have. Because he is scared. He's scared of everything. Everything frightens him. His parents' death, his own life, loving anyone, because they can go away, just like that, dying in front of his face on an operating table.

He can barely feel the alive, warm woman on his lap, the woman who is stroking him and murmuring a sound she must have made up for her children. He can barely feel her hot thighs clenching his, her warm, still-wet center against his belly. Maybe he's never known how to just be, not even when he's running, not even when he's making love.

"Oh," he sobs against Mia's throat, grabbing her back. "Please."

"Yes," Mia says. "Yes."

❧

Later, he leans against her as they sit in bed, her back against the headboard. They watch the local news, stories flitting past as they do—war, disease, robbery, murder—the day's events in second tidbits. Mia has undone his hair and is combing it with her fingers, starting at his scalp and then letting her hand pull through the entire length.

"If I only had a curling iron," she says, laughing against his shoulder.

"You want me in drag?"

"I never had a girl, you know. You're my last hope here. I can practice my braiding and ponytails. When I have grandchildren—not for years, God willing—I'll be ready for a granddaughter."

He closes his eyes and lets himself feel her touch, tuning out the noise from the television, forgetting what he told her a half hour before. Mia begins to hum lightly, a feeling more than a sound from her chest.

Robert closes his eyes just as the motel phone rings. Behind him, Mia tenses and then she pushes him away gently, leaning over to the phone. Before she answers, she looks at him, her face pale. Robert stands up and watches her answer.

"Hello? Oh, hi. What's up? . . . It went fine. . . ."

He wants to stand and listen to her conversation, scrutinizing each word for the affection he wants for himself. But he doesn't, putting on his jeans and shirt instead and stepping out onto the walkway outside the door.

The Bakersfield air hits him soft, like the cotton that grows along the highway. The pickup drivers have gone into their rooms, and now the parking lot lights reflect brilliantly off the truck paint. From this vantage, he can see the bright lights of the Buck Owens's Crystal Palace, the quick-flashing bulbs trying to draw in business. And, in fact, he can hear the country music, the twang and slow beat of a song that usually would make him laugh. But tonight, it seems to be the exact rhythm of his heart, slow and wistful and full of regret.

What do I want? he wonders. *Do I want Mia?*

He closes his eyes, smelling her on his entire skin. Yes, he wants Mia. He wants her off the phone and away from her family and with him all the time. But he also doesn't want that, knowing that having her will bring pain to other people. What is all this longing? All this feeling inside him? He knows it must have a name beyond midlife crisis, and it has to do with his career, his life's work, his life in general.

"Join our group," Jack would say. "You'll be happier here."

"Quit working at Inland," his mother would have said. "Do volunteer work. Help the people who need it the most."

"Get married," his father would have said. "You're alone too much. Settle down, for God's sake."

"Make us beautiful," some of his patients would say.

"Make us normal," others would say. "Fix what has made me broken."

"What do you want?" Mia would ask, always thoughtful, always going back to the source. "What do you really want, Robert?"

He doesn't hear the door open, but then there is her hand on his shoulder, sliding around to his chest. "I'm hungry," she says, and Robert nods. He's hungry, too.

☙

On Monday before going to the hospital, Robert calls Operation Grin. Two years ago, he and two of his Inland colleagues traveled to Norfolk, Virginia, and trained there for two weeks. They went over the procedures to repair cleft lips and palates. They studied cases of children born without noses, of women with facial tumors that impaired vision, of men slowly starving because they couldn't swallow, their palates gaping holes.

It had felt like camp, learning to operate without the machines and medicines and assistance that he'd come to expect in the United States, that most people in the Western world took for granted. He'd never made the commitment to go anywhere, but two of his colleagues had, coming home with pictures of Na and Felipe and Sofia from Vietnam and Honduras and Bulgaria. Robert looked at the photos, listened to the stories, but he never made the call to go, never felt—what? That he was ready? That he could do it? That he was good enough?

But today, Robert talks with Anna in Virginia, who puts him on the list for Honduras; he picks Honduras because he likes the way the capital's name—Tegucigalpa—sounds on his tongue. Robert hangs up the phone and stares at his e-mail, seeing MAlden. He clicks on her name, feeling the slight thrill her e-mails give him.

Dear Robert,

I loved seeing you at Buck Owens's Palace, standing next to that orange leather suit with fringe. In fact, I'm going out today to buy you a CD of Buck's best music. I want you to play it all the time.

Thank you for coming to see me in Bakersfield. Thank you for sleeping all night with me. Thank you for telling me the story.

Love, Mia

Love, Mia, Robert thinks. He does love Mia, but he's not sure how he knows this. He always thought love would take a long time, months and years to develop, and even then, it would be more of a habit than an emotion. For so long, he waited for something to happen, something that clichés defined so well: bells to ring, the sun to break free of the clouds, his heart to swell. Robert imagined, though, that he'd recognize love, remember the connection somehow, turn and suddenly see it. He would awake in the morning next to Leslie, or whomever he had been with at the time, and expect that the feeling would be there, like magic, suffusing his entire body. He'd blink a couple times, hoping that when he was truly conscious, he'd feel it, know it, want the woman next to him more than anything.

But until yesterday morning in the motel in Bakersfield, he'd never found his body suffused with more than affection, comfort, and then relief that it wasn't love. The woman wouldn't have to stay. He was free to let her leave.

Yesterday, though, he'd turned to see Mia next to him, her hair messy, her face slightly flattened by the pillow, and he wanted to weep because there it finally was, a feeling in every part of him, possessive and needy and wanting and hopeful and desirous and joyful. And he saw then more clearly than ever that she belonged to someone else.

Dear Mia,

Robert writes back.

I would really like to have the orange suit, too. Can you arrange that? I'll wear it while I listen to the CD. A total experience. Like you. I can't wait for Thursday.
    Love,

he writes, feeling the *L* and *O* and *V* and *E* under his fingertips,

Robert

Monday night after work, Robert has just enough time to make it to the brand-new Barnes & Noble in Emeryville, swiftly heading up the stairs to the second floor. He isn't even close to the reading area when he hears the laughter and then her voice. He's not going to let her see him, because he doesn't want to startle her, see her face flash red, have her lose her train of thought, shift uncomfortably, maybe even glare at him. What he wants is to see her without her knowing he's there, Mia in the wild, Mia natural, Mia as she is to everyone else.

Getting as close to the reading area as he can without entering her view, he leans against the self-help books and watches her. A crowd of about twenty-five people surrounds Mia, her books fanned out on a table that she stands in front of. She's wearing a longish black dress, and he imagines the smooth curves of her breasts and waist and hips under his hands as he stares at her. She's jangling with sterling silver bracelets and earrings, the same necklace she had on in Bakersfield, hanging between her breasts.

Robert closes his eyes and imagines he can smell her, her skin, her hair, her soap.

"That's a great question," she says to someone in the audience, and then she begins to talk about creating characters.

Everyone in the audience listens to her, except for a little girl, who has been dragged to the lecture by what looks to be her mother, a woman who writes down everything Mia says. The girl sits on her chair, swinging her legs and reading from a children's book. But the rest of the crowd is focused on Mia, who moves her hands, tells stories about her characters, describes how her character Susan ended up doing things Mia wasn't prepared for.

"The next thing I knew," Mia says, "Susan's off in a cabin in Tahoe with another woman. It was like I had to write to catch up to her. I told her, 'No, Susan. Don't do that!' But it wasn't in my control. Susan had a life of her own and she wanted to live it."

The audience laughs a little, surprised, like Robert is, by the idea of a character jumping out of an author's head to do what the character wants.

After the talk is over, Mia sits at the table, and some of the audience members stand in a line to have her sign books. Robert is about to walk up to the table when he notices the man in the back. The dark-haired man from Sally Tillier's hospital room. Ford. Or Rafael. Both. Ford, with whom Robert has been mentally conversing for weeks.

Ford doesn't see Robert because he's watching Mia. He leans against the wall, his arms crossed. Robert looks back at Mia and sees her glance up at Ford and smile. Ford raises his eyebrows, mouths something Robert doesn't pick up, and then smiles back at her. Mia shakes her head a little and then goes back to the book she's signing.

Robert's eyes burn. Mia smiles at Ford. They talk the invisible language of marriage.

Of course she smiles at him, he thinks. *She's known him for over twenty years.*

His heart leaps in a kind of neurotic arrhythmia. He thinks, *But she's sleeping with me.*

Robert looks again at Ford, who is now talking to the bookstore manager. By the way Ford's hands gesture toward Mia, by both the manager's and Ford's enthusiastic nodding, Robert can tell the manager is extolling Mia's virtues, giving Ford—the person closest to her in the world—what he can't say to Mia because she is busy. After all, doesn't the husband know more than anyone else? Of course, the manager knows this, asking questions, listening attentively, nodding and smiling.

Ford's the Mia expert, not Robert. Ford belongs here, not Robert.

Moving backward, Robert almost trips over the little girl who is holding the children's book.

"Sorry," he mumbles, turning away, walking quickly to the stairs and then out the big bookstore doors, needing air, needing to leave.

```
Dear Mia,
```

he writes later that night.

```
I don't think Thursday is going to work
out after all. I'll let you know what day
will.

Robert
```

THIRTEEN

Mia

The only one who calls her is an automated Cheryl Carr, the president of the California Teachers Association, who wants her donation in preparation for the big election in the fall. Teachers and their unions are fighting for money, the state in financial shambles, the elementary, middle, and high schools barely functioning, colleges turning away thousands of applicants. Mia hangs up without listening to more, even though she knows what Cheryl says is true and even though she cares about all the students. She wants to keep the line free, but she knows Robert won't call her at home. He doesn't even know her number here or at work. He hasn't called her cell phone, and he hasn't e-mailed since Monday night, telling her that Thursday afternoon wouldn't work out. She wrote him back, telling him about the reading in Emeryville and how she could barely talk to the crowd because he was in her mind the whole time. Mia suggested the following Tuesday, knowing that was his day without surgery, but he hasn't written back since then, and now it's Friday. Almost a week without seeing him.

She doesn't know why, but Robert is breaking up with her.

Mia decides she can't work on her current novel anymore, so she saves the sad three hundred words she's managed to compose and turns off her computer. She knows if she leaves it on, she will check and recheck her e-mail, wanting more than anything to see his address pop up on her screen. All the terrible behaviors she had while dating those millions of years ago before Ford are coming back: her obsessiveness, her need for constant reassurance, her desire for the body of her beloved. Maybe she was wrong to let loose all this terrible need. Maybe she would have been better served if she let herself go into middle age and beyond with only what she has. She could have made it, she thinks, as she begins to clean the kitchen, scrubbing the sink and counters with a soft-scrub cleanser. She could have been happy with Ford and the kids and her life. Eventually, she would be a grandmother, a grandmother who writes, Ford her lifelong partner, a man who knows more about her than anyone.

At the retirement home, they can sit on their patio overlooking the golf course and know that the life they now see is shared, understood by both of them. By then, he will have known her for three-fourths of her life, so much more of her experience with him than without.

Mia rinses the sink, watching the yellow, swirling water slip down the drain. But it's too late now. She opened the box, let all her lust and desire and hope and need fly out, closing the lid just in time to keep love safe in the small darkness. Love. Whatever love is, she thinks she is in love with Robert. From that very first moment, the door of the room opening. His ponytail, his slightly frayed sweater under his crisp white lab coat, the wild blush on his cheeks.

"Shit," she says, turning off the water and breathing in, the air catching on tears.

Mia shakes her head, wipes her hands on a dish towel, and wonders what to do. Go to his house and camp out until he comes home. Make an appointment with him. Forget about him.

Call Sally, Kenzie, even Katherine. Go visit Dahlia, traveling from her sister's house in Phoenix to her readings in Los Angeles.

Ask Sally if there is room for one more on the Celtic trip. Call her department chair and beg for a summer class. She'd take any class, anything, even English 1A. Go to New York and find a job as an editor, rent a Manhattan apartment, date no one because there are no available men there. Hide in the hills, sleep in a tent. Jump off the deck. Forget everything.

But then there is the *pound pound* of someone walking up the front steps. No, it's a *pound pound* and a second *pound pound*. Looking out the kitchen window, she sees it's Lucien and Harper, both of them now at the front door.

Mia puts down the towel and runs to the door, pulling it open. "What? What is it?"

Lucien smiles, his eyes caught in sunlight, a tumble of brown and green. "Hi, Mom."

Mia shakes her head. "Why are you here? What's happened?" Then she turns to Harper. "And why aren't you in school?"

"Jeez, Mom." Harper walks in the door, passing her but putting a hand on her shoulder. "Let us in, okay?"

Lucien comes in, kisses her cheek, and carries his bags down the hall. Mia closes the door and turns to Harper, who leans against the kitchen doorway.

"What's going on, Harp?" she asks.

Then Harper stills. "Wait till Lucien is with us."

Now more than ever, Mia is afraid. They know what she's done, and they are going to confront her. An adultery intervention. She'll have no choice but to jump off the front deck to the driveway below, her death the only possible solution to the mess she's created in all their lives. For the first time since reading Robert's e-mail, Mia begins to cry, a quiet, calm stream of tears coming from the corners of her eyes.

Harper reaches out a hand, and she leans into his shoulder. Does he know why she's crying? And if so, why is he being so kind? How does a sixteen-year-old learn this type of kindness?

"What did you say?" Lucien says to Harper when he sees them.

"Nothing." Harper pats her shoulder again.

"Mom." Lucien pulls her away from Harper. "Let's go sit in the living room."

Mia feels as if her brain has been carved out of her head and replaced with air and light. She's become one of those zombies in the movies the boys used to watch, mindless and evil. An evil adulteress mother zombie.

"Keep walking," Harper says, and she does, the rhythm of her feet making her solid, the lightness leaving her.

They walk into the living room and sit down. Mia knows she should take control because she is, after all, the mother, however inept. But she doesn't know where to start. She doesn't know what words will take away the pain of what she has to tell them.

Lucien looks at Harper and then starts, "Harp called me at school a couple of weeks ago. He heard some conversations. He didn't know what to do. Or who to talk to."

Mia wipes her face and looks at Harper, who meets her gaze. "What stuff? Talk about what stuff? About what conversations?"

She asks the questions but already knows the answers. He must have gotten into her e-mail. He managed to find the folder she'd hidden Robert's messages in, discovering her secret. It must have been something at the hospital. Or he saw her in Walnut Creek. Maybe that day at the restaurant. Maybe that instant by the Volvo when Robert kissed her.

"I can explain," she begins. "Listen—"

Harper looks confused. "You know? I thought you must. How could you not have noticed? It's been so obvious."

Lucien sits back. "When did you find out? Did he tell you?"

Mia blinks, her head light again. "What are we talking about?"

The boys pause and then look at each other.

"Dad," Lucien says finally. "His affair. With that woman he works with. Karen."

Mia swallows, tries to look at both Harper and Lucien, but sees nothing except the little lights that keep swirling in front of her. Something inside her body—a muscle, an organ—clenches and unclenches. Finally, she closes her eyes, and the lights slowly fade. Her breath finds a rhythm. Her body stops pulsing.

Of course. Of course. Karen. All Ford's late nights and sudden business trips. Of course.

Mia bites down on her lip and opens her eyes. Ford, her husband of twenty-two years, is with another woman. Ford. Her husband. So much betrayal.

She struggles to find the appropriate feeling. These words should burn and twist and scratch. She should feel the deep, keening pain. But the pain is not there. It's not there because for so long, she's lived in the tunnel of her own secret, a separate place in her brain, the place where she's admitted that she's no longer in love with her husband. The place she goes to when they make love and her body does not respond. This tunnel is the place of fantasies of other men, of hopes for another life. The tunnel is where she meets up with Robert, again and again and again.

At Harper's and Lucien's words, the wall between where she kept her "real" life and her secret tunnel collapses, and she knows, more than anything, she's relieved. Free.

Her sons watch her carefully, and she knows she owes them the truth about her own life. But how to tell it?

"This is a family problem," Lucien says, the exact words the counselors always told them during his drug rehab.

"A family disease. The denial. The excuses. The problems," the counselors said, righteous eyes on all the parents who had somehow missed the signs: the drop in grades, the listlessness, the weight changes, the new friends. "Don't blame the children solely. You all have to take responsibility for this."

But how could Ford's and her own adultery have anything to do with anything the children have done?

"Yes," Mia says finally. "And no. None of this is your fault, either of you. It's about your father and me."

Lucien shrugs, turns his head away. "I didn't help."

"No, Luc," Mia says, putting a hand on his shoulder. "It's not about you."

"But it affects us, Mom," Lucien says. He crosses his legs, and for a second she imagines he will take out a notepad and pencil.

"I know."

"You didn't notice?" Harper looks like he's about to cry, his eight-year-old boy face slipping through the new, solid bones of his sixteen-year-old one.

"I think I did," Mia says, finally feeling the pain she needs to feel. The pain she should feel. Harper is the person who will be torn up by what is happening, the last boy, the person who will need to jump from the sinking ship. He is the innocent, the unknowing, the one who will wish it could be fixed. For a second, she imagines that she feels her breasts let down, the prickly tingle of milk flowing to the ducts. When the boys were nursing, their cries, whines, upset would cause her milk to flow, drenching her blouses and shirts.

"His diaper is just wet," Ford would say. "He's not hungry. He just ate."

But it didn't matter; Mia's body responded to any discomfort, any pain. Like now, but Harper is almost a man, and somehow, he is going to have to survive this on his own.

"Did you notice, Mom?" Lucien asks into her pause.

Mia nods. She did notice. His refusal of counseling, his urgent lovemaking, his attempts to tell her something. His appearance at the reading in Emeryville, such a shock after a couple of years of no-shows. She felt responsible for him as he leaned against the far wall, needing to make him feel at home as he listened to her, watched her, waited for her. And she had to admit that it felt good to see him there, his dark eyes—the eyes that had always seen her—taking in her show, her talent, her shtick.

But all of the lovemaking and attention were a smoke screen for the understory, the true narrative of his desires. And her own.

"Are you okay?" Harper almost whines. "Should we have told you? Is it going to be all right?"

Mia reaches out and strokes his face, his skin smooth despite a whisk of stubble. "I don't know if it's going to be all right, sweetie. I don't know what all right is now."

Lucien leans forward, his elbows on his knees. "There's something I never told you."

She shakes her head, wondering if she can bear another truth, especially one from her own child. But Lucien, his gaze on his shoes, doesn't see her indecision.

"That last LSD trip? You know, the one with the musical notes?"

Mia nods. How could she forget his psychotic reaction in this very living room—his belief that he was the creator of all things, and the rest of humanity was nothing but musical notes that emanated from him. For hours, he begged them to call Gert Rouffler—a colleague of Mia's in the music department—to come to the house to prove his point until finally, Lucien came down off the drug and remembered they were all simply flesh.

"So when I looked at you and Harper and even my own arm, I saw that we were like the same sound, the same pulsing color. Sort of a red. Dad was like a blue, and he wasn't merging with the rest of us, kind of held back, the sound low and far away."

"Lucien," Mia begins, but he holds up his hand.

"I know, I know. You think it was only a hallucination. My whacked-out brain. But I saw it. I saw what was happening back then."

Lucien has been clean for three and a half years. For three years, Ford hasn't gone to her readings. For three years, he's been working late. For three years, he's been trying to tell her something she hasn't been able to pay attention to.

She thinks of Ford's hastily taken-off ties, looping the kitchen counter night after night after night. He must be waiting for Harper to leave for college. He must make love to her out of anger and fear and because she is there—to keep her there until it's safe to leave.

Mia rubs her forehead and then pushes her hair back, thinking as she does of Robert, his smooth, thick hair.

"I know this was hard to talk about," she says, "but I need to talk with your father, just he and I." Mia holds up her hand as Lucien starts to protest. "Luc, it's ours. You and Harper go out. See a movie. I'll call your father as soon as you leave."

"Mom," Harper says, "you don't have to."

"Harp!" Lucien says.

"You don't. Or it can be like your story, with Rafael and Susan. You know, how it ends on the deck. The way it ended?"

"You read it?" Lucien says to his brother. Then he looks at Mia. "It was that story—that's why I thought you might know."

Again, it's obvious. She's known everything all along, her stories like volcanoes bringing everything to the surface. At night in bed with Ford, she must have stolen into his dreams, his brain waves, taking in all the information she needed, just enough so she could find Robert. But not too much—who wants to see the destruction, feel the fire? Who wants to live through the time when the dead have to be buried, the village rebuilt?

Mia stands up, looks at her handsome, dark boys on the couch, the two who sought to save her.

"You go. I'll call your cell phone later," she says, and then she walks away, down the hall to her bedroom to call her husband.

Ford is pale, his tie clamped tight against his neck. He sits at the kitchen table, his hands folded as if in prayer. For a second, she thinks of how he used to sit at their first dining room table, so serious, reading a textbook or editing an essay. Back then, she'd walk into the room, and he'd look up, smile, say, "What's up?"

But now he doesn't smile or even really look at her. He sits back and then leans forward again, running his hand through his hair.

"Lucien came home from school to tell you?"

"Harper called him last week. He didn't know what else to do."

Ford shakes his head, shifts, stands up, sits down. "Shit. Shit."

Mia can't say anything, but knows that "shit" is exactly the right word.

"Really, I wanted to tell you. I've been trying to tell you." Ford watches her.

Mia stares back at him and knows he's not lying.

"Ford," she begins.

"No." He stands up again, walks into the living room and then back. "I wanted—I thought maybe I could . . . And there's Harper. He only has two more years of high school. I thought I could make it. And maybe I thought that one day, it would just be over. I'd be here, at home, with you. It's not like I don't love you, Mia. It's not like it's been bad."

"Ford."

He blinks, and she almost cries out. How many times has she seen him looking at her just like this, full of surprise and indecision? Through college and job problems and moves to new houses; when she was in labor, especially with Lucien, the whole event wondrous and strange. There he's always been, Ford in front of her, his shoulders straight, his mouth slightly open, his entire gaze begging her to give him the answer.

"I've been seeing someone, too," she says.

His body sags; he covers his eyes, sits back down in the chair.

For a long while, he is silent, his eyes cast down, his breathing slow and deep.

"What have we been doing, Ford?" she asks finally. "Why have we let it go so long? Why don't we know each other anymore?"

"I know you," he says quietly.

"But I didn't know this about you, the part that counts."

A breeze pushes past the open window, and a squawk and flutter of purple finches fills the air. Mia runs her finger over the oak table, waiting for an answer to her own question.

"I don't know what happened," Ford says softly, wiping his face. "Maybe we forgot how to know each other. Maybe—"

"You never wanted to go to counseling."

"It was too late. Way too late. I didn't think it would be—"

Mia interrupts, not wanting to hear aloud the truth, the idea that for so long something was wrong. "Are you in love with her?" she says.

Ford breathes in again, deeply, the sound wet and sad in his lungs. He nods. "You?"

She wants to tell him yes, but when her mouth moves on the word, she sees Robert's e-mail in her mind, sees "won't work out." "I don't know."

"Who is it?" Ford's eyes narrow, and Mia remembers his old love for her, a possessiveness pinching his face.

Mia looks at Ford, starts to cry, letting her tears fall onto the table. "One of my mother's doctors."

He sits back, breathing in. "So it just started."

She shakes her head. "It could have started earlier, with someone else. It hasn't been right with us for so long."

He wants to argue, lifting his hand, but then he doesn't. He sighs. "I know," he says finally.

Outside, Mia hears a squabble of squirrels, a high-pitched chatter, a scramble of claws. She suddenly feels like joining the animals, scrabbling up a tree, jumping away from the house, Ford, all of this. She hates that her long marriage can end this quickly, in one conversation on a sunny afternoon.

"It's too easy," she says quietly.

Ford looks up at her, his eyes wide. "Too easy? What are you talking about? Too easy. This has been hell."

Mia feels her tears pool in her chest. "What do you mean?"

"Mia, how do you think it's been living like this?" He waves a hand. "Here. Knowing I'm lying to you. To the boys. Every single day, I've just wanted to . . ." He can't finish, swallowing, his eyes full. "I've felt like I was disappearing into one of your stories. I would try to talk to you, but you weren't really paying attention."

For a moment, Mia feels like she is weightless, floating, her stomach the only thing heavy in her chair. Here's what she didn't know. Here's the story she could have never written because she wouldn't have wanted to see that Ford was so miserable. That living with her was killing him, draining him. All along, just as she'd thought, they'd forgotten how to know each other.

And he's right, of course. How easy is it to feel that you are only half, that the part that you've wanted to fit into yourself is nowhere in sight? For how many years has Mia awakened every day, understanding that that piece she wanted for herself wasn't available? That she could never have it. Because she was married to a man she liked and loved, she hadn't wanted to hurt him and she allowed whatever that part was called—love, happiness, fulfillment, completeness—to slip away each morning as she left her bed.

How many times had Ford held her, his body moving into hers, and she couldn't move into him, couldn't hold him close enough because even if she'd been able to, she'd be grabbing the wrong thing, the wrong man. Mia held his flesh but not his heart. He was pulsing into her, and she wasn't responding, nights and nights of the wrong movements with the wrong people. Years of time that wasn't wasted completely because they had their boys—both safe and strong—but wasted in their hearts.

Ford was right. It had hurt; a slow, long hurt.

"It's never been easy," he says. "It was the hardest thing I've ever done. And now I think I'm relieved. It's not easy. But I'm relieved."

"Wow," she says.

"I didn't mean—" he begins, but she waves away his words.

She hates how easily he can let go of her, even though this is exactly what she wants. She can't stand that she hasn't known his story, thinking that she was the unhappy one, the one who wanted to leave. For a strange minute, she wants to fight for him, to write the story differently. But the urge lifts and then falls, evaporating into the truth that today is the last day they will be together like this, married, in the same house.

"It wasn't easy," she agrees. "You're right."

Ford sighs, the sound loud in the quiet kitchen.

"What are we going to do?" he asks.

In the time that it took Ford to drive home from the city, Mia has figured out exactly what they will do. He will stay here at the house until the boys come home, and they will all talk, just like they learned to do in the days of rehab, each saying what is true. Because she has no choice, Mia will tell Lucien and Harper about her own affair. She doesn't want them thinking that their father was the one to ruin everything. She keeps hearing the words from rehab: "It's a family disease."

But after the talk and all the tears and the anger and disgust and feelings of betrayal, Ford will pack up what he can carry out of the house in one trip and leave. He will move in with Karen, and they can be business partners and lovers. He will hold her all night, and she will react to his body the way Mia's reacts to Robert's.

Later, Ford will come back and take the rest of his things, he and Mia arguing—but not too much—about what belongs to whom. Lawyers will take care of the rest of the details and the money, both of them being generous and fair, despite the flare of anger over discussions about when to sell the house and who will buy out whom.

When the divorce goes through, Ford and Karen can get married. Mia won't go to the wedding, but she will encourage the boys to.

In two years, Harper will go off to college. Soon after, Lucien will go to graduate school. Mia will keep teaching at Cal and continue writing, maybe finding someone to date, finding this person the normal way, through well-meaning friends and dating services and personal ads. She will never again expect another exam room door to open and her true love to walk through. She will never again expect her body to flood with feeling when a man steps into a room, looks at her, shakes her hand. This much she has learned. This much she will carry with her into her divorce.

"You'll leave," she says quietly. And Ford—this man she met when he was still a boy, who grew up right in front of her, who gave her two children—looks up and agrees.

☙

Lucien asks smart questions and nods through the entire discussion, but Harper sobs. He doesn't let either Ford or Mia touch him, holding himself to the edge of the couch.

"I'm so sorry," Ford says over and over, his hand trying to decide what part of Harper to try to touch now: shoulder, arm, knee. But Harper jerks away, mumbling,

"You suck. You both suck."

Mia starts to cry then because she knows he's right. She sucks. She is a coward, was a coward. But she won't be anymore.

"Harper," she says, "how your father and I did this was wrong. We should have talked to each other. But it's hard."

"How hard is the truth?" Harper cries.

"Impossible," Lucien says. "Worse than anything."

Ford rubs his forehead. "We lied to ourselves, too."

"What's going to happen to us? What's going to happen to me?" Harper asks.

Ford looks at Mia and says, "You'll live here. Except for me being gone, your life will stay the same. Then you can come and see me." He stops, bites his lip, and then breathes in. "If you want."

Harper sits up, wipes his eyes. "I'm never getting married."

"If I never got married, Harp, I wouldn't have you and Lucien," Mia says. "You wouldn't be alive. I would have never written what I wrote. I wouldn't have been able to live in this house I love so much. I would never have been able to know someone like I know your father, even if it ended this way." She leans over to Harper now, who lets her touch him. "This is a horrible ending. A terrible way to stop. But there were years in there that will always be the best I ever had. I've been able to live a certain way because of my marriage, and I don't regret most of it."

Ford stares at her, his old expression on her, the one she remembers from when they first met, full of surprise and interest. It's the same way he looked at her when she walked out of her apartment door and he was locking his bike against a post. "Who are you," the look said. "I want to know."

They watch each other for a moment, and then his face settles into the truth of now.

"That's right," Ford says. "All of that is right."

Harper wipes his face, pulls in a ragged lungful of air. Lucien pats his shoulder.

"I hate this," Harper says, his voice flat.

Mia nods. But even though she is sad and knows that this first night alone without Ford in her bed will feel like sleeping on knives, she doesn't hate it.

"One day at a time," Lucien says, whipping out the constant refrain from rehab.

Mia wants to bark out a laugh, but he's right. Tonight and then tomorrow and then the next day. Nothing more than living through them until she can walk out the door that today's truth has opened.

"Fuck that," Harper says, standing up and walking toward his room. "I hate you all."

❦

Ford throws some clothes and shoes into a duffel bag; lays a few suits into a garment bag. Then he stands in front of the closet, his hands on his hips, and cries.

Mia sits on the bed, looking out the bedroom window at the bay and oak trees, an empty toiletry bag in her lap.

"You're going to Karen's." She turns the bag in her hands and then puts it on the bed. She's not going to fill it for him this time, making sure he has razor and shaving cream and lotion as she has done so many times before.

"Yes," Ford says. He wipes his eyes, turns back to the garment bag, and zips it up.

"This is horrible." Mia can't look at him.

"Yes," he says. He picks up the toiletry bag and walks into the bathroom. She hears drawers open and close, the sound of him putting containers and bottles and jars on the sink counter. After a couple of minutes, she hears the zip of the bag, and then he's back in the room.

"I've left her number by the phone," he says.

"Okay."

"Mia," he says, and she looks up. She wants to hug him, hold him tight, tell him that it's still not too late. It's all a mistake that they can fix. They'll be one of those couples who renews their vows and then has a midlife baby, a happy, spoiled child who will graduate from high school when Mia and Ford are in their early sixties. She wants to tell him there is still time to start all over again, make it right this time. Somehow, Mia will fix that part of her that wants something else. He can, too. Maybe through antidepressants or weeklong tantric workshops or twice-weekly counseling appointments they can stand to live together for the next forty years. Whatever it is, she'll do it in order to save them from this transition. In order to save Harper. To keep them all from having to change.

"I'm going to go," he says.

"I know," she says.

వ§

After Ford leaves, Mia picks up the phone and begins dialing. She thinks she is calling Kenzie, not able to believe that so much has happened in her life that Kenzie is unaware of, when Katherine answers the phone.

"Katherine?" Mia says, surprised, looking at the phone.

"What is it? Is it Mom?"

"Yes," Mia wants to say, "yes, it's all about Mom and not about me."

But she doesn't. She breathes in and exhales. "No. It's about me."

"What did he do?" Katherine says.

"Who?"

"The doctor. The one in the hall."

"How did you know that?" Mia feels her face burn, her throat tighten. Just the thought of Robert that day in the hall makes her want to weep. There he is, pushing his hair back, looking at her. There are her lips on his cheek, his skin soft and warm.

"Mia, I've been single as long as you've been married."

Mia nods, begins to weep.

"Meesh," Katherine says, using her old nickname for Mia; *Meesh,* the way she pronounced her sister's name when she could barely talk. "It's okay."

"Ford left."

For a second, Katherine stops, and then she clears her throat. "That's been coming for a while."

"How do you know that, too?" Mia stands up, walks around the living room. "How could you have possibly seen that?"

"I know you think I'm the family loser relationship-wise, but, Meesh, you and Ford, your staying together—it was about the kids, wasn't it?"

Mia wants to hang up on her sister, the doctor who seems to have known the truth about everything all along. How irritating! How annoying! Just like Katherine to come in with the facts when they won't do any good at all, the same way she sailed in and then out of Sally's illness, barging forward with pronouncements and ideas and then flying home before any of the real healing had even started. The way she left for med school and never came back to the Bay Area, leaving Mia to do it all. And now she says she could see what Mia couldn't? Wouldn't?

But then Mia sits on a chair. She's never told anyone except Kenzie how she felt about Ford.

"Yes," she says. "The kids."

"Then this is good. It's a new start."

"Once I start, where do I go?"

"Look, who in the hell am I to say? I can't even find the starting line, with either sex."

Mia hears Katherine's breathing, the soft sound of music in the background. It's a weekday and Katherine is home from work, alone in her big house, preparing dinner, listening to jazz, talking with her cats. Then she'll eat and watch a movie on the VCR and go to bed. Alone, at least tonight.

Mia will be alone tonight, too.

"I don't know how to do it," Mia says.

"Who does? But what about the doctor? What was his name? Rosen-something? No, Groszmann? Anyway, I saw that. I don't think I've ever seen you with, well, such an expression."

"We were— we had an affair. But he ended it. Something freaked him out."

"You told Ford?"

"Yes. And the boys."

"The boys? They know about this?"

"They told me about Ford."

"Shit," Katherine says. "The kids told you? Christ. How did they find out?"

"Harper overheard Ford on the phone a couple of times, and then Lucien pieced it together."

"You damn writers. Always working on what makes people tick. He'll probably write about that later in life."

"Maybe."

"Look, are you going to be okay? Do you want to come out here? Just come. Get on a plane tomorrow."

"I can't," Mia says, knowing that she literally can't make it to her own front door right now, her body heavy and dull and immobile. Besides, she needs to be here for Harper and Lucien, staying put to make it seem that she is not destroyed by their choice to tell her. And really, she's not destroyed by that truth. Or by Ford's affair. What she's destroyed by is Robert's silence and her reaction to it.

"Okay, but listen. Call me if you need me. I know— I know you think I'm a pain in the ass, but you know I care."

"I know," Mia says, meaning it.

"And before you go, tell me what in the hell is going on with Mom. This Celtic Adventure thing? And Dick Brantley? Now without her breasts, Mom feels free to start dating? What's the symbolism in that?"

Mia smiles through the ache in her face, the sound in her throat almost like laughter.

F O U R T E E N

Sally

Sally learns how to vomit, the arc of bile and food and liquid neatly plopping in the toilet just so. All she has to do then is reach over and flush. And then it's a simple turn to the sink and the faucet, a whoosh of water, a quick rinse of her face, a quick brushing of her teeth. Then she goes to her bed and sits on the edge, waiting for the next wave of nausea to rumble and the pulse to her stomach. Finally, after exactly three rounds, she will sleep, her face clammy, her body sore. If she's lucky, she will sleep for hours; if not, she will awaken in an hour or two and start the process over.

"Take the pills Dr. Gupta sent you," Mia says on the phone. "Don't be brave. Take the pills. Or we can get you the marijuana, Mom. Seriously."

"Goddammit, Mom," Katherine says, her voice a slim, stringent, long-distance chord. "Why are you being so stubborn? Take the damn pills. But if you don't like the pills, there are injections, too. They work better. What's wrong with your doctor? Do you want me to call him?"

Sally doesn't tell Katherine this, but the pills make her woozy, sleepy, duller than usual. There's no way she wants an injection, because the pills alone give her dreams of David.

In one dream, Sally sat up in bed to see her husband, her young, beautiful husband sitting on her bed, his legs crossed, his hands folded in his lap. Even in her dream, she gasped. Sally hadn't seen him in so long, his face now only a memory, a photograph, a jumble of remembered traits.

He looked at her, smiled, and said, "Where have you been?"

"Here, David. I've been here."

"Hardly," he said, stretching out his legs.

Before he could say any more, nausea shook her awake and she ran to the bathroom, clutching her chest, her incisions pounding as she moved.

In the next dream, she pushed a baby carriage, but she didn't know whose baby was crying inside it. Dahlia's? Mia's?

"Can I see?" David asked, bending over the carriage, his face hidden by the hood.

After a moment, he looked up, his face drawn. "Have you seen this? Have you been paying any attention at all?"

Then he was running down the hill, his unfurled umbrella behind him.

That time, Sally didn't wake up right away, but in the early-morning hours, she found herself asleep on the bathroom floor, her face pressed onto the cool tile.

Pushing herself up and off the floor, she took Dr. Gupta's pills downstairs and hid them behind the Morton salt so that Mia wouldn't find them, knowing that nausea wasn't any worse than seeing David's young, confused face.

This morning, though, Sally feels better, days three and four passing into day five, her body strung out, wired, exhausted. She's been on the couch for about an hour, Dick in the kitchen making soup. Mitzie sits next to Sally, looking up at her expectantly, as if any minute Sally will morph into Ellen.

The shadows remain, she thinks, knowing that David is still here, as is Ellen. And in a way, Ford must still be in the house with Mia, even though he's packed up all his belongings and moved in with his girlfriend. She can hear his ghost in Mia's voice; Sally heard Ford's absence when Mia called and said, "I've got some bad news," the day that Ford left the house.

How can all of us ghosts and humans live together on this plane, she wonders, all of us packed together, stuck to each other by memory?

Dick carries in a bowl of soup and places it on a tray next to Sally, unfolding a napkin and smoothing it in her lap. She watches his long, slender hands, notices as she looks at his face how his ears have grown large and flappy, like all ears seem to as people get older. Like noses, ears keep growing when everything else stops, the rest of the body shrinking. Sally smiles, imagining them both at ninety, Dumbos with huge ears and no bodies.

"What?" Dick blinks, sits down, smiles back.

"Nothing," she says, picking up the spoon. Then she puts the spoon down and places her hand on Dick's knee.

"I'm going to stop the chemo," she says.

Dick jerks, sits back against the couch. "No, Sally. You can't."

"Yes, I can. I'm not going to do this to myself. That two percent Dr. Gupta kept talking about? Well, it's mine. My two percent."

Dick shakes his head, sighs. "But it could mean—"

She interrupts. "It could mean I live a little bit longer, or it could mean I'm suffering all this pain for nothing. Even without the chemo, the chances are in my favor that in ten years, I won't get it again. Ten years, Dick! Think! That's a long time. That's a lot of trips."

He watches her, his eyes swimmy, and she hopes he won't cry. He's seeing Ellen, Sally knows, in her wheelchair at the home, no good news for miles around. He's seeing everyone he's ever given encouragement to, wanting all of them to take his quiet advice: Be careful. Live.

"Look, it's not going to happen to me like that," she says quietly. "It's a different story."

Dick puts his face in his hands, and Sally hears the sadness in his throat. Slowly, she moves toward him, leaning against his back, feeling his fear under her cheek.

"Think of Scotland," she says. "Think of Ireland. Green hills, blue sky. Think of the Celts battling back the Saxons. Think of a language we don't understand."

He nods, and Sally closes her eyes. They sit unmoving on the couch for so long, Sally slips into a dream of sunshine, a village, people in thick wool clothes. In her dream, the villagers speak to her in Gaelic for so long she almost learns to understand their message. It's so clear, so obvious, but then Dick shifts, sits up, moves her gently into a sleeping position.

"Rest," he says, pulling the afghan up over her body.

Sally thinks she nods, but then she's not sure if she does. It doesn't matter. Dick will be here when she wakes up, she knows that, and he will reheat the soup and they will eat together. Mitzie will wag her tail and yap. The day will turn to night, the night into day, and Sally will no longer be a chemotherapy patient.

She breathes in, hears the kitchen tap run, and then falls asleep.

✍

Sally and Dick are in Target looking at bath mats. After the time Sally has spent close to her bathroom floor, she knows she needs a new one. Dick picked her up early so they could beat the Saturday crowd, but even so, the store is busy, especially the bathroom aisles.

"Excuse me," a woman says, brushing by them, clearly irritated, probably because both Sally and Dick have big red carts blocking the aisle.

"Blue is nice," Dick says, not noticing the woman.

"Dick," Sally says, "my bathroom is green. I think I might get a migraine if I saw the two colors in close proximity."

"Oh," he says, smiling. "You're a little artistic, huh?"

"No, just not color-blind. Are you color-blind?"

"I most certainly am not. A true color connoisseur."

"Well, then, use your discriminating tastes."

"Fine," he says. "What about beige? Goes with everything."

"A very safe call," Sally says. Another woman pushes past them, mumbling, and Sally takes the beige mat from Dick.

"What about new towels to match? Then let's go to the nursery." Sally nods, and they walk down the aisle, their carts bumping, and turn the corner to linens.

&

"I told you," Katherine says to Sally as they talk on the phone. "You didn't need it. That doctor of yours is not progressive. But you need to talk to him about tamoxifen. Or about one of the new aromatase inhibitors. Anastozole is one of them."

Sally is on her back patio, potting three new red geraniums she and Dick bought that morning at Target. She holds the phone between her cheek and shoulder as she pulls the plants out of their plastic containers.

"This is the color I see when I look at you," Dick said, holding up a pot. "But when you're in a mood . . ." He picked up a dark purple pansy. "Watch out."

"Pansies, that's for thoughts," Sally said.

"*Hamlet,*" Dick answered. "Don't show off to me, missy. I was the English major here."

"But all those years at Voyager Insurance knocked it out of you!"

"You don't even want to know what's inside of me," Dick said, raising his eyebrows up and down.

Sally smiles at the memory, digs in a terra-cotta pot with her spade, tries to focus on what Katherine is saying.

"Mom," Katherine says. "Are you listening to me?"

"Yes, of course, dear," she says. "And don't you worry. Dr. Gupta has already sent the prescription to the pharmacy. Dick is going to pick it up this afternoon."

Katherine is silent for a moment, but Sally knows what's coming.

"Mom," Katherine says. "Are you— I mean, how is it going with Dick?"

Sally shakes her head, pats down the soil on top of the first geranium. "After not dating anyone for over thirty years, I think it's going very well."

"And he's . . ." Katherine stops, and Sally wants to laugh. Her daughter, the ballbuster, can't find her words?

"Look, Katie, it's fine. It's nice. He's a good friend, and we're figuring things out. It's what we all have to do with each other if we want to go further. I just never found someone I wanted to be with until Dick. It's what—" Sally feels her next sentence in her mouth and then holds it against her tongue, its bite pushing on the roof of her mouth. "It's what *you* have to do if you want to go further— unless, of course, you don't have a choice. Sometimes, like with your father, it's there. In front of you, knocking you on the head. There's nothing you can do about it. Sometimes, though, you have to choose to move closer. It's what you could do with someone. A man . . . or a woman."

Now Katherine is truly silent, and for a quick second, Sally wishes she hadn't said the words, the truth. But then she's glad. She wants Katherine to know she's always known—and Sally wants her daughter to know she loves her, no matter whom she chooses.

"Mom."

"It's all right, dear. Truly. I know why you didn't tell me. I seem very old-fashioned. But after all, I've lived in the Bay Area for a lot of years now. We have a lot of gay couples at the bridge center."

"Mom."

"Katherine."

Katherine sighs. "I'm sorry."

"Don't be. There's nothing to be sorry about. It's who you are."

"It is who I am. I just didn't know . . ."

"Didn't know if I could take it."

There's silence on the line, and then a slight rustle, as if Katherine is nodding. "Well, maybe. Or I was just scared. In a way, I knew that if you were okay with me and who I was, that meant I would have to do something. I could actually bring someone home. That I'd have to commit."

Sally understands. Saying words aloud like "I'm unhappy" makes things happen. Look at Mia and Ford. One day they were in a marriage that wasn't working despite all the signs to the contrary, and then the words were out and things changed. One sentence, and poof! Life is different.

"I'd love to meet someone you were committed to," Sally says.

"Well, first I have to actually find someone. Most of the people I work with don't say much," Katherine says, and both she and Sally laugh a little. Sally puts her hand to her chest, liking the feel of her amusement, the vibration in her body.

"Listen, come home for a visit," Sally says. "Visit your sister. I don't think she's doing well. Visit your old, chemo-free mother before she heads off to the United Kingdom. Come see how I kept most of my hair."

"Okay," Katherine says. "I will. Soon."

After a few more words, they hang up, and Sally puts down the phone. For a moment, she's engrossed with her plants, tamping down the dirt, soaking them with water from the watering can. Then she hears her own words to Katherine.

"It's what you have to do if you want to go further."

Good advice, she thinks, knowing that she hasn't truly followed it herself. Sure, there was that strange, surreal moment of Dick touching her incisions. And they are good friends, constant companions. A couple in many ways. Also, there has simply been her recovery and then her chemo. Now, her body almost hers again, Sally knows that there are things she needs to do, wants to do.

Sally pulls herself up and slaps the dirt off her hands. Looking around the patio, she nods. She needs some snow-in-summer, a few zinnias, and a couple of cosmos. More dirt, a little compost.

But more importantly, she needs to change the sheets and take a shower. Then a little mascara. Her new silk blouse that Dahlia sent her with the pockets over the breasts. Some music. Reservations at that new restaurant on Main Street, Kenitos, the one Mia said was so good.

≈

"That was a fine meal," Dick says as he takes her coat and hangs it up in the coat closet.

"Mia said that chicken dish was the best she'd ever had." Sally walks into the kitchen to start the coffee. "I'm glad I ordered it, too."

Dick follows her, picking up the *Newsweek* and flipping through it as she scoops coffee grounds into the basket. She can feel him behind her, all the energy that he is, the pulse and heat of his body. Sally smiles, shakes her head, presses on the machine and turns to him.

He looks up and she opens her mouth, knowing there are words to say. She's heard them on television and in the movies, and maybe once, a million years ago, she said some of them to David. She said, "Let's go upstairs" or "I'm feeling a little frisky, honey." Was that how it had always happened? Or had it been just a roll over in the bed, arms around each other, a pressing of flesh? Who knew? Who besides her is here to remember?

"Sal Gal," he says, before she can remember what she's forgotten. Dick walks around the counter and takes her in his arms, just like that. Then he looks down at her, brushing her wispy hair away from her face, the hair she's just managed to save.

"Yes," she says, and then he leans down and kisses her.

Upstairs, he sits down on the edge of the bed, pulling her down so that they are next to each other. He unbuttons her blouse, the fancy silk one Dahlia gave her. What would Dahlia think if she knew that the most important thing about her present was that it was being taken off by a man? By Dick, who now pulls it off her shoulders, whisking it along her arms and then putting it gently on the chair next to her bed.

Sally brings her hand to his face, holding his jaw in her palm. Then she leans into him, pressing her flat chest against his shirt, his hands on her back. Wherever he touches her feels like tears, as if her very skin will cry from the feeling of him against her, as if they are talking in a language she now recognizes.

She moves away, and he takes off his shirt, and there is his older man's body, a body David never grew into: white chest hair, a belly a bit pooched out, his shoulder and collarbones prominent.

Sally loves the way Dick feels, her hand running along the flat ridge of his sternum, and like he did before, he brings his hands to her chest, running his fingers lightly over her scars, the small puckers of extra skin, and then trailing to her belly. Then he is no longer touching her lightly; hugging her tight instead, and they lie down on the bed, kissing, their flat chests pressed together.

Inside herself, Sally feels another story beginning to form, and for a little second, she wonders if Mia got her talent directly from her mother. Sally knows how to create a narrative, the beginning and middle, though she's never been too good with ends. But now as she kisses Dick Brantley back, one old story ends.

She can see the story's ending even in the darkness of her closed eyes. David gets up from this very bed, the bed they used to sleep on together, and walks to the door. He turns, smiles, gives her a little wave, and then disappears into the hall and walks out of the house he never actually lived in, the one he only inhabited because Sally wouldn't let him leave.

Opening her eyes, she looks at Dick's face, his closed eyes, his hair hanging over his forehead. She doesn't see David. He's not there at all. She sees only this, them, and she closes her eyes. His hands move; so do hers, finding the terrain she thought she'd never travel again. He sits up, turns off the light, and they take off the rest of their clothes and get under the blankets, old bodies, old bones, their flesh hot and warm.

❧

That night, spooned up against Dick's back, Sally dreams of Scotland again, sees the same green hills, the little village with thatched roofs, the villagers in their wool clothes, the women wearing big white aprons. She tries to find herself in the dream, but she's not the observer, really, she's one of the villagers. But where? Which one? She scans the entire village, the doorways, the windows, the barns. But then, there! There she is! An old woman picking vegetables and putting them in her basket, her long gray hair tucked up in a bonnet. And then Sally's in the body of this village woman, her hands on small brown potatoes and then long green beans. She moves down the rows, talks with other women, feels the dirt on her palms, the sweat at the back of her neck.

Oh, this is hard, good work, and she puts the basket down on the tilled earth and stretches, her arms held high, breath tight and full in her body.

FIFTEEN

Robert

Robert has never been to Honduras, so he very carefully reads the extensive list Operation Grin sent him. Lightweight shirts, drip-dry shorts, sandals. Mosquito repellent. Water purifiers. First aid kit. All things he hasn't used since camping two years ago with Jack and a couple of other guys from Jack's practice.

Last week, he went to REI, a local camping and sports-supply store, and bought all his travel supplies. With all his purchases, Robert felt like he was moving to another state, country, world, all for only two weeks.

And this list is just for getting to and from the airport, the brief time he will be at the International Tegucigalpa Hotel, and the small slip of time he might do some sightseeing before and after his work. One of the other lists is for the operating-room donations Operation Grin would like Inland Community Health Center to make: a standing anesthesia machine, a portable vaporizer, oxygen regulator, Leibinger cleft lip/palate instrument, or portable suction machine.

Then there is the request for the incoming staff to bring their own scrubs, gloves, masks, all the things Robert tears off his body daily without really thinking about them—without thinking of the money and human energy required to manufacture them, to clean them, to fold them, to stack them, to start all over again.

He puts down the list and looks at his duffel bag and sighs. He wants to go, he needs to go, but he still hears Jack's voice in his head from last night.

"Fucking liberal do-gooders. Fine. Fix all the cleft lips in the world, but at least they should put you up somewhere." Jack slapped his hand on the table. "Where are you going to be?"

"I put myself up, Jack. At a good hotel, too."

"Oh, but where is this good hotel? Somewhere in the jungle? You'll get Chagas' disease. Or malaria, cholera, or dengue fever. And then what about all the wild creatures? Snakes and what? Vampire bats."

"Vampire bats live in the Amazon," Robert said, smiling, enjoying the sight of angry Jack, righteously indignant Jack. Jack after one too many martinis.

"So why in the stories do vampires always live in Romania? Shit. Nothing makes sense."

"Artistic license," Robert said, thinking of Mia, pulling her memory close and then pushing her away. "Writers. You know."

In the long pause, Jack raised his eyebrow, sipped his drink. "All over, huh?"

Robert nodded, shrugged, fell still. "I don't want to talk about it."

"What else is new?" Jack said. "Unlike vampire bats, you are wholly unsurprising."

"I wouldn't want to disappoint." Robert sipped his beer, knowing that "disappoint" was his middle name.

"Aw, man, shut up," Jack said, hitting his shoulder with his palm. "Knock it off. When do you leave?"

"A couple days," Robert said. "For two weeks."

"Do you think you'll escape it by going farther away this time?" Jack stares at him.

"What do you mean?" Robert tilts his beer into his mouth, but there's nothing left.

"You're running away."

Robert puts the bottle on the table, slouches down in his chair. "I can't handle it."

"Yes, you can. You've handled a lot in your life. Your parents. What happened to your patient. You've been on your own too long, though, man. Maybe this time you should try to stay and figure it out." Jack shakes his head. "I try to stay out of it."

"Yeah," says Robert. "By talking to Leslie at the gym? She called me, you know."

"I'm just worried about you. That's all." Jack finished his drink. "But who knows. Maybe this is the adventure that will change everything."

As he packs, Robert wants to believe Jack. This is the trip that will save him, that will show him the light. Maybe he will meet someone perfect. But he knows that Jack's first assessment was probably closer to the truth. He is running away.

Whatever is true, there's no time to think about it now. He's going to leave in a day. Inland has given him the time off, happy to publicize the good works of one of its doctors, grateful for the opportunity of shipping an oxygen regulator and a portable suction machine to San Felipe Hospital. In fact, the marketing and publicity departments even called him for an initial interview, wanting to use his story in a round of commercials. Inland loves to pick ordinary doctors to profile, showing them in lovely, well-lit exam rooms, talking with happy, satisfied patients whose illnesses are not apparent.

"No," Robert told them. "Absolutely not."

He can see the commercial in his head: Here's Dr. Fake in his fake office talking to a patient about fake breasts. The voice-over will explain how Dr. Fake travels to third-world countries to help poor and destitute children, but if you are by chance looking for augmented breasts, please stop by. Dr. Fake truly cares.

Phyllis jumps up on the bed and begins to sniff at his duffel bag, prodding his new mosquito hat with her paw. Robert shoos her off, and then the doorbell rings. The cat sitter is going to come over this afternoon to get the Phyllis tour, but she's a half hour early.

Robert zips up his bag and walks out of the room, down the hall, and then opens the front door. But it's not the cat sitter, the teenaged girl who lives down the street. It's Mia.

She blushes, smiles, and then her face falls. "Hi."

Robert's body feels confused. His heart is racing, pumping blood everywhere, but he doesn't think he can move, his legs wooden, his arms leaden. They haven't seen each other since Bakersfield over a month ago—or, at least, she hasn't seen him—and the body memory of that time rushes through him.

"Hi," he says back, holding on to the door. "How are you?"

She cocks her head, watching him. "Not very good."

Robert doesn't move.

"Can I come in?" she asks, and he starts.

"Of course. Yes."

His arms somehow move, and he opens the door wider. Mia walks in, and he can see how she's trying to make herself smaller, maybe as if she wishes she weren't here at all. He knows what she's going to tell him, of course. It's the news he tried not to hear before. That everything that happened between them was a terrible mistake. That she's worked it all out with Ford. He already knows this because of the way she looked at Ford during the reading.

Together, they walk into his living room. He tries not to glance down the hall to his bedroom, that being their usual path: the front door closing, the kiss, the pull to the bed, the sex. And then the talking and the holding. She's really only been in the living room once, that first time they were together here. Robert can still see her looking out to the courtyard and still see his vision of her typing there, writing, working. Living.

Mia sits on the couch, her face still aflame. Robert wants to lean over and smooth her pale skin with his hand, but instead, he sits on a chair opposite her.

"So," she says and then bites her lip. "What happened, Robert? Why did you change your mind?"

He swallows, looks away, too much in his throat to say a word. Slowly, he brings forth the words he subintonated to himself for weeks. "It wasn't going to work out, Mia."

She shakes her head. "Where—how?" She stops, breathes in, holds back words he can almost see inside her. She bites her lip, breathes out. "Why?"

Robert lifts his hands, lets them fall to his knees. "You know, Mia."

"No, Robert," she says, her face fading, her eyes glittery. "I don't. We had a good time in Bakersfield, didn't we? I thought— I thought we got through some stuff."

He nods, crosses his legs. Phyllis jumps on the couch and steps onto Mia's lap. Mia pets her absently with one hand and wipes her eyes with the other.

"You're married, Mia. You have a life that I can't really be in, except on schedule."

For a second, Robert imagines that the room has been sucked dry of air and sound. Mia opens her mouth but says nothing, her mouth a small *O*. Finally, she says, "Is that it? Me being married? It didn't stop you in the beginning. Is that the only reason you stopped writing? Calling?"

Robert looks at the tile floor. "I don't think that it's right."

"Right? Like moral? Or good between us?"

He can't say anything because whatever he says would be a lie. And he can't tell her the truth. He doesn't know how.

"Robert, isn't this about you? About you not being able to—to love me? Don't hide behind my marriage. Just tell me the truth."

He should just say yes to it all. It would be easiest, wouldn't it? How can he articulate to her the feeling of being on the outside, removed, not understanding, not knowing how to really move into someone else? She knows it's really not about her or her marriage or Ford. She can see through him because he's shown her how during their afternoons together. He gave her a map in Bakersfield. He rubs his forehead quickly, hiding his eyes from her gaze.

"I don't know."

Mia picks up Phyllis and puts her on the couch and then stands up. She walks back to the window and looks outside, brings her hand to the wood on the French door. *A portrait,* Robert thinks. *Mia thinking.*

"You're scared," she says so lightly that he almost misses it. He wonders who she's talking to, him or her.

But she doesn't know the half of it. She doesn't know anything. Yet she does. That's the problem. She knows it all.

"I'm going to Honduras," he blurts out before she can say anything else.

She turns to him, surprised. "Honduras? For how long?"

He wishes he could say six months, a year, something that would make it easier for them to never see each other again, something that would keep her from seeing him as he really was.

"Two weeks."

She sighs, shakes her head, turns back to the courtyard, and mumbles something.

"What?"

Mia walks back to the couch and stands by it, her hand touching the armrest, the pillows, her fingernails scratching the soft fabric. In the afternoon light that fills the room, her hair seems golden, her eyes almost yellow. He can't help himself and lets his gaze move down her neck to her breasts, waist, thighs. He closes his eyes. For a second he's with her in his bedroom, the sunlight on the bed, her arms around him.

"I think you're wrong. For a lot of reasons, Robert," she says. "And things have changed for me. In my life. You don't even know what's been going on."

Looking up at her, he wants to ask what things she's talking about. For a quick second, he imagines that she's going to tell him that she's left Ford. That she has all her possessions in the back of her car. That's she moving in with him now.

Robert wants to know what she means, but then he sees Ford in the back of the bookstore, smiling, mouthing incomprehensible words to Mia that she understands. What can change the fact of the *knowingness* in that marriage, even if it is over? How can he, Robert, ever be as close to someone as that?

What would Ford say to Robert now?

Mia sees his confusion, and she shakes her head again, turning to look out the window, into the light. She begins to cry and she doesn't hide it, letting her sadness show on her lips and in her eyes, letting her tears fall.

Stand up, he thinks. *Go to her; hold her tight.*

But he doesn't move.

"I know I can't expect— I want to . . . Never mind," Mia says when she finds her breath. She looks up at him, holds his gaze for a moment as she says, "I thought you were someone else."

"I wish I were," he says, and he means it.

"Have a good time in Honduras," she says, and then she's walking away, out of the living room, down the hall. The front door opens—a wide swath of light fluming into the house—and then it closes.

Because he can do nothing else, Robert sits in his living room, numb and still. The sun moves a little, settles behind a tree, the living room shaded and full of shadows.

When he was finishing second grade, his teacher wrote on his report card, "Robert needs to engage more with the class. Learn to share what he knows."

His teachers and attending doctors in medical school said the same thing. "Goddamn it, Rob," Jack said. "If you'd just talk, you'd have it all. Show them what you can do. Show them what you know."

What does he know? He's failed on so many fronts, let so many people he's liked and loved leave, as if too much connection could kill.

But he wants to share something with Mia. He's told her more than he's ever told any woman, never discussing the story of Joyce with anyone except for Jack. He's moved into her body—her body took him in. He's looked into her eyes and seen some part of himself come back—reflected, refracted—through her gaze. And he liked what he saw. He didn't cringe or run away or pull back. Until that day in Emeryville, all he wanted was more.

When the doorbell rings again—the sound jarring in Robert's head, his heart pounding—he jumps up, adrenaline pumping into his legs and he runs down the hall. She's so brave, his Mia. She's the one who can come back, start over, give him a second chance. He's going to tell her he finally understands. He knows what it means to love. She's taught him. She'll walk in the house and he'll hold her, press her against him. This will be it, the instant when everything is perfect.

Robert pulls open the door, wanting to say it all to her. But it's not Mia. It's Monique, the teenaged cat sitter from down the street, smiling, her pants low-cut, a turquoise jewel glinting in her belly button.

"Sorry I'm, like, late," she says, and moves into the house.

Robert lets her in, blinks into the brightness of the empty street. And then he shakes his head, looks back at Monique, who is already in the living room, and closes the door behind them.

❧

If Robert thought he was going to have time to sightsee outside of Tegucigalpa, he was mistaken. After landing at Tegucigalpa Toncontin Airport at seven in the morning, he went immediately to San Felipe Hospital, where he was introduced to the staff—doctors, nurses, dentists, med students, college and even high school students—in an overwhelming, long, intense two-hour meeting that detailed the entire two-week process. Then they were broken up into teams—students and nurses and translators to screen the patients; doctors and dentists paired with nurses and translators to examine the patients to determine the types of procedures necessary.

After each screening, the patients went to classes the students had prepared—lectures on proper dental hygiene and the importance of fresh vegetables and fruits in a country where eating, for many, was a daily struggle.

And now, dressed in one of the lab coats he brought with him, Robert stands by an exam table with a nurse and a translator. The line to reach him and the other doctors is enormous, whole families slumped together against the hospital corridor walls, seeming to have walked for miles to get here, carrying almost all their household goods.

"They *have* walked that far," the translator, Manuela, said when Robert made a comment earlier. "Sometimes, the families, they walk for sixty miles to bring their children here. One man tried for three years to get here on time, traveling by foot and by cart with his little boy, and each year he made it too late. Someone heard about it and flew him to the States. But most . . ." She moved her arm to indicate the line. "They leave early, and they stay until it's finished."

❧

Ramon wiggles on the table, his mouth and palate open, yawning, glistening red. His mother watches Robert with serious, steady black eyes, flicking her gaze away only briefly when Manuela translates.

"Next week," Manuela says in Spanish. "Surgery to the lip, here. And inside the mouth, here. Maybe more than one procedure, señora. Maybe you will have to come back next year for more."

The woman nods, doesn't smile, even though Ramon tries to. In all his time as a plastic surgeon, Robert has never seen a cleft lip and palate this horrible, and as he looks quickly down the hall, he sees one after the other, open mouths leading wide into the body.

"Surgery," he agrees, writing down Ramon's age and weight and his mother's name: Elena Maria Garcia de Torrez.

Manuela tells Señora Torrez where to sign the forms and how to schedule the appointment, and then there is another patient and another. Dasha, the nurse, takes vitals, and then Robert examines them all. Most are like Ramon, cleft lip, cleft palate, or both. But one woman's mouth is twisted and melted from a cooking fire; a little girl with a nasofrontal enceophalocele—a bony defect that allows brain material to push out from the skull—has to be referred to the surgery team back in the States; twin girls hide identical facial hemangiomas—benign facial tumors—behind their small brown hands.

Mostly, the stream of children has cleft lips and palates, operations that in the States are done when the child is ten weeks old. During his internship and residency, Robert performed a number of these procedures on infants, their clefts smooth, seemingly small. How different those American babies looked in comparison to these children, who grew from infancy to childhood with these holes in their faces. These clefts are developed and deep, Robert imagining he can look forever into the welling darkness.

At first he grits his back teeth, trying not to see how the defect has twisted the face, turned the smile into a sneer, the mouth into a sieve. But then as he studies his patients, he focuses on how the cleft in the lip flows into a nostril, the skin red and full and slightly glistening. Almost ripe, welling thickly around exposed, white front teeth. With gloved fingers, he presses gently on the full flesh and imagines the lips like flowers, the folds of lip like puffy petals.

Even with the congenital defects, these patients smile, their eyes hopeful, their need so great, so desperate. Just like his.

Despite the six teams that are evaluating patients, the line in the hall stays long. And even though he stops for lunch and takes a short break late in the afternoon, Robert is exhausted by six, his feet sore, his back stiff. Manuela looks at him, her eyebrows raised, when he asks at what time they stop for the day.

"When you can't go on anymore," she says flatly.

And so they work together with Dasha until eight, when Robert's eyes start to blur and all the patients seem to have the exact same problem, without variation.

Manuela clicks her tongue and straightens the pages on her clipboard. "Tomorrow, then," she says, walking toward the people who still slump against the wall.

❧

Back at the hotel, Robert unpacks, orders up some room service, and then showers. Under the water, his body feels weightless, his consciousness seeming to float above him in the tiled shower stall. Afterward, he isn't sleepy but wired, anxious, nervous, and he keeps having to flick away at memory. Mia under him, Mia loosening his ponytail, Mia laughing with him. Mia all the time.

So he puts his key and wallet in his pocket and leaves the room, heading downstairs to the bar that is filled with mostly international people, businessmen, foreign officials, and probably hidden CIA folk among the tables. He nods and waves to a few of the doctors he met at the early-morning meeting, and then sits at the bar and tries to think of a drink that doesn't require added water. Finally, he looks at the bartender and says, "Bourbon *solamente, por favor. No quiero hielo.*"

The bartender nods, pours Robert's drink, doesn't add ice, and then Robert stares at the brown liquid, wondering if it will help.

"Did you know drinking is the worst thing of all for travel fatigue?" Manuela says, taking a seat next to him.

Robert puts down his glass and looks at her. She has become another woman, her long brown hair loose on her shoulders, her face relaxed. She wears a pair of pants and a soft blouse, and now, without her white lab coat on, he can see the smooth column of her neck.

"I'm sure it isn't," he says, taking another sip, letting the sting of alcohol fill his mouth. "I thought I would fall into bed, but I'm so wired."

"It's exciting work, in a strange way," she says, nodding as the bartender hands her a drink.

"You don't even have to order," Robert says. "You must not be on your first tour of duty."

"No." She shakes her head. "I first came down about five years ago, and I can't stay away. I come twice or three times a year."

"So you know all the sights to see," he says. "Your way about town."

She shrugs, sips her drink, something clear and thick in a small glass. "There are only so many times you can go to the Iglesia de Nuestra Señora de los Dolores or the Comayagüela market. Even the jungle has lost its charms. Mostly, I know this hotel and the hospital."

"What do you do in the real world?" Robert asks. He feels the bourbon already, the reaching, electric hand of potential intoxication.

"You and I don't live in the real world." She shakes her head, her gold necklace glinting on her chest.

"How do you know that?" he asks. "Why is what I do at home or how I live there not the real world?"

"The real world? With all that we saw today, how can you even imagine that anything in the States is real?" She licks her lips, runs a finger on the slick side of her glass.

"Because of Maslow and his hierarchy of needs."

"Do expound," Manuela says, crossing her legs.

Robert breathes in, glad to talk about steps and stages and levels, anything to take himself away from the lightness in his body and the memory of Mia. "All humans are motivated by unsatisfied needs. Basic needs need to be satisfied before higher needs can be satisfied. I want to eat and sleep before I worry about what I am eating and where I am sleeping. But once I am full and rested, I move to a safer place with better food and cleaner water. Then I want someone to live with me at the safe place. Next I want to feel really good about this place where I am living. Finally, I want to understand my choices for living there so I can understand who I am."

"Interesting."

"This is real and home is real. I'd want my cleft lip repaired so I can eat before I'd want to buy a new house in a better school district. But it's all the same thing. The same need."

The bartender drops a glass, whispers a string of curses that makes Manuela smile wide, her teeth luminous in the darkened bar. She reminds Robert of something that has been warmed all day in the sun.

"So," she says. "When you are home, the nips and tucks and tweaks you do on people's noses and necks and breasts are the same need as having one's mouth whole."

Robert shakes his head. "I don't perform elective surgeries. Mostly breast reconstructions."

"Why?"

For an instant, he's on the bed in the Bakersfield hotel room, Mia watching him. The words come out then, the whole story. Robert bites his lip, turns to Manuela.

"I lost a couple of patients. I only want to work where there's physical need."

"So," she says, ignoring, it seems, what he said about all the death. "Your work doesn't always fit in with Maslow?"

He wants to ask her if she heard him, but from the bright look in her eyes, he knows she did. "Touché." Robert raises his glass. "So, back in the States, where some things are not as important as here, what do you do?"

"That's better." She smiles again, her lips lightly coated with a soft red color and the liquor. "I'm a professor of Spanish literature at the University of Texas at Austin," she says.

A professor, Robert thinks. *Like Mia.*

He nods. "So this work fills the . . ."

Manuela laughs, pushes her thick hair back with her hand. "The blank. The void. The gap."

"Married? Kids?" He turns to really look at her. She can't be more than thirty-five.

"Once. Divorced. No kids. You?" He can see a faint blush on her cheeks, and his heart pounds, feeling Mia's hot skin under his palm.

"Never for both."

She raises her eyebrows, smiles. "You plastic surgeons. What is it? Are you all perfectionists?"

"I guess you've made a study of us," he says. "You're on a mission to save us from our own profession."

Manuela doesn't say a word, waiting for the answer to her other question.

Robert takes another sip and pushes away his empty glass. The bartender refills it. "No. Not a perfectionist. An idiot."

Manuela nods. "What's your void?"

Now Robert laughs, imagining a game show, contestants full of a special, secret emptiness they slowly reveal during the half-hour contest. The one who catharts the most wins whatever is behind door number 2. A washing machine. A stove. A brand-new car!

"Mia."

She sits back. "What?"

"My girlfriend. My—" There is no word for what Mia is to him because there just isn't. Lover? Paramour? Friend? Soul mate? All of the above? Or none of the above because he let her go? Because he was a coward who watched her close the door?

"It means 'mine,'" Manuela says. The blush has paled on her cheek, and her face is closed to him now, the easy bar openness folding back into the tough translator stance of earlier in the day.

"What does?"

"*Mia*. Spanish for 'mine.'"

Robert tries to hold back, but the liquor and the jet lag and his exhaustion since the reading in Emeryville slip over him. His eyes start to water, and he rubs his eyebrows.

"Of course it does," he says finally. He said Mia's name so often without remembering his seventh-grade Spanish, the few small sentences he'd learned from Señora Bernal. Or he just never thought in the feminine, his nouns, everything that was his, *mio*.

"So, is she?"

"What do you mean?"

"Is she yours?" Manuela asks, her dark eyes on him. Her pulse beats in the sweet brown hollow of her neck.

"Not yet." And there Mia is, walking away from him. There is his front path, empty again, just like always.

Manuela leans forward. "If you see a way to fill your gap, you *are* an idiot if you don't. I'm sure Maslow would agree."

She finishes her drink, puts a couple of bills on the smooth wood, and stands up. "You should get to sleep. We'll be doing what we did today for another six days. And then you'll start to operate. It doesn't really get any easier."

Robert nods, hands her the *lempiras* she put on the bar. "My treat."

She shakes her head but takes the bills, and he can see that if he were the person he'd been before Mia, he would want to be with Manuela, feel her body under him, let her run her hands through his hair. But now, in Tegucigalpa, he knows he has changed. He's found something, someone he wants for his own, someone he can love even though he knows that one day he will lose her in the way that everyone loses everything in life.

He doesn't care about loss now. He wants her. Someone he can say is his. He just didn't know he was saying it before. He'd ignored the word "mine" that long.

"Good night, Robert," Manuela says.

"Good night," he says back, and she walks away, but not from him. She's not angry or upset or disgusted with anything he's done. In fact, he knows that Manuela was looking for something to fill the void. His body, his attention for two weeks. And even though he's rejected her, he hasn't hurt her, hasn't said anything wrong. He hasn't ignored her. So this walking away from him seems true, real, just a walk away from him in general.

Robert follows her with his eyes until she disappears into the lobby. He's going to have to learn a walk—but another kind, the kind that moves toward, near, closer, in. The kind that will lead him to what he needs and wants. To what is his.

Mia

"Did they get to the airport okay?" Dahlia asks on the phone, a slight crackle of static between them. "Did Mom make you take her there about four hours in advance?"

All their lives and long before extra security requirements at airports, Sally has believed in being at the terminal at least three hours in advance. For days and then hours before her flight, she would call the airline, double-checking on the time of departure and the gate. Earlier this week when Mia told her she can confirm any flight on the Internet, Sally didn't care, wanting to dial up British Airways herself, over and over again.

"I like to speak to a human," Sally said. "Humans are better than machines."

"Maybe in some ways," Mia said, knowing that at least machines are predictable.

Now Mia smiles at Dahlia's question and then sneezes, holding the phone away from her mouth as she does.

"Bless you," Dahlia says. "Your immune system must be damaged from all the excitement of getting them there."

"Probably. I dropped them both off about three hours before

their flight. Mom brought three suitcases, making Dick claim one of hers as his own."

"What are they like together? Does she ride right over him?"

"Not really. Actually, no. She wanted to get there four hours in advance, but Dick put his foot down."

"Really?" Dahlia says. "And she let him?"

"Barely. But I checked their flight status online, and they've departed. Sally and Dick are somewhere over the continental United States."

In the background behind Dahlia, Mia can hear the kids splashing in the pool. During the long, blazing Phoenix summer (which coincides with the slow tax season), Dahlia and her children are either in the pool or inside, the heat outside oppressive, flat, white with unrelenting sunshine.

"So, how are you?" Dahlia asks softly, as if the question won't hurt in a quiet tone. "How are the boys? Harper?"

Mia stands up and walks out onto her deck. Spring turned into summer all at once, the green of March, April, and early May morphing all of a sudden into a blond June. In a week, Mia will start teaching a summer school class, "Introduction to Fiction Writing," which filled the first week it was offered on the schedule.

Mia sighs, thinking about all the incomplete, half-written stories she will be reading. About the hours of time when she will have to push Robert out of her head as she tries to concentrate on words. "I'm okay, Dahls. I start teaching soon. It'll keep my mind off it. Well, a bit. Lucien is fine, but Harper's still kind of a mess. He pretends he's fine, but I know he's really upset. He even agreed to go see someone to talk about it. When he gets back from backpacking in Europe."

"When does he leave? And Lucien's off for somewhere too, right?"

The phone clutched between her jaw and shoulder, Mia leans down to deadhead a bushy lavender plant, crunching the dried flower heads in her palm. "Harper leaves in about three weeks. And Lucien is working for a couple of months and then is going to hitchhike across the country to the Republican convention. He wants to protest there, and then head up to Maine to see a friend. Both of them will really be gone."

As she says the words, Mia realizes that when the boys leave, she will be here alone. For the first time in over twenty years, she will be living by herself.

"Look, come visit me after your class," Dahlia says. "Bring Kenzie. You two would have a blast. You could drive to Sedona. Have a 'mystical' retreat. Talk with aliens or spirits."

Mia rubs her nose, trying to keep back another sneeze. Her eyes are watering and her throat feels full of needles. "I don't know. I've got a lot to do here. Things to fill in. Replace the furniture that Ford took."

"That asshole," Dahlia says.

"Then there are two of us," Mia reminds her. "I'm an asshole, too."

"No, you're not. You haven't been having an affair for years." Dahlia sounds to Mia like she did when she was five, belligerent and close to tears at the same time.

"But I may as well have been." Mia knows this is the truth. She hadn't been fooling around, but her characters had been, cheating and betraying for years and years, longer even than Ford. Both of them felt their marriage shred and rip, and neither of them could say the words, manage the truth. Both of them hid behind the bodies of others.

"Look, I've got to go," she says before Dahlia can argue with her. "I think I'm going to call Inland. I haven't been feeling very good, and I don't want to start teaching sounding like a frog."

"Okay," Dahlia says. "But—but take care, okay? And say hi to the boys for me."

"You, too. Say hi to everyone. Bye," Mia says, hanging up the phone and staring out into the valley spread before her in grass and oak and pine and finding her breath, which seems to get lost these days, hiding under and between her ribs. Sometimes air itself seems like a gift. So does food, or at least her enjoyment of it. And sleep, too. It is as if divorce or betrayal or loss—and she isn't exactly sure what she is mourning: Ford or Robert or both—came with its own specific symptoms. Nothing any doctor at Inland could give her could cure them. Not even Robert at this point.

But this cold! Inside the house, Mia grabs tissues out of the box on the kitchen table, blows, and wipes her nose, and begins to rummage through the spice cabinet, looking for the cold medicine she bought last year when Harper was sick. But it seems to be gone. Maybe it was something else Ford wanted.

Mia shakes her head and closes the cabinet door. What Ford wanted. What hadn't he wanted? Not unexpectedly, he'd grown attached to all the things Mia had—plates and cups and pillows and paintings and silverware. Furniture and beds and books. Just as she had predicted, they'd sniped at and argued with each other, both of them holding back words when Harper walked in the room they were hunkered down in, grabbing silver or picture frames or vases from each another.

Now the house seems like a set. It is as if someone has hastily put together rooms that resemble Mia's house, but forgot some of the most crucial details: the candlesticks they bought together in Big Sur, the watercolor of California hills that used to hang over the mantel, the large stuffed chair Ford found at Macy's.

Leaning against the stove, Mia blows her nose, coughs, and looks at the phone. She has to go to the doctor, even if it means going to Inland and chancing a meeting with Robert. She can't start the summer quarter off this way—deaf from fluid in her ears, squealing from a sore throat, wheezy with mucus. She needs to try to wheedle something miraculous from her doctor, not that she's ever actually seen her "primary care physician." Whenever she makes an appointment, he's too busy, so Mia ends up with a nurse practitioner. But at this point, she doesn't care.

Mia looks at the phone and then at the phone number list on the bulletin board next to it. She sighs, knowing that she has to take care of herself now. No one else will tell her to go to the doctor. No one else will run down to Rite Aid for cough syrup and echinacea. No one will heat a bowl of soup and bring it to her on the couch.

She starts to laugh at her melodramatic riff and then dials Inland's customer service center, wanting to get this part over with. After about ten minutes on hold, Mia finally is able to make an appointment for the following morning with yet another nurse practitioner.

"If you don't want to see the nurse, I can schedule you with Dr. Rutsala next Tuesday at twelve?" the woman says in a question, already knowing how Mia will answer.

Mia writes down her appointment information and hangs up. She sighs and walks down the hall past the bedrooms—Harper's, Lucien's, Ford's and hers. Now just hers. She leans against the doorjamb and stares at the bed. It's not the bed either boy was conceived on, that one a cheapie they bought in college at a mattress discounter, with student loan money, and later gave to the Salvation Army.

No, this king-sized bed was a much later purchase, thick and high and cozy, fluffy with a feather mattress and goose-down pillows. When Mia wakes up in the morning, she finds herself at the edge of what used to be Ford's side, as if she's spent the night searching for him. She walks in the room and sits down on the bed, rubbing her hand along the comforter. Mia loved sleeping with Ford, the hours against his warm back sometimes the best part of a hard day. Maybe she'd forgotten who he was, what they were— maybe she didn't long for him in the way she wanted to—but she desired his knownness, his warm, known ass. His familiarity.

But all that knowledge and all that comfort weren't enough.

Mia lies down, her head almost whirling as she does, her nose and eyes and forehead feeling like they are going to burst. So does her heart, all the blood in her body pulsing in her chest with memory.

What she wants is to sleep for a long, long time and to wake up feeling better. Whole. Completely different. Except, of course, she thinks as her mind starts to wander, everything is completely different already.

৶

"I saved a little kid today," Lucien says, passing the salad to Kenzie.

"What happened?" Mia asks, as she sits down and pushes in to the table. She cuts the lasagna into hot squares and begins to serve it on plates as Harper passes the sliced sourdough bread.

"No one was watching him. He just sort of walked into the pool and then walked all the way to the bottom. He sank like a rock. Usually little kids float a bit longer."

They all look up at Lucien, and then Mia laughs. "What? There's some kind of guideline? One-year-olds float for five seconds? Five-year-olds a minute? What about adults?"

Lucien holds out his plate for lasagna. "Adults sputter and flail, but they float for a long time. But they're more dangerous. Like octopuses when you try to save them. The next thing you know, you're the one on the bottom of the pool."

For a second, her head pulsing from cold and fear, Mia wants Lucien to quit being a lifeguard. She sees him limp on the wavery bottom of the pool, his tan, strong body pale under the gallons and gallons of chlorinated water. But she looks up at him and sees how strong he is. He's conquered drugs. He's gone from imagining he was the center of the universe to knowing he is just a man. He will save children all summer and then go to protest the Republicans.

And what about Harper? He will fly to Europe, where trains are

exploding and militants and terrorists are plotting, and will em-
bark on an adventure in the mountains. He will be surrounded by
good kids and trustworthy adults, but angry people don't care who
they kill as long as they make a point.

So much to worry about. So very much to worry about, and yet
nothing to worry about, because worrying won't change a thing.

"Well, tell the parents of those kids to pay better attention."

"Why don't you go up there and give them a good lecture,
Mia?" Kenzie says. "I bet you could run some seminars. Call them
something like 'Learn to Pay Attention or I'll Kill You' classes."

"Don't tempt her, Kenzie," Harper says. "She'd do it."

"I know," Kenzie says. "She'll do anything."

For a second in their laughter, Mia catches Kenzie's eye and they
both stop and look at their meals. Harper and Lucien begin a conversation, and then Mia looks at Kenzie, shrugging. Kenzie winks,
and they turn to the boys and listen.

❦

While Harper and Lucien watch television, Mia and Kenzie sit out
on the front deck. Kenzie is smoking one of her illicit cigarettes
from the pack she always carries around in her purse. Mia would
like to have a glass of wine, but she's a little high from the cold-
and-flu formula she found in the back of her medicine chest. If she
takes anything else, she might slip into a coma.

"Why is something so bad, so good?" Kenzie exhales a white triangle of smoke.

"I don't know. Ask Lucien. He can tell you all about addiction.
In fact, he might do an intervention on you this second."

"Bitch," Kenzie says, taking in a huge drag.

"Well, it's true. You need help."

Kenzie shakes her head. "I know. But at least it's only one cigarette a week or so."

"So only a part of one lung looks like charred hamburger."

Kenzie laughs. "Do we have to go through this every time?"

"Probably."

Mia sits back in her wooden chair and wipes her nose. Kenzie smokes her cigarette as the night turns from purple to black. One bright star rises and blinks over the waves of oak trees covering the hills. The boys turn off the television and go back into one of the bedrooms to play computer games. A bat swoops over the deck, twirling in a food-chase dance.

"Has he called?" Kenzie asks.

"Yeah. He's all settled in with Karen. He wants Harper to come over next weekend."

"Not Ford. Robert."

Mia knows that if she starts to cry with this cold, her face will indeed explode, so she breathes through her mouth and closes her eyes. She hears Kenzie's deep smoker's inhale.

"No. And he must have come home from Honduras by now. At least I think so. I hoped he'd call. But no."

Mia bites the inside of her cheek, willing her feelings to stop. Stop. She doesn't have the energy to think about Robert. How can she? She has a divorce, two boys, a summer school class, her writing, and her wounded heart to care for. Robert didn't call, didn't officially break up with her, didn't e-mail. Robert doesn't deserve one tear or sigh or moan or sleepless night.

"I was wrong," Kenzie says, stamping out her cigarette.

Wiping her eyes, Mia turns to Kenzie. "What do you mean?"

"About Robert. I'm sorry."

Kenzie's eyes glint in the darkness, the light from the house a fire in her pupils. Mia sighs. "It seemed wrong, I know. There was nothing truthful about it. You were—"

"I was the bitch," Kenzie interrupted. "Jealous. I was thinking, *Why does she get all the love?* Ford at home, and Robert outside of it. But I didn't know about Ford."

"Kenz, I told you all along how I felt about Ford."

"No, about how he felt. About what he was doing. I guess I wish that if someone loves you, that's enough. It doesn't have to be reciprocal totally. Like that's a myth. A dream. Some kind of fantasy that writers have made up."

Kenzie stands up and walks to the deck rail, looking up into the sky. "Because for me, just finding that has been hard. Impossible."

For a terrible instant, Mia is in Robert's bed, feeling his body next to hers, looking into his eyes. She sees him in Bakersfield, hears his story, feels the tears on his neck. But then the truth pushes into that bedroom memory, the motel memory, showing her what is real: Robert sitting on his couch in his living room. Robert letting her leave.

Mia blows her nose and swallows. "Maybe it is a dream. Do you see it happening now?"

Turning from the rail, Kenzie shakes her head. "Mia, I couldn't say this right away because of Ford leaving, but if you really love Robert—" Mia tries to interrupt, but Kenzie says, "Stop. Listen. If you really love Robert, you should try it again. Talk with him. Maybe he was saying something you couldn't hear that day. Maybe there is more to the story than you know."

Because Mia's ears are full of fluid, Kenzie almost sounds like she's talking underwater. Mia stares at her friend, her best friend.

"It hurts," Mia says finally.

Kenzie walks over to her, kneels down by the chair. "I know."

Now Mia starts to cry, unable to stop the wave of feeling she's been tamping down all day. She leans onto Kenzie's shoulder and her friend hugs her, lets her cry, not caring about catching her cold. In the dark night, Mia finally feels it all. In the room of her sadness, she sees Ford and Robert and her mother's flat chest. She sees her boys and herself. She sees Kenzie smoking a cigarette alone.

"No," she moans into Kenzie's shirt.

"Yes," Kenzie says, squeezing her tight. "Yes."

"I cannot prescribe anything for this but rest and fluids," the nurse practitioner says. "You have a cold."

Mia wants to tell her that she has more than a cold. In fact, she wishes she could force the woman to check her heart. All night, her chest ached, right through to her back. As she lay alone in her king-sized bed, she imagined she was having a heart attack. Like the book that she read to Sally during chemotherapy, Mia has a hole in her heart. In the morning, the boys would find her stone-cold and pale, a victim of her own inability to see her marriage, to pay attention to what her heart needed. So instead of going on, her heart was trying to quit. To jump ship. To bail out while there was time.

"What about my ears?" Mia says. "I can't hear. It hurts."

The nurse sighs and picks up the ear scope, attaches the pointy tip, and then looks into Mia's right ear.

"Oh. Well," the nurse says.

"What?"

"Looks like you do have an infection. Do you get these a lot?"

"No," Mia says. "Never. It's a year of firsts."

The nurse takes the scope from her right ear and looks into the left. "Just the right ear. Well, it looks like antibiotics, after all."

Mia nods and watches the nurse write on the chart. *How different this is,* she thinks, *from all the appointments with Mom.* Look how slim my chart is. By the time she and Sally were in oncology, Sally's chart looked like a tax code manual, thick and incomprehensible.

"Let me go get a script from the doctor. I'll be right back. You can get dressed."

The nurse leaves, and Mia slides off the table and takes off her gown. She shivers in the cool exam room air and her skin prickles, gooseflesh everywhere. Mia is dressed and waiting when the nurse comes back in and hands her a prescription.

"You'll feel better soon," the nurse says. "Make sure you take them all."

Mia nods and then walks out of the exam room, feeling her feet hit the same Inland floor that she walked so many times with her mother. Every time they left an exam room together, Mia felt heavy, weighted down with news and information and statistics. She can't believe how much has changed. Sally is in Scottland, happy, traveling with a man. A boyfriend. A gentleman caller. Her postcard to Mia was almost exuberant: *It's beautiful here! Dick and I are loving it. Everything is green—the hills go on forever. I might just stay.*

Mia has an image of her mother whirling around on hills, sort of a *Sound of Music* move, but more subdued. More Sally.

Clutching a piece of paper that will lead her toward health, Mia can almost smile, and she pushes out into the waiting room, feeling lighter—as if she isn't clogged with cold—and there is Robert, sitting on a chair, looking at her.

Mia stops moving but her body seems to rush forward, and she almost staggers, trying to find her balance. Robert puts down a magazine and stands up, walking to her, grabbing her arm.

"Are you okay?" He looks at her, and the color of his eyes and the closeness of his face make Mia want to weep. If she were someone else or if she were in a movie, she'd wail and fall to the floor of the waiting room, disregarding all the sick people and her new cotton slacks.

But she's who she is, and even as she is looking at Robert, she knows she's angry. Her head pulses, her ear throbs.

"Yeah. Ear infection."

"No wonder you're wobbly." He smiles, and Mia looks away.

"I've got to go to the pharmacy," she says, showing him the prescription as if she has to prove it.

"Let me take you," he says, as if the health center is his home and he's giving her another tour, just like that first time at his house.

They start to walk, and then Mia stops. "How did you know I was here?"

Robert blushes and pushes his hair away from his forehead. She watches him smooth his hair, and she wants to touch his head, feel the soft strands under her fingers. But then she wants to yank hard on his ponytail and storm off.

"Well," he begins, his face completely red, "I happened— Look. I went into your file on the computer. I saw this appointment."

Mia blinks. "You spied on me."

He nods. "Yeah."

"Why did you wait so long?" she asks, a flare of anger racing along her jaw. "Why didn't you find me sooner?"

"I was scared," he says quietly.

She turns to him, her jaw aching. "Who isn't?"

Robert nods, keeps his eyes down, but he touches her wrist quickly. At his touch, all the tiny hairs on her body rise, and she swallows back her embarrassing desire.

They reach the bank of elevators, but neither of them presses a button. Instead, they walk away and stand by the back wall, leaning against it. Mia breathes through her mouth, knowing that she must look terrible. Maybe she does look better because of the weight she's lost since Ford left, but her eyes and nose are red, her hair washed but not styled. In all the fantasies she'd concocted of how she'd act and what she'd look like when she saw Robert again, this was not one of them.

"How was Honduras?" she asks finally, filling the space between them with sound.

"Great. I'm going back next year."

She nods, watches two women at the elevator door talking, and then she sighs. "Robert."

"I'm sorry," he says.

She nods and begins to cry. "What happened?"

Robert starts to say something, but then he pushes off the wall and takes her hand, leading her to the stairwell. "Let's go outside. Let me tell you there."

They walk down the three flights of stairs and step out into the late-spring morning. Already, it feels like it's ninety degrees, the concrete sending up waves of trapped sunlight. Robert leads them to a bench that surrounds a giant oak, and they sit, not facing each other, thigh to thigh.

Mia wipes her eyes and breathes in. "Ford and I are separated. We're divorcing."

Robert jolts and then softens, taking her hand. "Were you going to tell me that the day you came over?"

She nods because she can't talk.

He brings her hand to his mouth and kisses it, his lips soft and warm. "I'm glad I didn't know then."

She nods again, swallows.

"I found out something in Honduras," he says.

"What?" she mumbles.

"About your name. What it means."

"Oh, that," she says.

"It has meaning," he says.

She shrugs. "I always thought that my mother made a mistake. She named me 'mine' when it always seemed I wasn't hers at all. But I think I'm hers, after all."

"No," Robert says, kissing her hand, turning her palm to his mouth. "You're not hers. She named you for me. You're mine."

For a moment, the air seems to cool and still around them. For a tiny second, her nose and head seem to clear, and Mia believes she will die now because she can't breathe or hear or speak. Her heart will finally stop, too full and too empty both at the same time. She will die at this moment, as if the gods will choose her instead of Sally. She will die at this moment because she is finally completely, perfectly happy. In this second of time, she's found that piece she longed for every morning of her long marriage, and she can't believe that she's been allowed to touch it here, right now. She wonders if it will suddenly disappear.

But the seconds keep passing. Robert continues to kiss her hand and then wrist and then arm. Then he lifts her chin and kisses her lips, not worried, it seems, about her cold or anything. He isn't running away or hiding or sitting still and letting her leave him.

"I've started your new novel," he whispers against her neck.

"How do you like it?" she asks, kissing his forehead.

He pulls her tight against him. Mia closes her eyes, listens into his body with her own, feeling all of him next to her, with her, not leaving her. And for the first time, she's with him, in the open, under a tree in the middle of a public place, loving the man she loves.

"So far, it's been a very intense read," Robert says, his lips by her good ear. "A little scary. I had to put it down for a while. But now I know I love it. I don't ever want it to end."

Jessica Barksdale Inclán

The
INSTANT
WHEN
EVERYTHING
IS PERFECT

This Conversation Guide is intended to enrich the
individual reading experience, as well as encourage us
to explore these topics together—because books,
and life, are meant for sharing.

A CONVERSATION WITH JESSICA BARKSDALE INCLÁN

Q. Many of your previous novels were inspired by specific events in your life. Is that true for this novel as well?

A. Most writers do follow the old adage "Write what you know." But, actually, most of my novels have been inspired by either something I've read or something a friend has gone through—or experiences that many people I know seem to be having. For instance, both *One Small Thing* and *Walking with Her Daughter* deal with infertility issues. As I've rounded into my forties, many of my friends have gone through infertility treatments, and being so close to so many who have, I've let reality seep into my stories.

On the other hand, *Her Daughter's Eyes* and *When You Go Away* were inspired by small articles I ripped out of the newspaper because the stories—one about a teenaged girl who hid her pregnancy and the other about a mother who neglected her special-needs child—horrified and intrigued and interested me. Later, I realized I had to try to get to the bottom of the story in order to understand it. And the only way to do that was to write about it.

Yet all of my stories have snippets of my real life in them—

teaching, for one, shows up in this novel and in *Walking with Her Daughter*. I have two full careers, and my other life can't help but influence my writing.

What is true in this novel is cancer—my mother was diagnosed with breast cancer in 2004, and one of the ways that I dealt with the situation is by writing about it. She is absolutely fine, by the way, Sally's prognosis and hers were quite the same. And since I lost my father to cancer when I was fifteen, I do seem to want to explore and discuss the impact of losing a parent—either as an adult or as a child. But loss, and how we come to grips with loss, fascinates me, probably because I haven't really figured it out as a human being.

Q. Like Mia, you're a novelist and teacher who lives in northern California with two sons and a husband. Of all your female characters, is Mia the one who comes closest to being you?

A. She has both of my jobs—that's certain—but I don't think Mia and I are alike in terms of temperament. She is slower-paced, willing to hang out in the uncertainty a bit longer than I am. I would have gotten on the phone and demanded that Robert tell me what was happening. I would have said something to Ford earlier. When Harper started asking strange questions, I would have jumped all over them. I am sure I would have gotten on the phone a few times to my sisters to demand that they help out more with Sally. I think I'm much more impatient, so it was very interesting to hang out in Mia's head and let her watch what was going on. She tended to respond rather than react, and I often react and then wish I'd waited and responded more thoughtfully.

My friends who have read all my novels seem to think that Jenna in *Walking with Her Daughter* is the character who is most like me.

Q. Through Sally, you explore the blossoming of love that comes later in life, something that we rarely see in fiction. Why was it important to you to include this aspect of the story?

A. Sally has a great deal of unfinished business, unresolved grief from the death of her husband years ago. So I'm not sure if it's that I wanted to explore late-in-life love or that I wanted her to be able to finish her grief, to move into another stage, to find a way to keep growing. Also, I thought that the parallel between Sally falling in love and Mia falling in love was important, as both of them begin to understand their fears and worries about moving on.

Q. Adultery is a tough subject to handle in fiction, partly because it's challenging to keep the characters involved sympathetic. Why were you drawn to this subject and what choices did you consider as the novel took shape?

A. Adultery can seem like the biggest betrayal of all. Yet the truth is that adultery is a symptom of something wrong in a relationship, and what it can do is signal that help is needed. No one has an affair if a relationship is full and growing, if the two people in it are committed to each other and to nurturing the relationship. So if one person or both turn to someone else, that's a pretty clear sign that things need attention.

I also feel that marriages can be developmental. For instance, Mia and Ford certainly developed in their relationship. They grew up, had children, cemented their careers, worked together to create a life for their boys. But I think that their relationship has already fulfilled what it needed to: They helped each other and brought up two wonderful children. Their affairs show that they have stopped needing each other to grow. They are hanging on to the skeleton of their old relationship to avoid hurting each other.

Many people can turn back toward each other after affairs and heal the problems in their relationships—and some can't. Some don't want to. Some know they need to move on to continue to grow as people.

Q. Why did you choose to tell the story from three different points of view—those of Mia, Sally, and Robert?

A. The first scene in the exam room created the point-of-view scenario for me. I realized that I was equally interested in all three characters and wanted to follow them through the whole story. So I just kept going, developing each through the story that was connected from the first lines.

Q. Last year, you took a sabbatical from your teaching position. Was that time off a period of great creativity, or did it involve lots of afternoon naps?

A. I wrote a couple of novels, worked out a lot, taught for UCLA, wrote a textbook, and gardened. Like Mia, I was rejuvenated by my sabbatical and needed very few naps!

Q. What is keeping you busy and creative these days?

A. Life keeps me pretty busy. I have just finished writing the draft of a novel and completed the revisions for another novel that will come out in 2006. I've actually been writing more poetry these days, which has been wonderful.

Q. You meet many of your readers via reading groups, e-mail, and bookstore appearances. What is the most surprising or most touching response you've received?

A. Probably the most touching response occurred recently. While doing research for *Walking with Her Daughter*, I learned about Karri Casner, one of seven Americans who died in the terrorist attack in Bali on October 12, 2002 (as does my character Sofie). When I finished the novel, I realized I wanted to dedicate the book to Karri. Her youth and vivacity strongly influenced much of what I wrote about Sofie.

One of the most popular questions I was asked on the book tour was if I had told Karri's parents that I had dedicated the book to her. I said no. I wasn't sure how to broach the topic with them, not knowing where they were on their trajectory of grief. I wasn't sure they would understand. I just thought hopeful thoughts for them. Somehow, they found out about the novel and wrote to me. Here is what Susan Casner wrote:

> *I want to thank you for dedicating your book to our daughter, Karri. I'm sure after reading the many articles about Karri in magazines and on the Internet, you were able to*

get a sense of what a special young woman she was. Karri was an old soul—much wiser than her years. She visits us often . . . but that's another story!!

I felt a great deal of gratitude for their generous response, and I also greatly admired how Karri's parents seemed to be healing and growing from this horrible experience.

QUESTIONS FOR DISCUSSION

1. Mia is different from her sisters in both appearance and profession. She's big-boned and fleshy while they're tall and slender; she's artistic while they're scientific. These differences have sometimes made her feel estranged from her family. Have you, or someone close to you, ever struggled with similar feelings of being disconnected to your family?

2. Does Mia and Ford's twenty-two-year marriage remind you of other marriages you have known? Do you think it's an accurate depiction of many longtime marriages? Comment on Mia's realization that after she and Ford achieved the dreams of their early years, they "forgot to think up later dreams, other goals, future plans" (page 23).

3. Mia was never sexually fulfilled in her marriage, yet she accepted that loss and learned to live with it because Ford brought many other positive qualities to the marriage—excellent parenting, for example. Do you know of other women who have made the same or similar compromises? In your opinion, are those trade-offs acceptable, or not?

4. Robert has been involved with many women, but has not been able to make a commitment to any of them. Do you think that will change with Mia? Why or why not?

5. Sally chooses not to have reconstructive surgery and she stops her chemotherapy treatments, preferring to live more fully right now despite the slightly increased chance that her breast cancer will return. In her situation, would you make the same choice? Drawing upon the experiences of women you've known, discuss the many choices open to women who are fighting breast cancer. Do you think some choices are more socially accepted than others?

6. After Robert lost two patients on the operating table, he decided to focus his work on "serious" reconstructive plastic surgery rather than on cosmetic surgery. Do you find him more admirable because of his choice? How does his work in Honduras change your impression of him? Share your thoughts and opinions about the popularity of cosmetic surgery today. Does changing how people look really change who they are inside?

7. When Robert first meets Mia, he seems to recognize her as a "kindred soul." Jessica Barksdale Inclán writes: " 'There you are,' he almost said. 'Where in the hell have you been?' " (page 39). Do you think that immediate sense of recognition is a common experience among people who fall in love? If so, how do you explain it?

8. Mia's younger, high-school-age son brings the family situation to a crisis by telling his mother that his father is having

an affair. Do you find this development realistic? How do you feel about the boys' direct involvement in their parents' adultery?

9. Jessica Barksdale Inclán devotes quite a few pages to dramatizing the doctors' appointments and medical treatments that involve an entire family when one member is suffering from a serious illness. Discuss the family dynamics described in the novel. How do your own experiences compare?

10. Do you find the end of the novel satisfying? If so, why? If not, how would you change it?